Home in Detroit

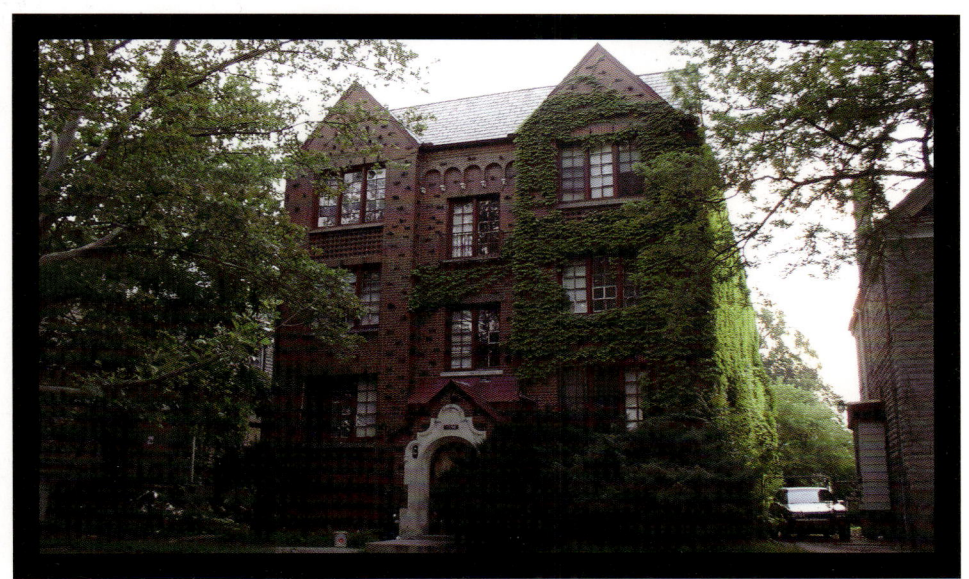

T. Burton

Shaking the Tree Publishing

Shaking the Tree Publishing LLC

Special thanks to Mark Patrick, and his staff, at the Burton Historical Collection of the Detroit Public Library.

Photo Credits:

AP Images: Pages 4, 8, 22, 24, 28, 32, 36, 38, 40,44, 48, 50, 56, 58, 60, 62, 64, 66, 68, 70, 72, 76, 78 80, 82, 84, 86, 94, 96, 102, 104, 106, 112, 116, 120, 122, 124, 126, 130, 132, 138, 140, 142.
Walter Reuther Library: Pages 6, 10, 12, 14, 16, 18, 20, 26, 30, 88, 90, 92, 98, 100, 108.
Nadine Joy: Page 118
Jackie Kallen: Page 54
CharlesBush.com: Page 46
Lynn Goldsmith: Page 52
Philip Levine: Page 42
Sonny Eliot: Page 34
Fox Sports Net: Page 136
Topps: Pages 128, 134
Ray Parker Jr.: Page 114
Kyle Artiste: Page 110

Cover - AP Images - Rosa Parks, Tom Selleck, & Eminem. Walter Reuther Library- Aretha Franklin, Smokey Robinson, Malcolm X, Walter Reuther, Stevie Wonder, & Henry Ford. Jackie Kallen - Jackie Kallen. Lynn Goldsmith - Lynn Goldsmith. Nadine Joy - Ted Nugent. CharlesBush.com - Dr. Wayne Dyer.

Front Dust Flap Image - AP Images

All "Home" Photos by T. Burton, all rights reserved.

ISBN: 978-0-9801696-0-7

Library of Congress Control Number: 2008902066

Printed in Canada

FOREWORD

My name is John J. George, a life long Detroiter. Twenty years ago we started the Motor City Blight Busters in an effort to help stabilize, revitalize, beautify, and repopulate the city of Detroit with homeowners. Our aim is to restore the city to the state of great prominence it once held. We believe that inviting everyone to participate in this worthwhile effort will add up to Detroit's rebirth.

"Home in Detroit" details the lives of the most talented Detroiters with current day photographs of where they lived in Detroit. While the book celebrates their lives, we feel it also celebrates the neighborhoods where they lived and the memories attached to their homes. Through the charity's website, www.blightbusters.org, you will be able to join in the effort to revitalize Detroit; you can volunteer or make donations of resources or dollars. We have a car and home donation program that allows you to participate in this program. By supporting Blight Busters, you will possibly help the neighborhood where you grew up, or maybe where your loved ones lived, or maybe an area that has been forgotten, we need your involvement!

If you need assistance in finding where family members may have lived in Detroit, please visit the Burton Historical Collection at the main branch of the Detroit Public Library downtown, or contact them at (313) 833-1480. If you are unable to visit the Burton Historical Collection, you can e-mail your family's historical information (full names, approximate years in Detroit, spouse's names, and or line of work) to us at home@blightbusters.org and we will do our best to locate where they might have lived and get back to you with that information.

This book represents the best who have lived in Detroit, it is all our challenge to ensure that Detroit neighborhoods continue to produce great people for generations to come, together, we can accomplish anything! A portion of the proceeds from this book will be donated to the Motor City Blight Busters so that we can expand and continue our work here in the city of Detroit. You can contact Blight Busters at (313) 255-4355 or www.blightbusters.org.

John J. George

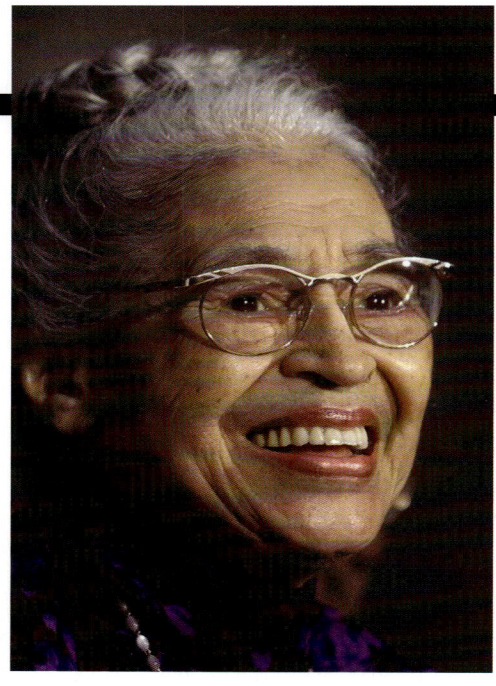

Mrs. Parks

The "Mother of the Civil Rights Movement" was born Rosa Louis McCauley on February 4, 1913 in Tuskegee, Alabama. Rosa became famous when she refused the order of bus driver, James Blake, to give up her seat for a white passenger, in 1955. Her arrest would lead to the Montgomery Bus Boycott, which was one of the most successful civil rights movements against racial segregatation.

In 1957, she moved to Detroit along with her husband, Raymond, and mother, Leona, to escape constant death threats. They lived with a friend at 13528 Fleming (which is no longer standing) for a month until they found an apartment on Euclid Avenue and later moved to the pictured flat on Virginia Park in 1961. Rosa passed away on October 24th, 2005 at the age of 94.

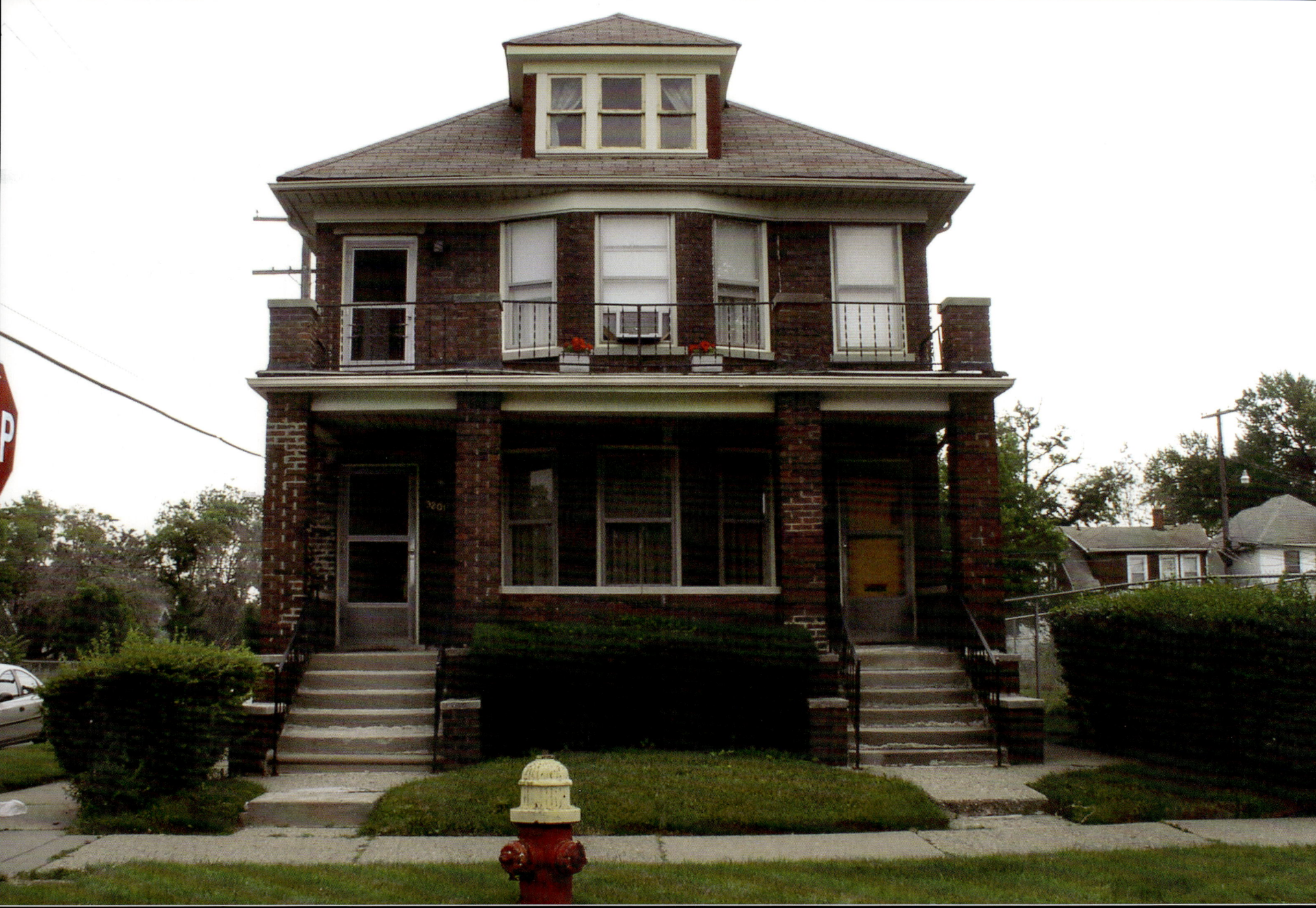

3201 Virginia Park

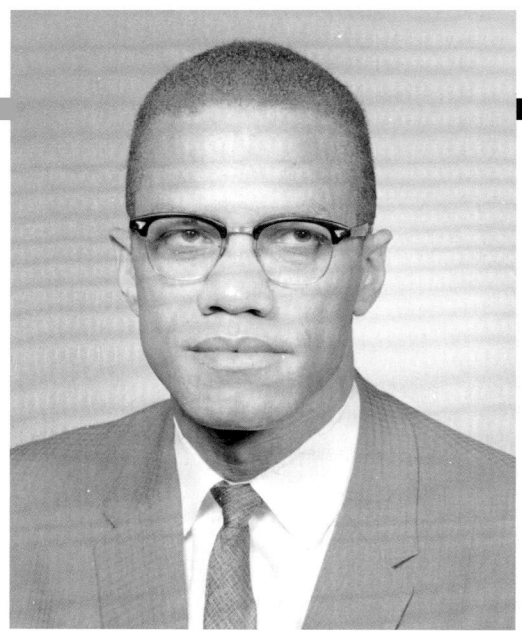

Malcolm X

Malcolm Little was born in Omaha, Nebraska on May 19th, 1925. In 1931, his family moved to Lansing, Michigan where his father was murdered, although police reported it as a suicide. While living in Boston, Malcolm was convicted of larceny and was sent to prison for eight years. After his release in 1952, Malcolm moved to Detroit to live with his older brother Wilfred. Malcolm quickly became one of the most influential leaders of the Nation of Islam under the leadership of Elijah Mohammad, who bestowed upon him the "X" designation.

Malcolm lived with Robert Davenport (Robert X), a former Negro League baseball player and member of the Nation of Islam, and his wife Dorothy in the pictured home. The address of the Davenport's home was 18827 Keystone; it was incorrectly identified in Malcolm's 1954 FBI file as 18887 Keystone, an address that does not exist. Malcolm X left the Nation of Islam in 1964 and was assassinated on February 21, 1965 in New York City.

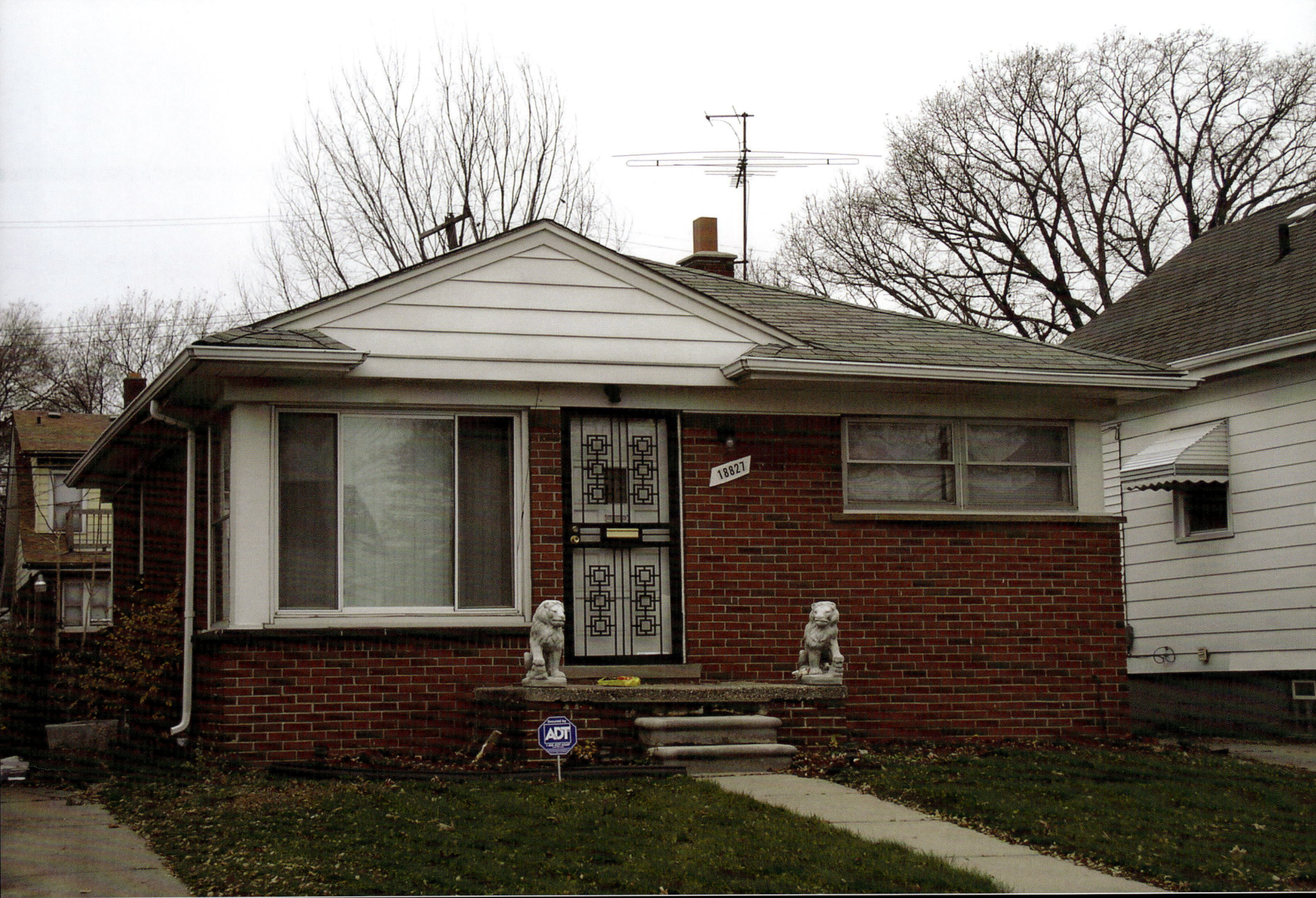

18827 Keystone

Betty Shabazz

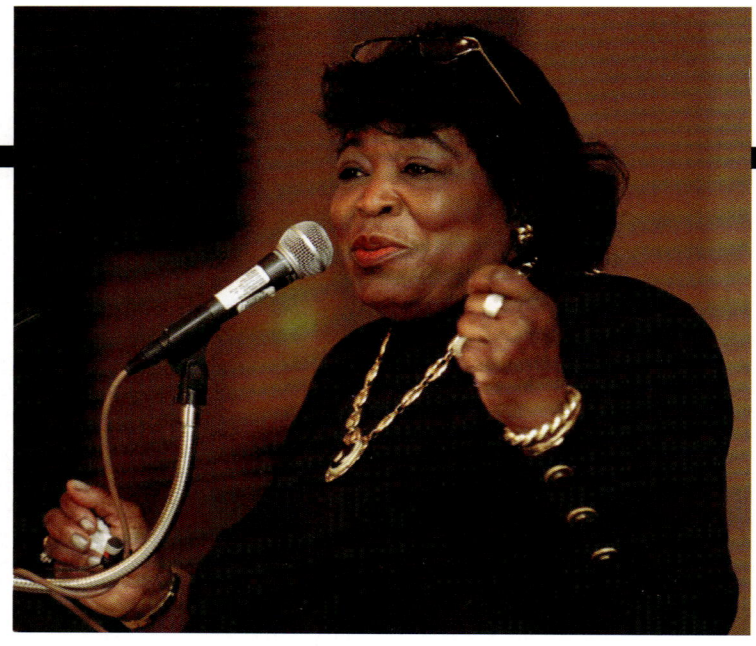

Bahiyah Betty Shabazz (Betty X) was born Betty Jean Sanders on May 28th, 1936 and was the wife of Malcolm X. Betty was taken in by foster parents Lorenzo and Helen Malloy and lived in this home on Hague, located just east of Woodward in the center of Detroit. She graduated from Detroit's Northern High School and enrolled at Tuskegee Institute in Alabama, she later earned a degree in nursing in New York.

Betty and Malcolm were married in 1958, after his assassination in 1965; she raised their six daughters. Betty Shabazz died on June 23, 1997 from third degree burns suffered in a fire set by her grandson, Malcolm Shabazz. Before they met, Betty and Malcolm may have both lived in Detroit at the same time. Betty may have been living in Detroit preparing for college when Malcolm came here after his parole from prison in August of 1952.

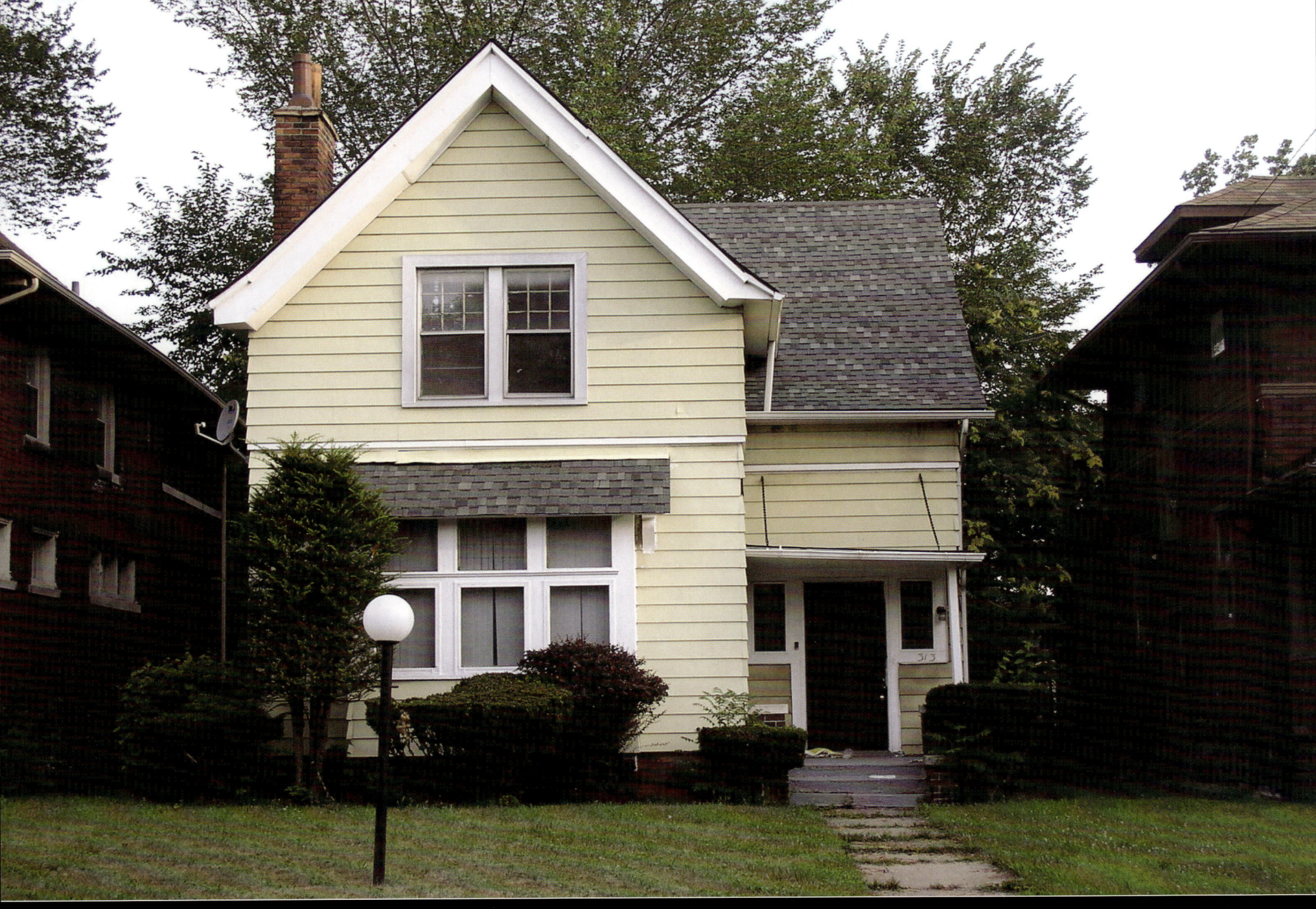

313 Hague

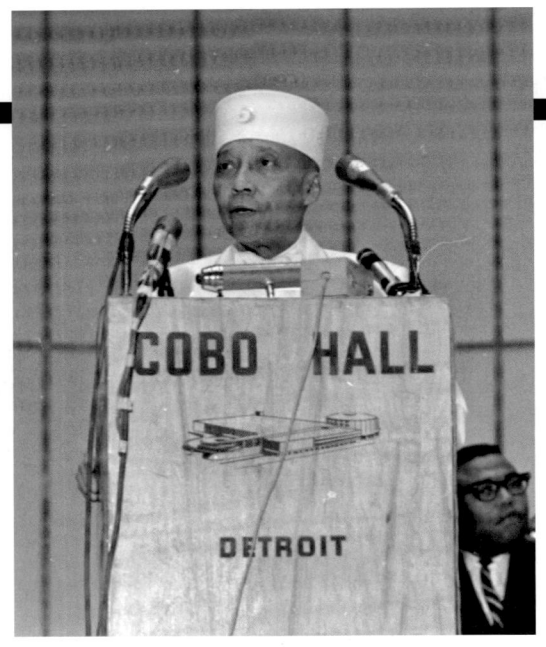

Elijah Mohammad

Nation of Islam leader, Elijah Muhammad was born Elijah Pool (he would later add the "e" to the end of his last name) in Sandersville, Georgia. Elijah married Clara Evans in 1917, started a family and moved to Detroit in 1923. After hearing Wallace D. Fard preach, Elijah quickly became one of his trusted disciples and when Fard disappeared, he took leadership of the Nation of Islam. He moved to Chicago in 1934 and was on the run from authorities until 1941 when he was arrested in Washington D.C. for sedition.

After his release, he continued to lead the Nation of Islam, which started to gain popularity in the African-American community with the help of a charismatic follower by the name of Malcolm X. Malcolm X left the faith in 1964, and was assassinated in 1965 by three members of the Nation of Islam. Elijah was suspected in the plot of Malcolm's murder, but no charges were every brought. Elijah Muhammad passed away in 1975. Around 1932, his family rented this home on Yemans in Hamtramck, which is a separate city located within the center of Detroit.

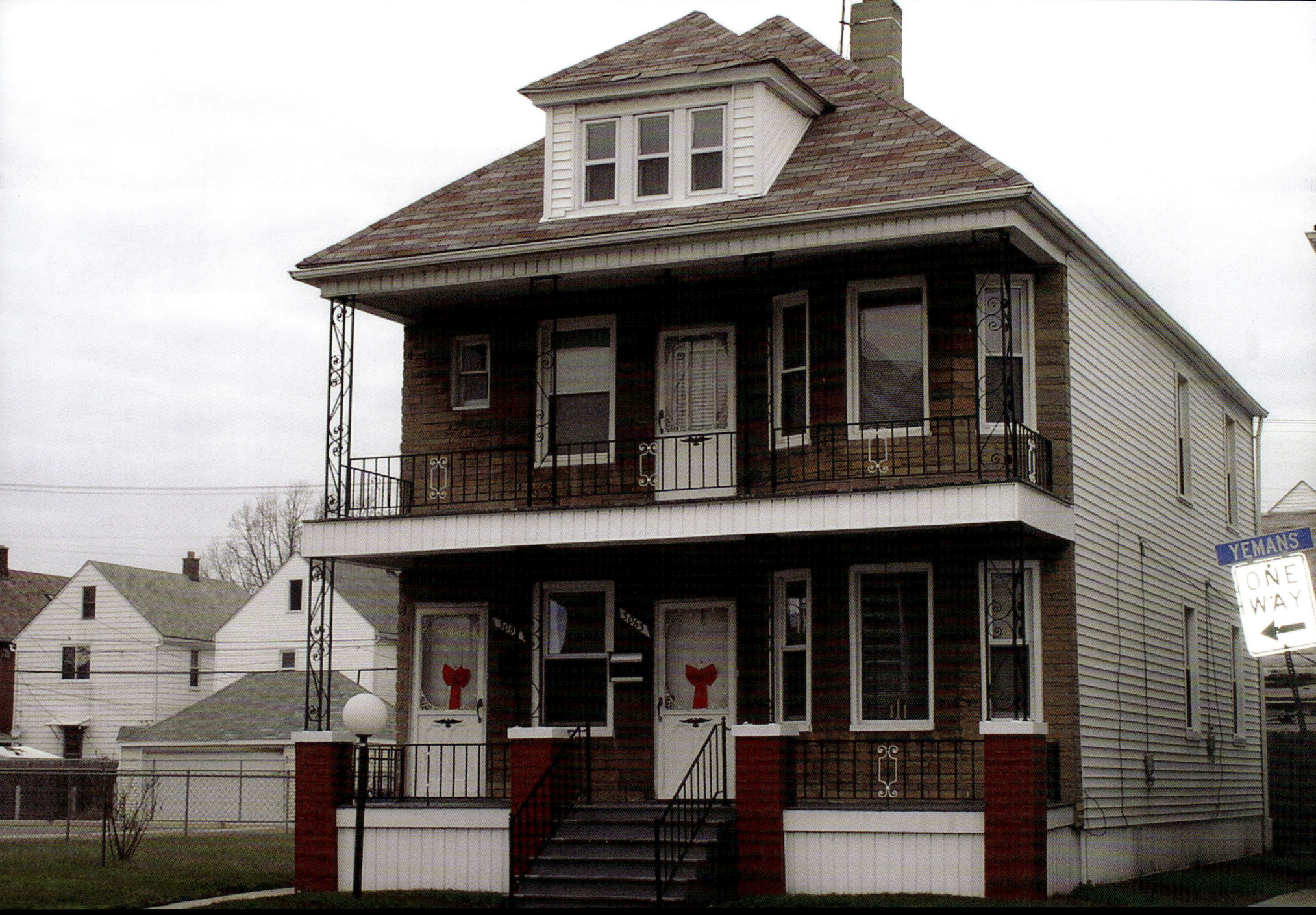

3059 Yemans

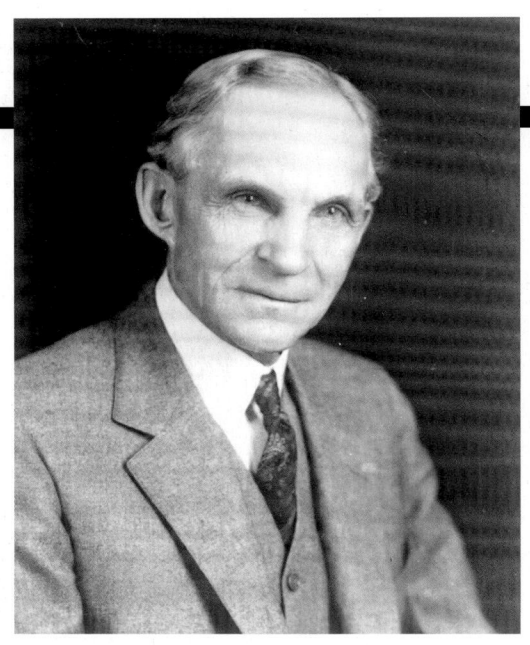

Henry Ford

Henry Ford was born on July 30th, 1863 in Dearborn, which was known at the time as Springwells Township. At the age of 32, Ford went to work for the Edison Illuminating Company, but later left the company to pursue a career in the automobile industry. In 1903, Henry and eleven partners, with $28,000 in capital, incorporated the Ford Motor Company and produced the Model T at the company's Highland Park assembly plant on Woodward Avenue, which is a national landmark.

Henry relinquished control of the company to his son Edsel Ford in 1918 but continued to be the driving force behind the scenes, at that time; half of the cars driven in the United States were Model T's. Henry Ford died at the age of 83 in 1947; he is recognized as the most influential person of the 20th century. The home is located just west of Woodward in the Boston-Edison neighborhood.

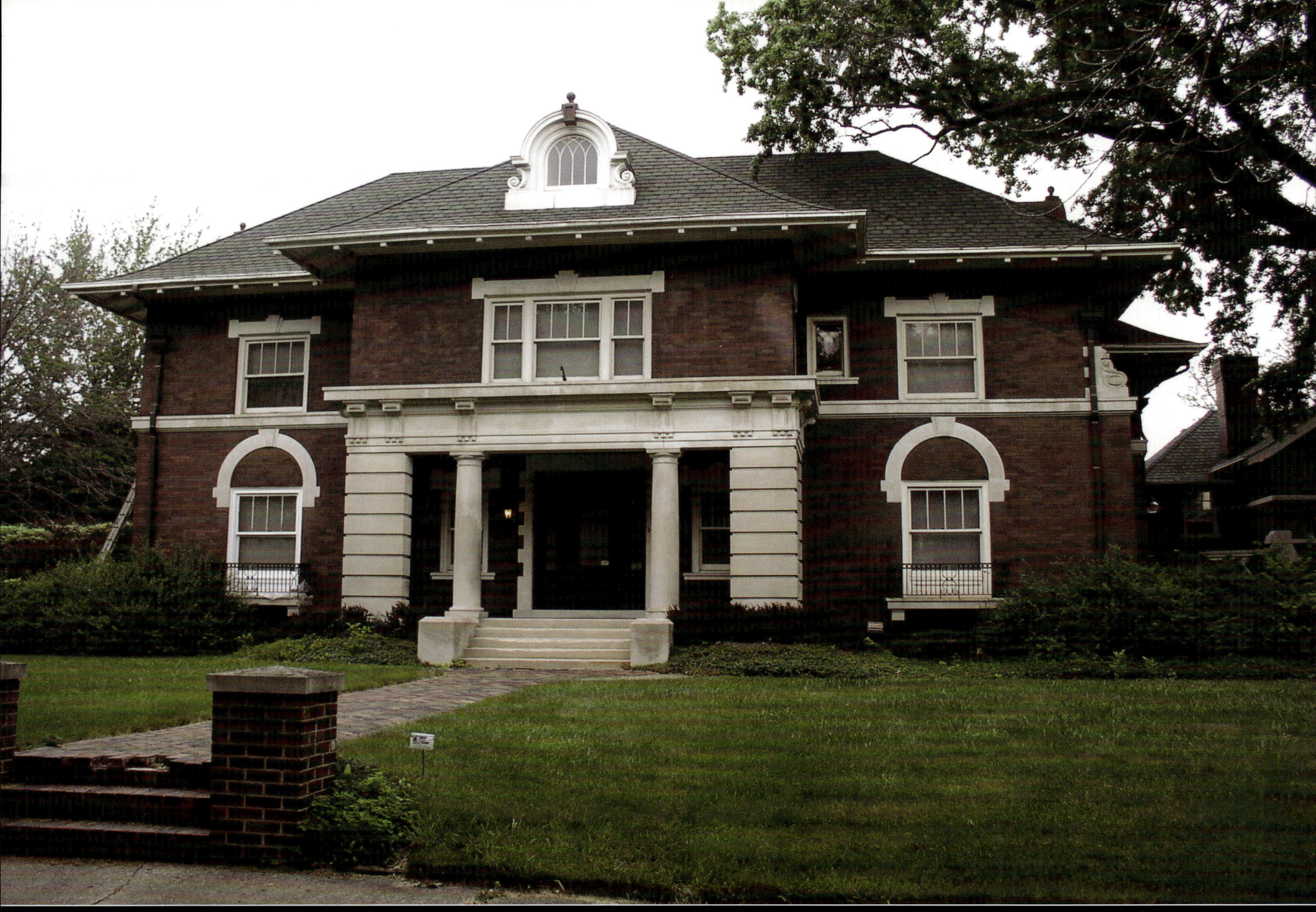

140 Edison

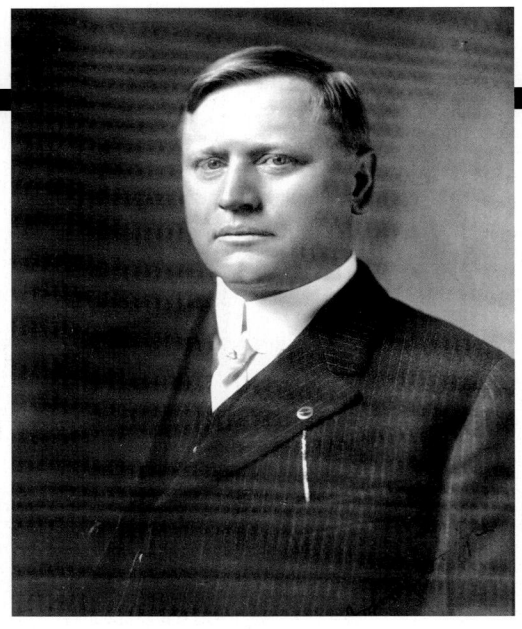

John Dodge

John Dodge was born in October 25th, 1864 in Niles, Michigan where his father owned a foundry and machine shops. John and his brother, Horace, came to Detroit in 1886 in search of employment. The brothers started a company that built bicycles and later transmissions. After being suppliers to the Ford Motor Company, they formed the Dodge Brothers, Inc. in 1914, and built their own line of automobiles.

In 1920, John died from influenza, his viewing was held at the pictured home on East Boston Boulevard because his wife Matilda, who also had contracted influenza, was too ill to leave the house. John's brother, Horace, died a year later; after which both Dodge widows sold the company for $146 million. John's home is now owned and occupied by the Detroit Catholic Archdiocese.

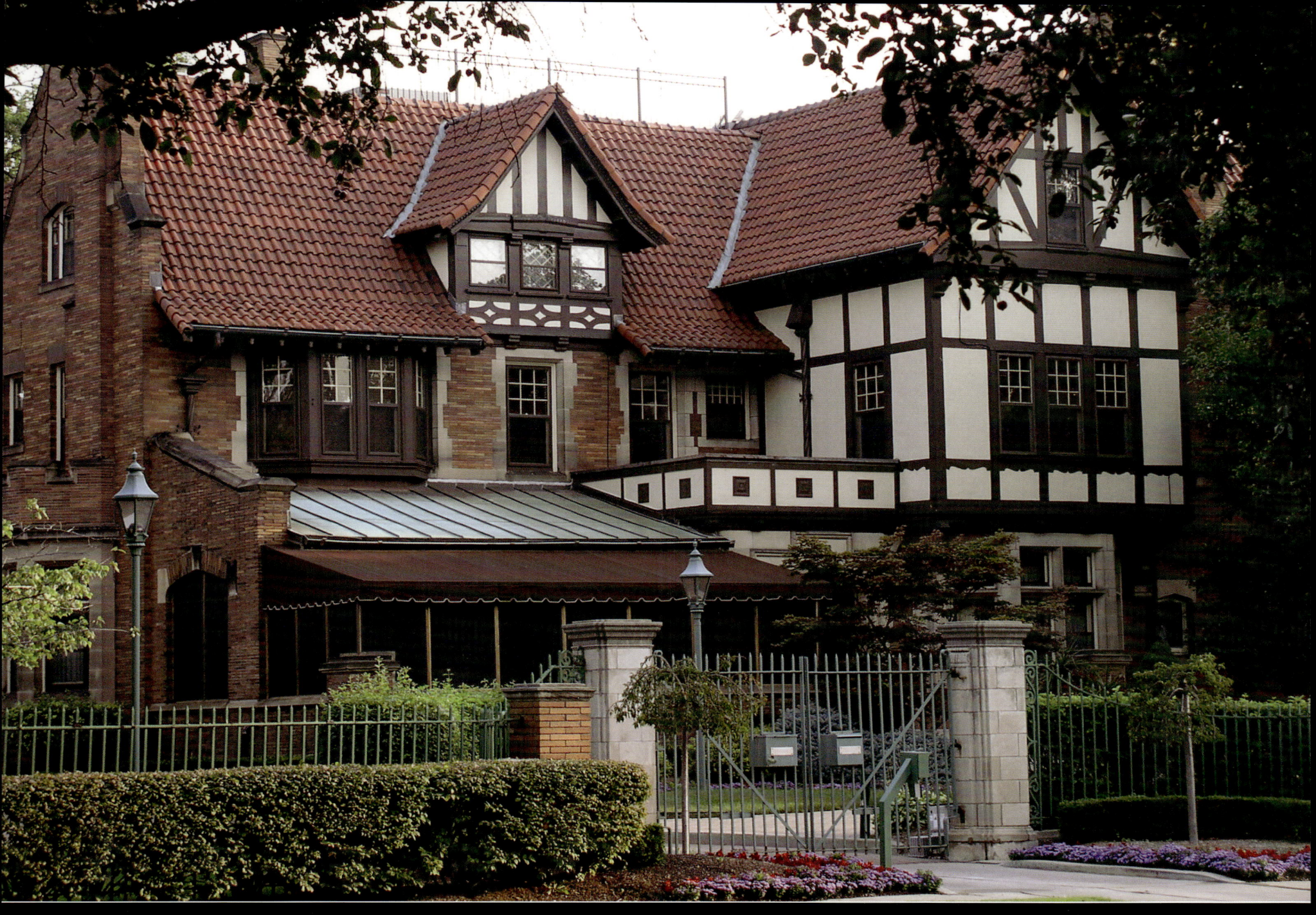

75 East Boston

John DeLorean

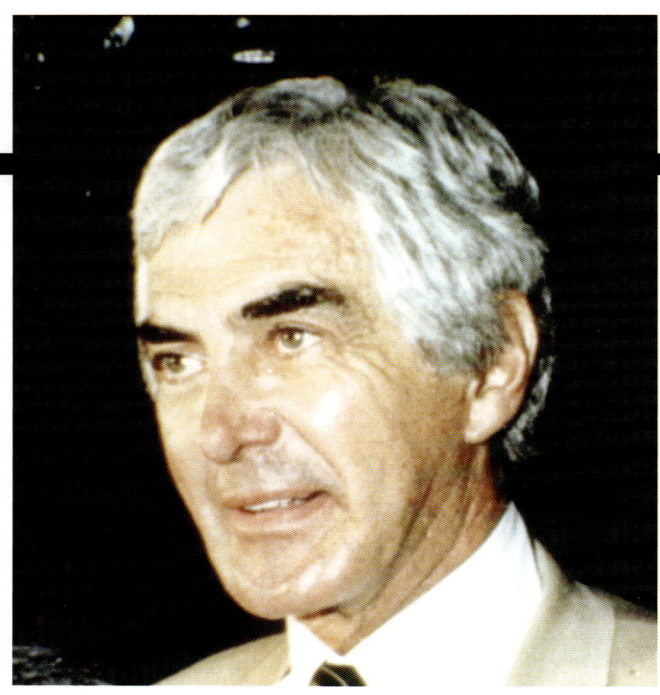

John was born to Zachary and Kathryn Pribak DeLorean on January 6, 1925 in Detroit. He started his auto career with Chrysler, which ended a year later when he took a job with the Packard Motor Company. As the Packard Company began to decline, John left and went to work for General Motors. In the early 1980s, John started the DeLorean car company, which was in receivership by 1982. Later that year, he was charged with cocaine trafficking by the United States government. He defended himself and was found not guilty due to entrapment.

Throughout most his childhood, DeLorean lived in the pictured home on Marx street, which is just east of I-75 and north of McNichols Road. He attended Cass Technical High School in Detroit, where one of his teachers was Evangeline Lodge Land, mother of legendary pilot, Charles Lindbergh. John died at the age of 80 in March of 2005.

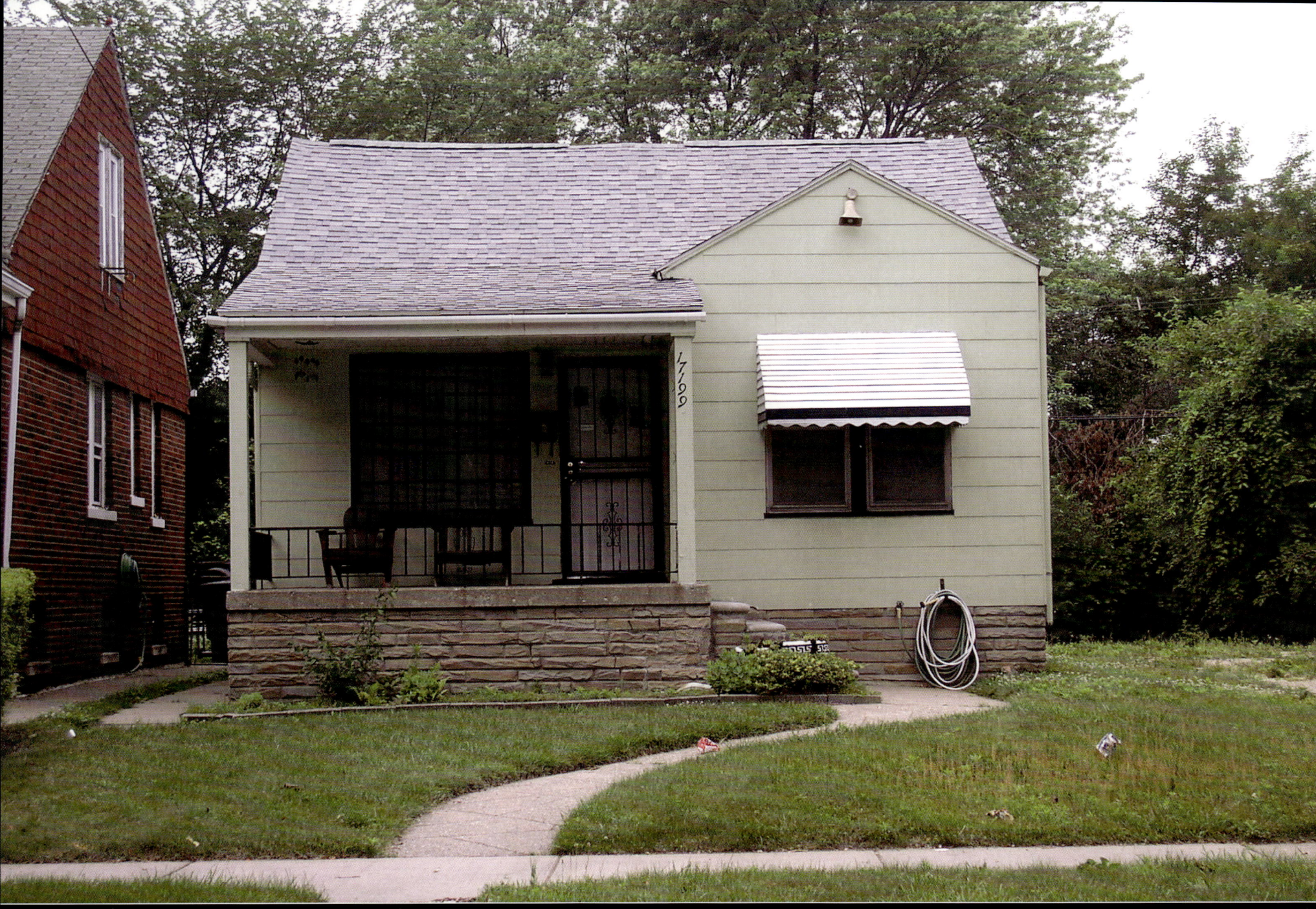

17199 Marx

Walter P. Reuther

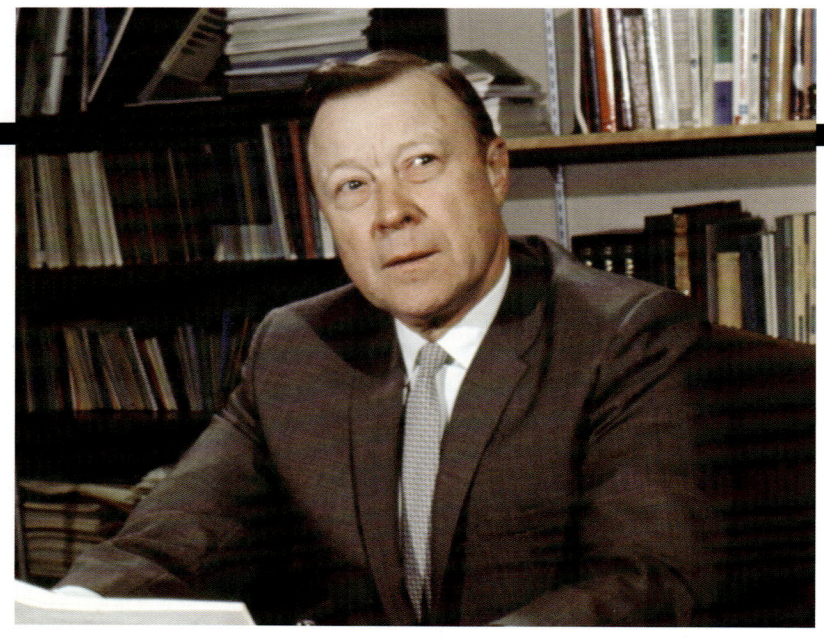

Born on September 1st, 1907 in Wheeling, West Virginia, Walter went on to become the leader of the United Automobile Workers union (UAW) and was a major influence in the auto industry and the Democratic Party. Walter left the United States during the Great Depression to work at an auto plant in Gorky, Russia. Although he was a socialist, he never became a communist while in Russia. He moved back to Detroit in the mid-1930s to work for General Motors, where he became an active union member.

Reuther became president of the UAW in 1946 and held that position until he died in a private-plane crash in 1970. His family believed the crash was not accidental, but the FBI refuses to release documents regarding the circumstances surrounding his death. The house is located on the west side of Detroit between Linwood and Dexter, north of West Grand Boulevard. Several photos supplied by the Walter P. Reuther Library, located on the campus of Wayne State, were used in this book.

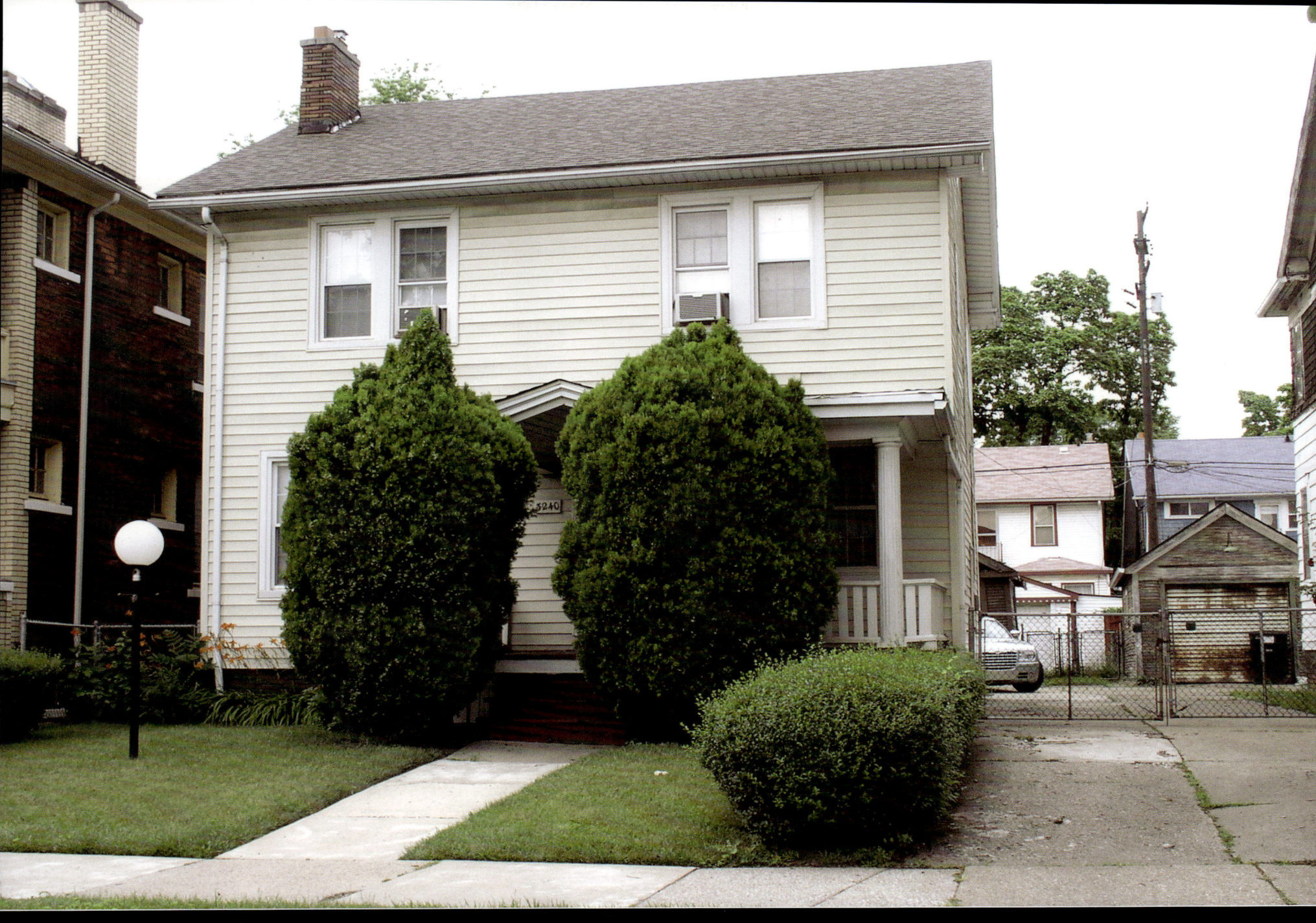

3240 W. Philadelphia

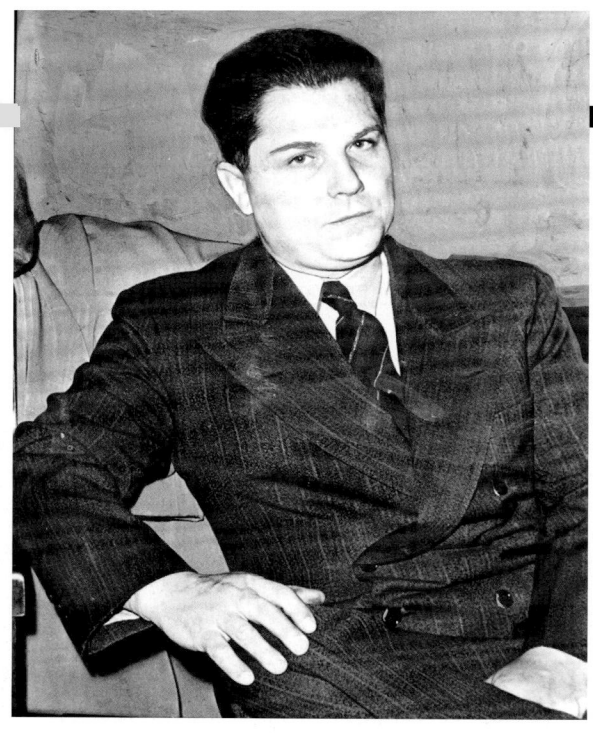

Jimmy Hoffa

Jimmy was born on February 14th, 1913 and lived in Brazil, Indiana before moving to Detroit after his father's death in 1920. At 14, Jimmy lived with his mother at the pictured home and quit school to work as a warehouseman for the Kroger Company. He organized a union at Kroger that would eventually be admitted into the Teamster's Union.

He became president of the Teamsters in 1957, but in 1967, Hoffa was convicted of fraud for the illegal use of the union's pension fund and received a 13-year prison sentence. President Nixon commuted his sentence in 1971. Jimmy disappeared on July 30th, 1975, he was last seen at the Machus Red Fox restaurant in Bloomfield Hills and was declared legally dead in 1983. Jimmy's childhood home is located on the Detroit's southwest side, near the Mexican Village area.

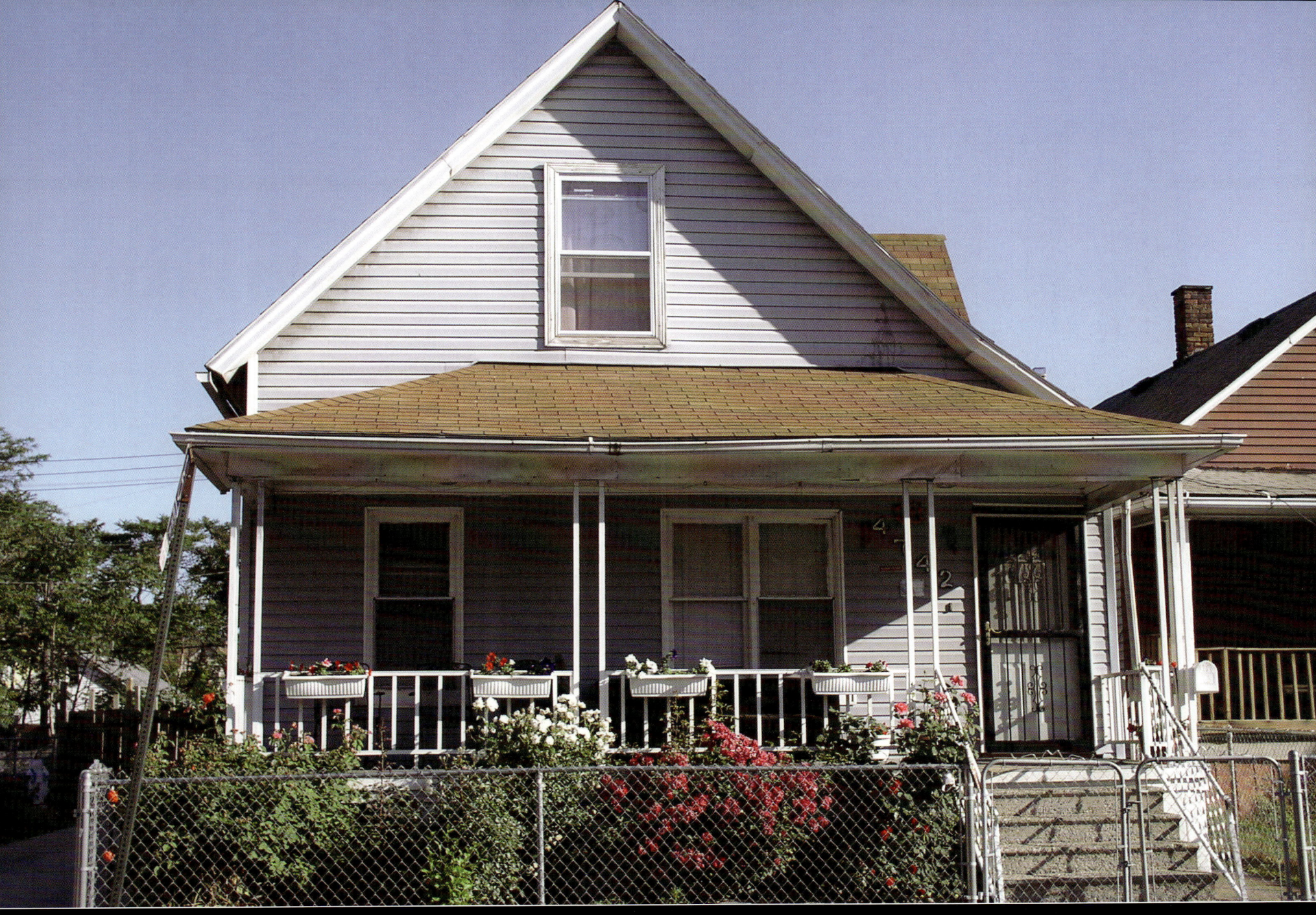

4742 Toledo

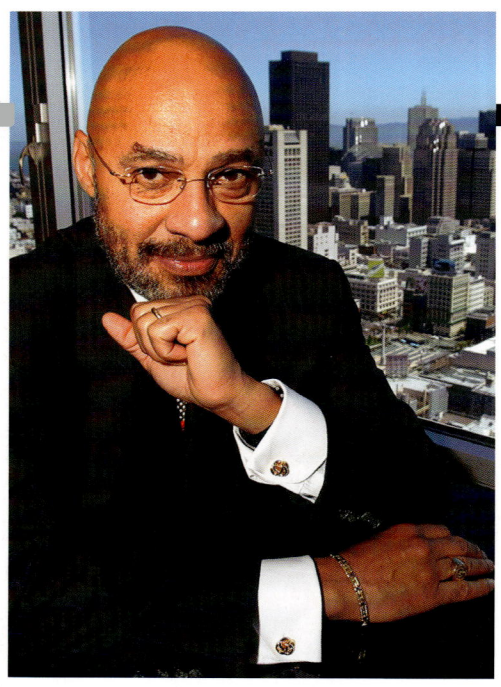

Dennis Archer

Dennis Wayne Archer was born on January 1st, 1942. He was raised in the small town of Cassopolis, Michigan and graduated with a degree in education from Western Michigan University. Dennis moved to Detroit and taught in the Detroit Public School System in the late 1960s before graduating from law school. He was a Michigan Supreme Court Justice from 1985 until 1993 and was mayor of Detroit from 1994 until 2001, Dennis is currently the chairman of the Dickinson Wright law firm in Detroit. Dennis lived for several years in this home on Lincolnshire, located in the Palmer Park neighborhood, before he was elected mayor in 1994.

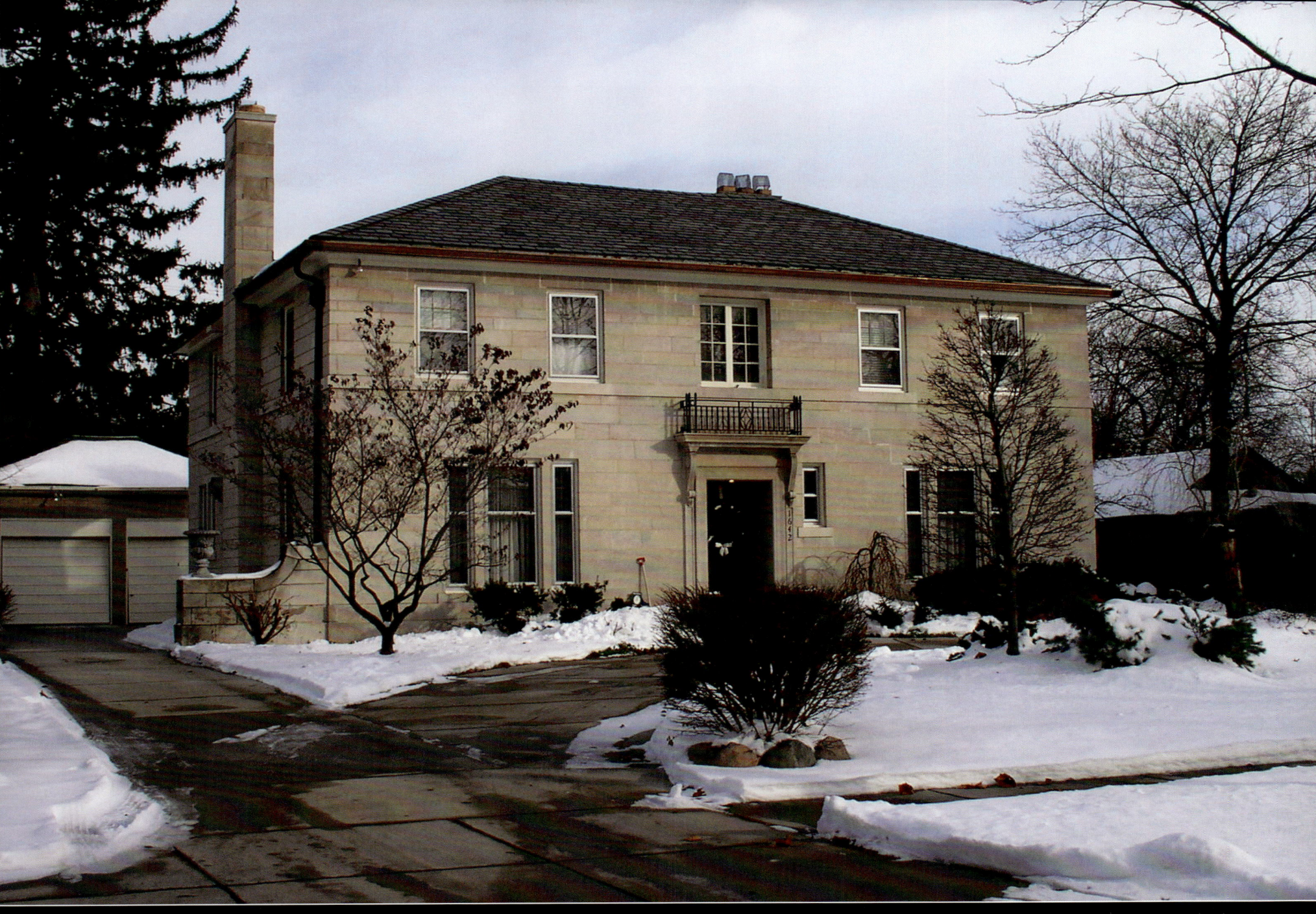

1642 Lincolnshire

Carl Levin

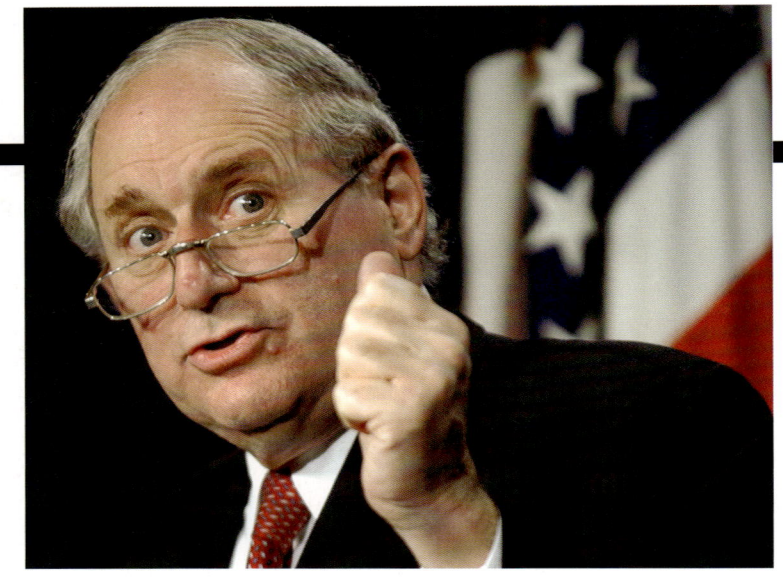

Born to Saul and Betty Levin on June 28th, 1934 in Detroit, Carl has been a United States Senator from Michigan since 1979. Carl was born and raised in Detroit; he attended Detroit Central High School and went on to graduate from Harvard School of Law in 1959. Carl has served on the Armed Services Committee since 1997 and has been very outspoken on the Iraq War. Carl comes from a family with a long line of elected positions. His brother, Sandy (Sander), is a member of the House of Representatives, his uncle, Theodore, was a judge and his cousin, Charles, was a Michigan Supreme Court judge. Carl's home is located on La Salle, just south of Clairmount and east of Linwood Avenue.

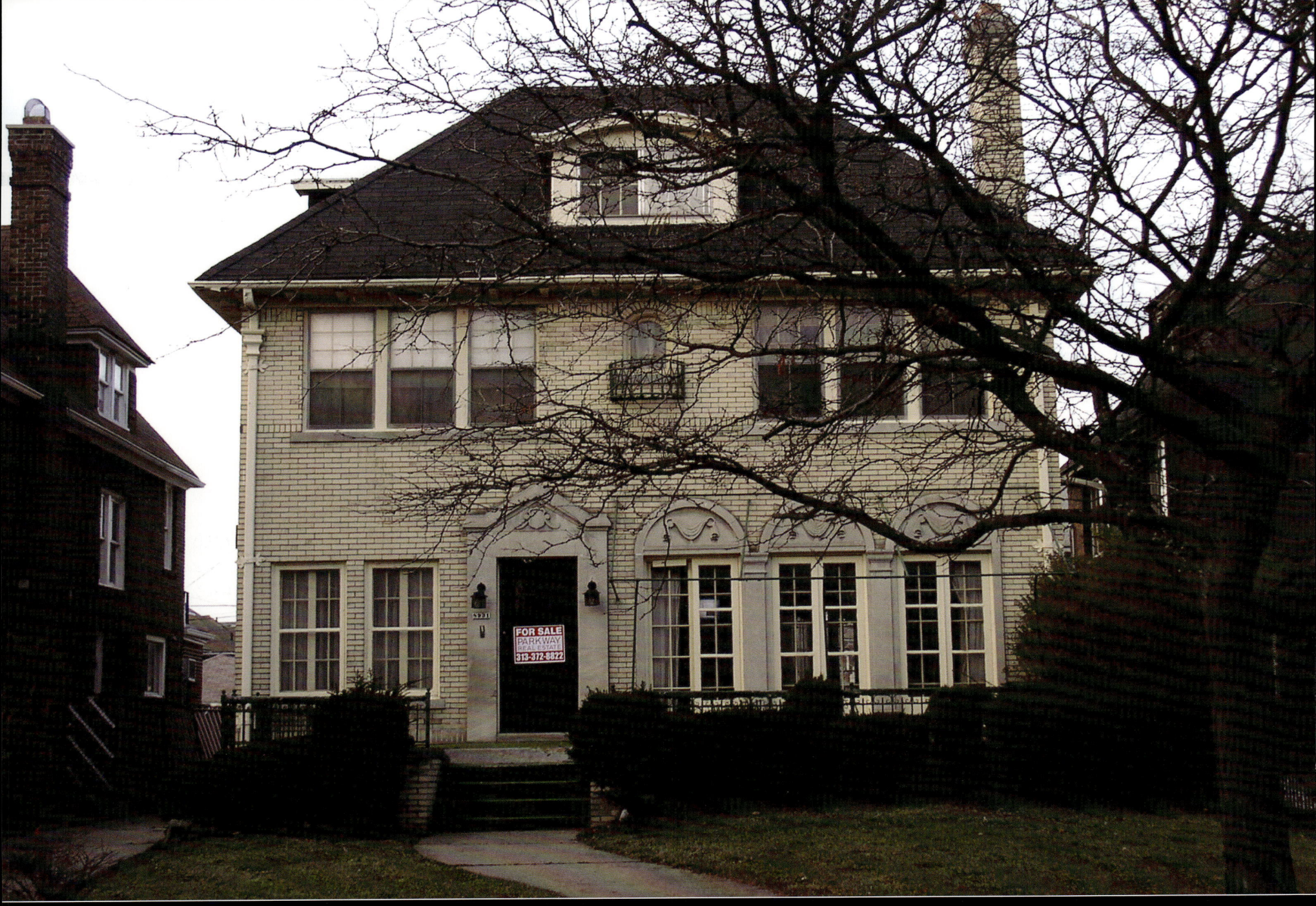

8931 La Salle

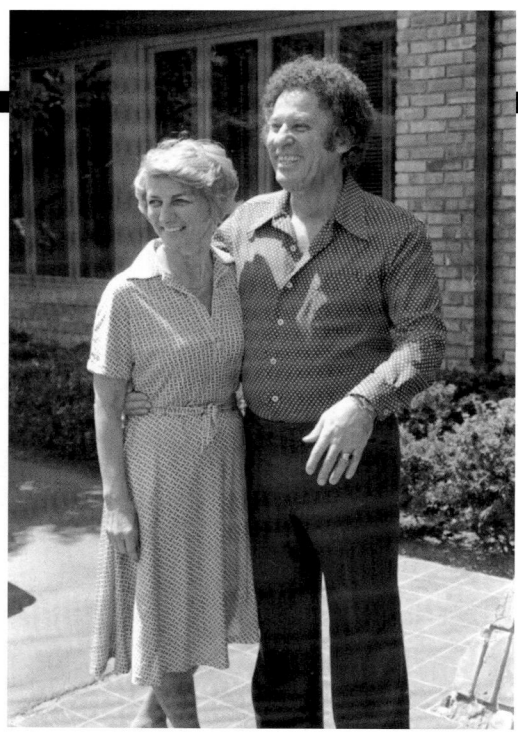

Mike and Marion Ilitch

Michael Ilitch was born on July 29th, 1929 in Detroit MI, he was raised on Detroit's west side. He lived at 8216 DeSoto and graduated from Cooley High School in 1944. Mike joined the Marines in 1948 and returned home to play baseball in the Detroit Tigers' farm system. Marian grew up working in her father's restaurant and graduated from Dearborn Fordson High School. Mike and Marian went on a blind date set up by Mike's father and the two were later married in 1955. In 1957 they lived in the pictured home on Chalfonte; Mike's parents lived next door.

In 1959 they open their first restaurant, Little Caesars Pizza Treat in Garden City, Michigan that would later become the Little Caesars Pizza franchise chain. Mike Ilitch owns the Detroit Red Wings and Detroit Tigers, and Marian has an ownership interest in the Motor City Casino. Their home is located just west of Livernois and only four blocks south of the Lodge Freeway.

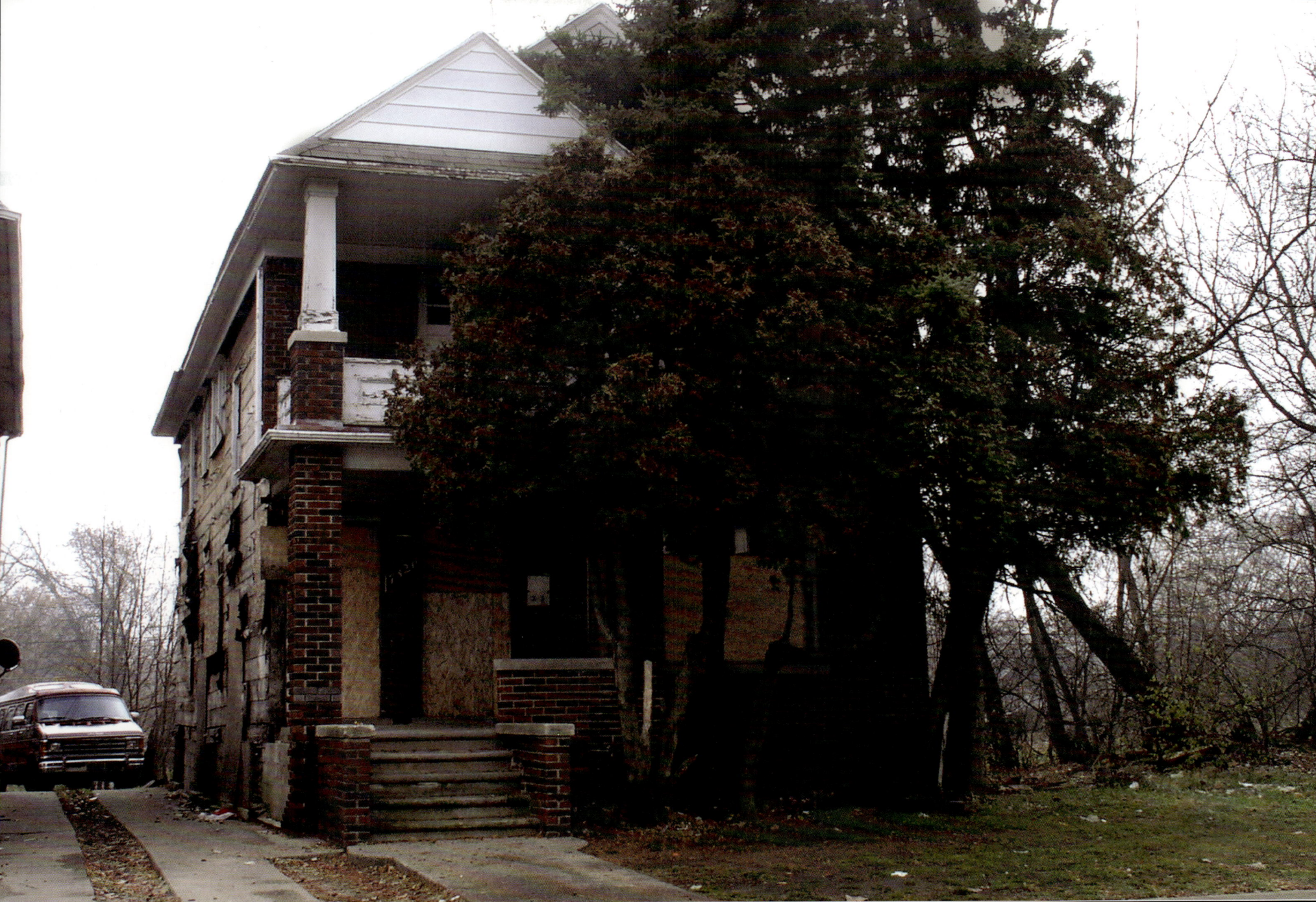

7321 Chalfonte

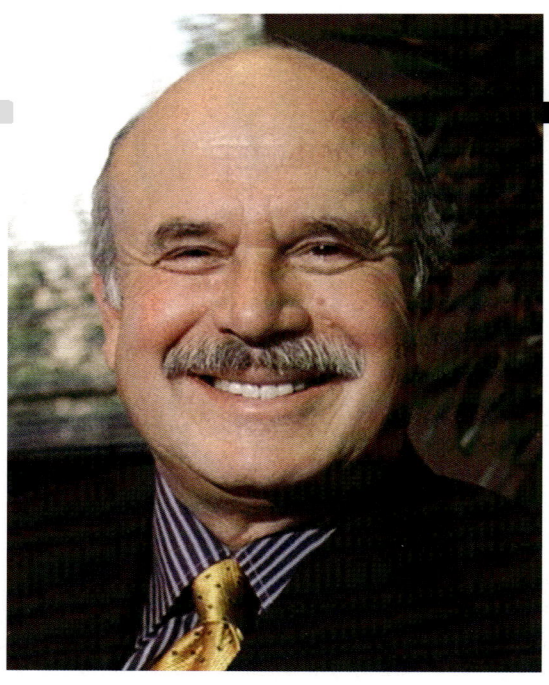

Peter Karmanos

Born and raised in Detroit, Peter's parents, Peter Sr. and Fonette, were both Greek immigrants. He attended Detroit Henry Ford High School and then graduated from Wayne State University. In 1973, Peter and two friends pooled their tax refunds together and started the technology services company, Compuware.

Peter donated $15 million to the Prentis Cancer Center, which later became the Barbara Ann Karmanos Cancer Institute in memory of his first wife, Barbara, who died of cancer in 1989. In 1994, he purchased the Hartford Whalers, and moved the team to Raleigh, North Carolina, naming them the Hurricanes. Peter's childhood home on Asbury Park is located across from Crary Elementary, between the Southfield Freeway and Greenfield on the city's west side.

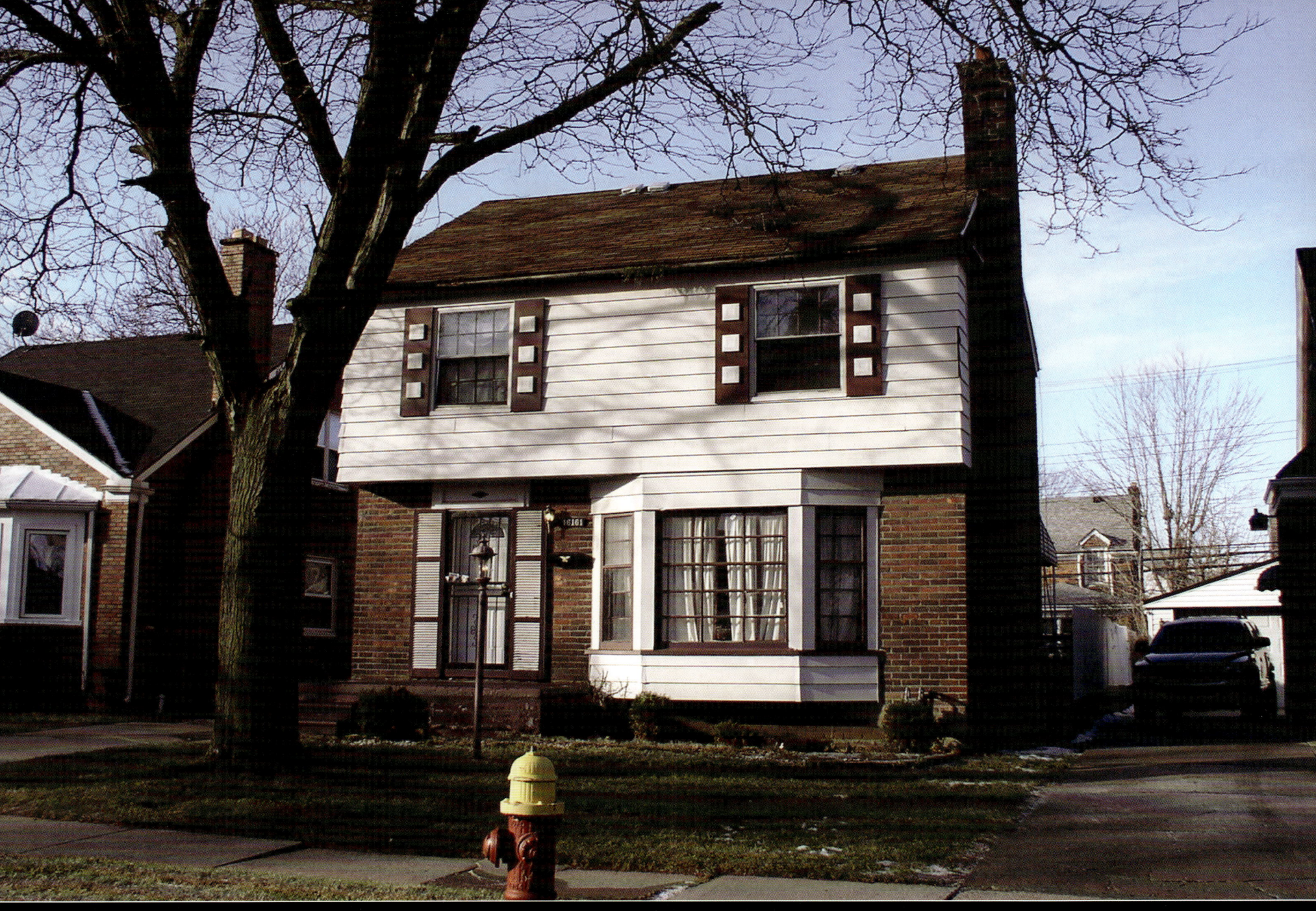

16161 Asbury Park

Charles Lindbergh

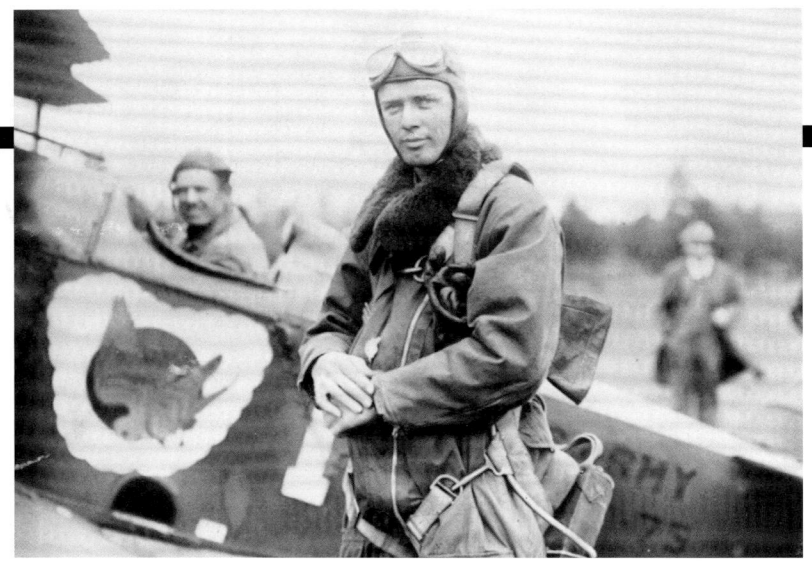

Charles Augustus Lindbergh was born on February 4th, 1902 to Charles and Evangeline Lindbergh in Detroit. Nicknamed "Lucky Lindy," he was the first person to fly solo across the Atlantic nonstop when he flew from Long Island, New York to Paris, France in 1927. Charles spent most of his early life growing up in Minnesota. His mother, a native Detroiter, came back home to deliver Charles under the care of her grandfather, Dr. Edwin Lodge, in her parents' home at 258 W. Forest, which was changed to 1120 W. Forest in 1920 when Detroit changed street numbers across the city.

Charles lived at this residence for the first few weeks of his life. Yes, I know this is a stretch, and no, Charles did not live in the pictured apartment, but it is the actual address of his birthplace. The house actually sat across the parking lot to the left of the pictured complex, which is located on the north side of W. Forest, just west of the Lodge Freeway. There was a celebration at this location when Charles returned to Detroit in 1927 to a hero's welcome. You can see pictures of the celebration and the birthplace home of Charles Lindbergh in the Virtual Motor City tour at *www.reuther.wayne.edu*. Charles died of cancer at the age of 72 on August 26th, 1974.

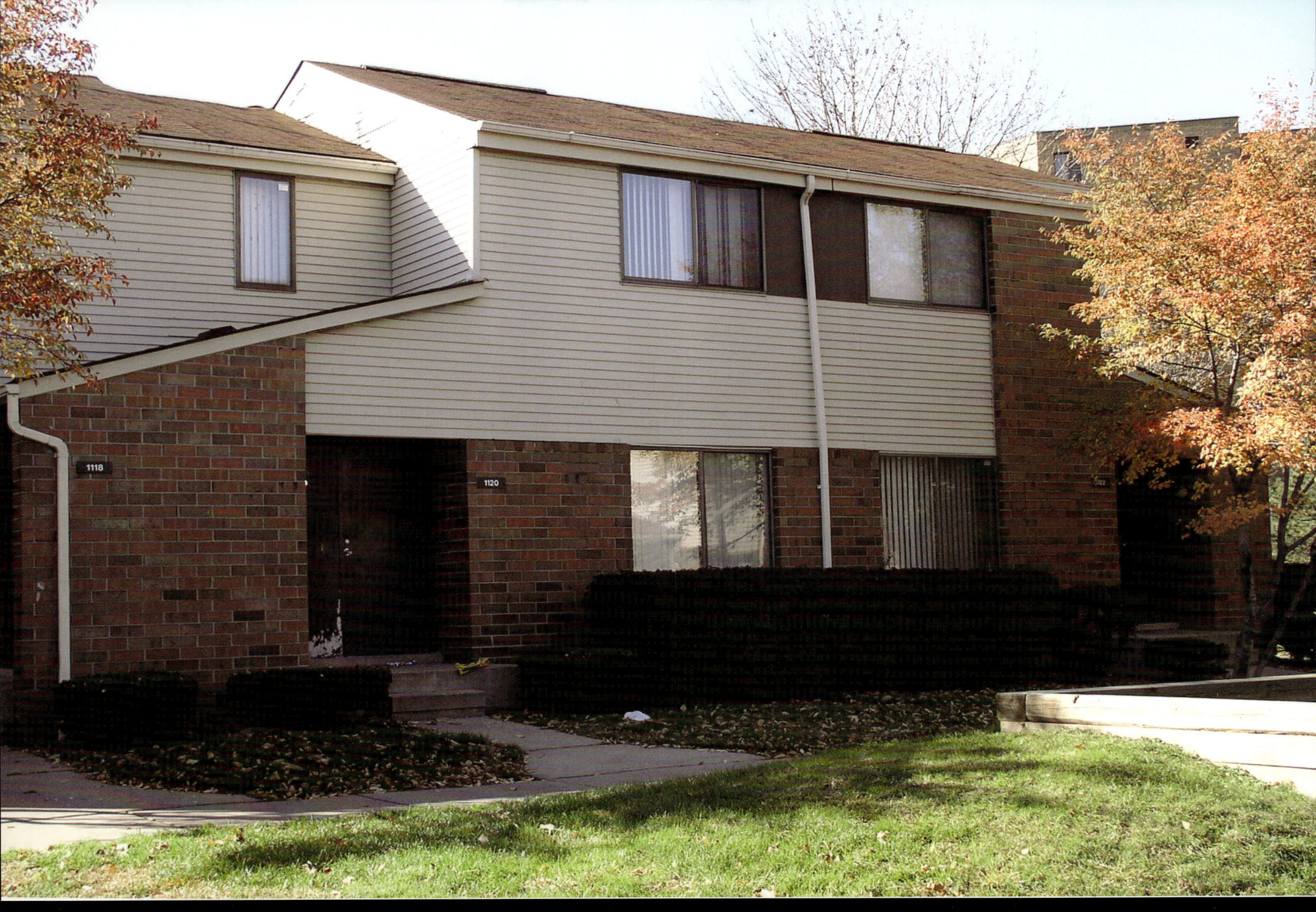

1120 W. Forest

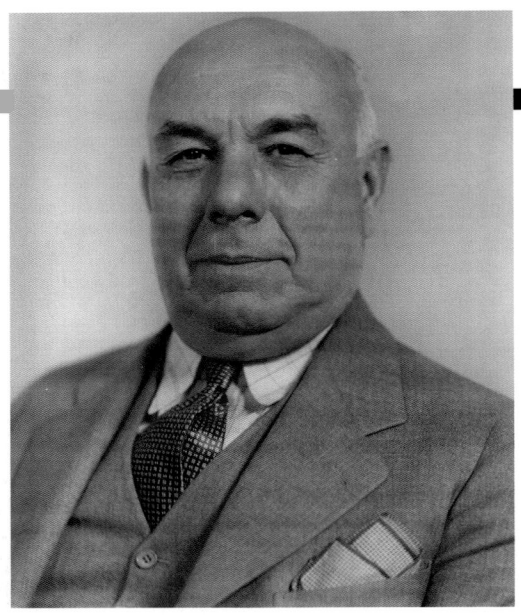

Sebastian Kresge

Born Sebastian Spering Kresge on July, 31st, 1867 in Bald Mountain, PA. He opened a small store in 1899 in downtown Detroit that would sell items for five and ten cents. The S.S. Kresge Company expanded to 85 stores by 1912. He opened his first Kmart store in 1962 in Garden City and established the world headquarters for the Kmart Corporation in Troy, Michigan. In his later years, Kresge became quite a philanthropist, giving away over $60 million through his Kresge Foundation that was established in 1924. Sebastian passed away in 1966; his home is located in the Boston-Edison neighborhood, just a few houses west of Woodward.

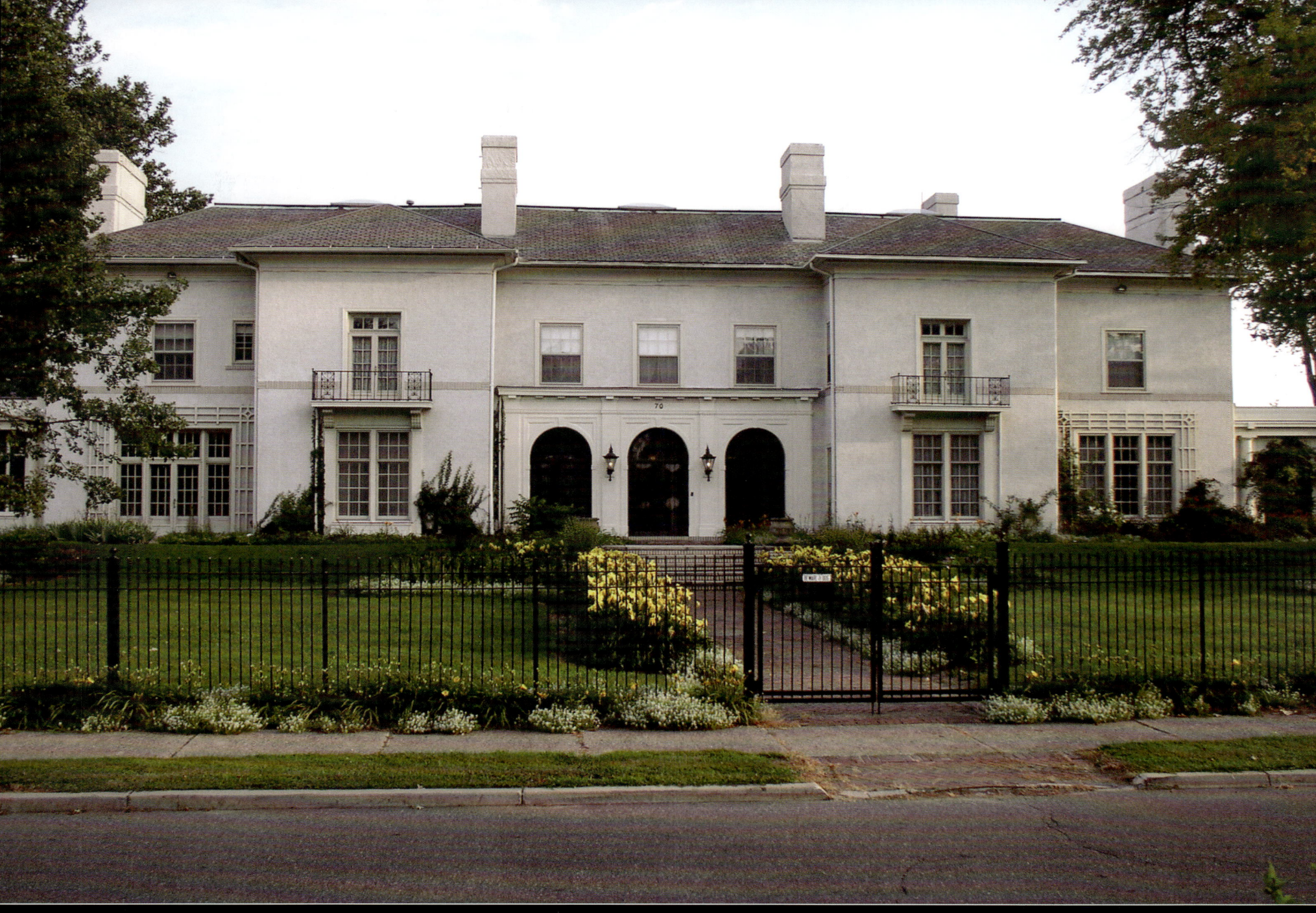

70 West Boston

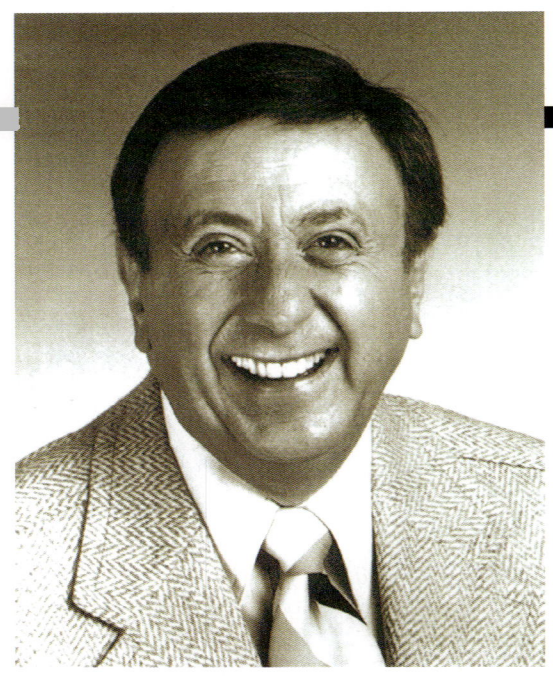

Sonny Eliot

Born Marvin Eliot Schlossberg to Jacob and Jenny Schlossberg in Detroit. Sonny's parents owned a hardware store located at 5140 Hastings. He attended Detroit Central High School and then Wayne State, where his broadcasting career began. Sonny served his country in World War II as a bomber pilot and was shot down during the war. He spent a year and a half in a prisoner-of-war camp in Stalag Luft I.

He retuned to Detroit in 1945 and started a broadcasting career, which continues today at News Radio 950 WWJ. Sonny is Detroit's most famous weather forecaster, but he also hosted *Channel 50 Movies, At the Zoo*, plus several Thanksgiving Day parades. Sonny still occasionally stops by his home on Calvert, which is located just north of West Chicago and east of Dexter.

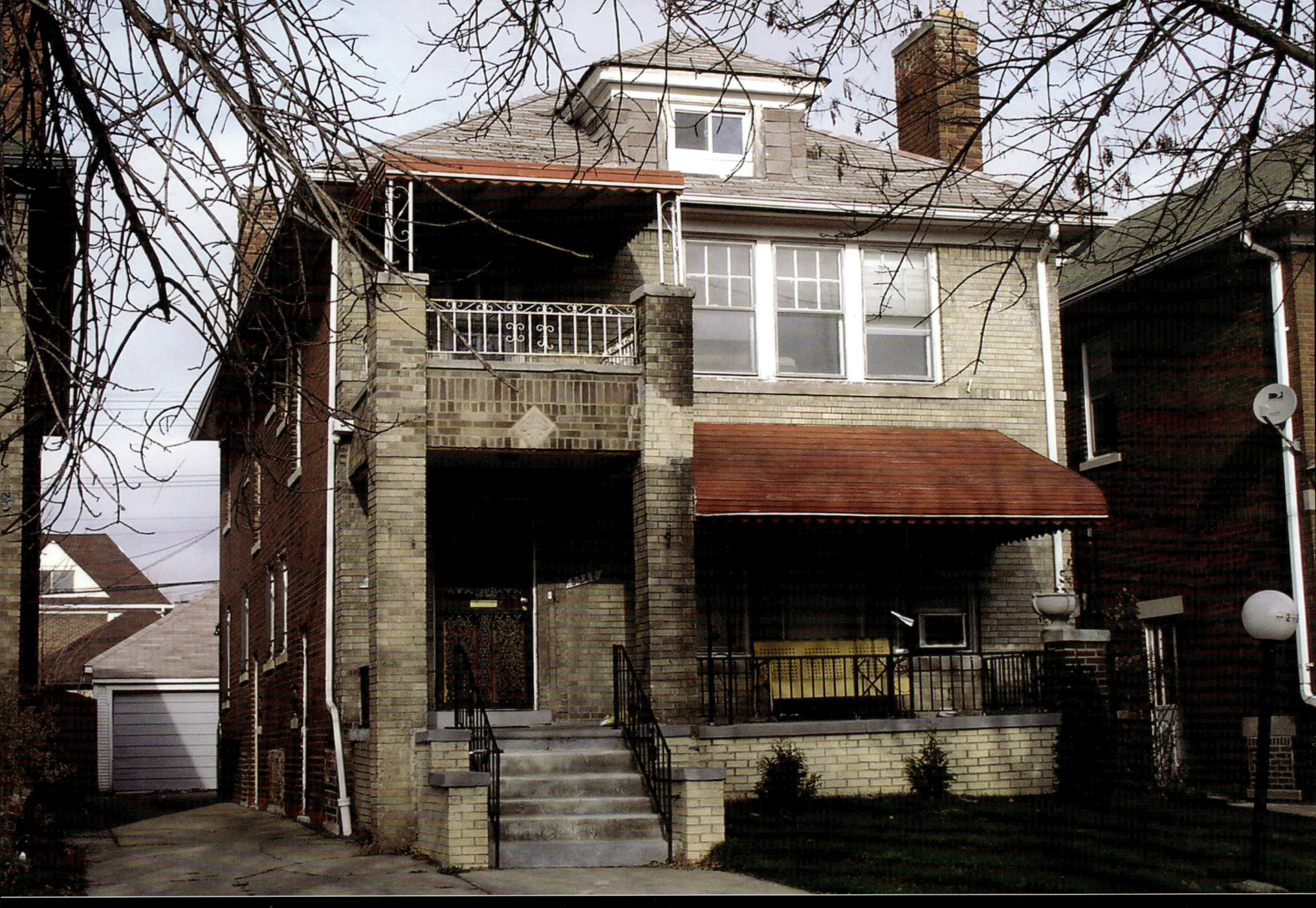

3242 Calvert

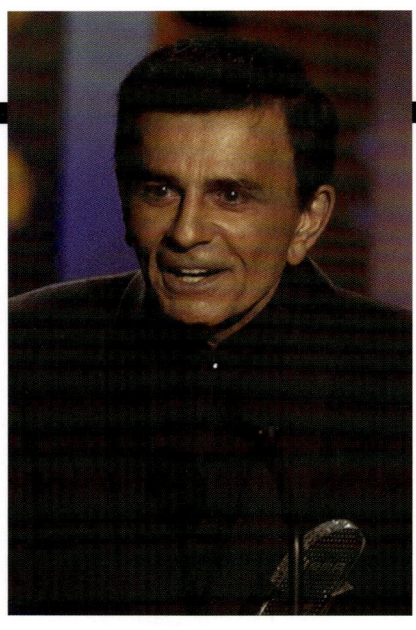

Casey Kasem

Born Kemal Amin Kasem to Amin and Helen Kasem in Detroit, Casey is best known as the host of *American Top 40*. Casey was also the voice of Shaggy in the *Scobbie-Doo* cartoon series and has done many voices for Sesame Street. In 1992, Casey was inducted into the Broadcasters Hall of Fame.

Casey lived in apartment thirteen in the pictured apartment building at 454 Alexandrine, located west of Woodward in the Mid Town area. He also lived down the street at 646 Alexandrine, which is no longer standing. When Casey returned from Korea in the late 1950s he worked as a DJ for WJLB and lived at 3230 Taylor, located on the west side of Detroit. Casey is a proud graduate of Wayne State University and avid supporter Lebanese-American causes.

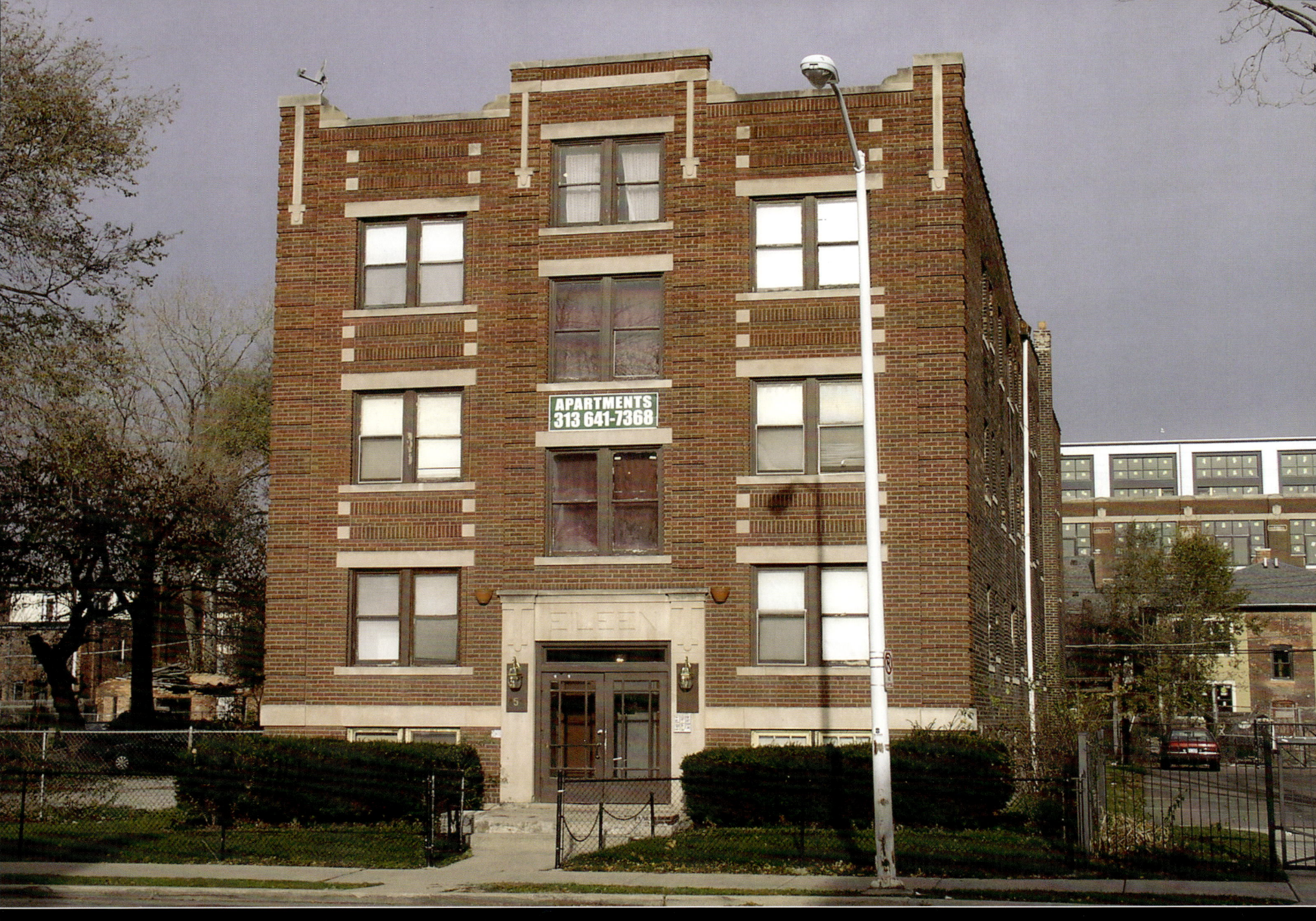

454 Alexandrine

Marvin Mitchelson

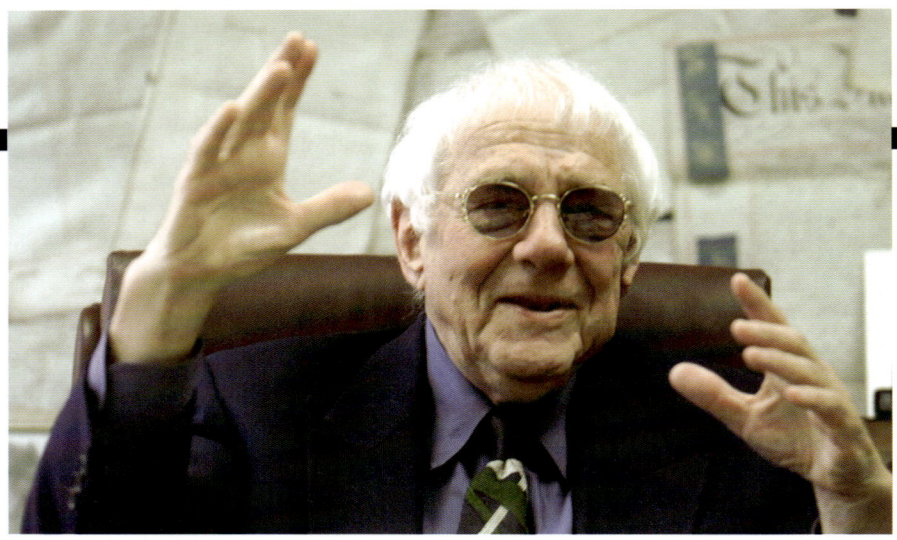

Best known for being the lawyer who developed the concept of palimony, Marvin Michelson was born to Herbert and Sonia Michelson on May 7th, 1928 in Detroit. The family would move to Los Angeles when Marvin was only about a year and a half old. He would go on to become one of the most powerful divorce attorneys in the country. His highly successful career had some speed bumps and he did prison time due to a tax-evasion conviction, resulting in his filing for bankruptcy. Michelson was married to his wife Marcella, for 45 years, until he passed away in 2004. He often joked that his matrimonial success was a bad example for his law practice. Marvin's home is located just north of Davison Avenue, between the Lodge Freeway and 14th Street.

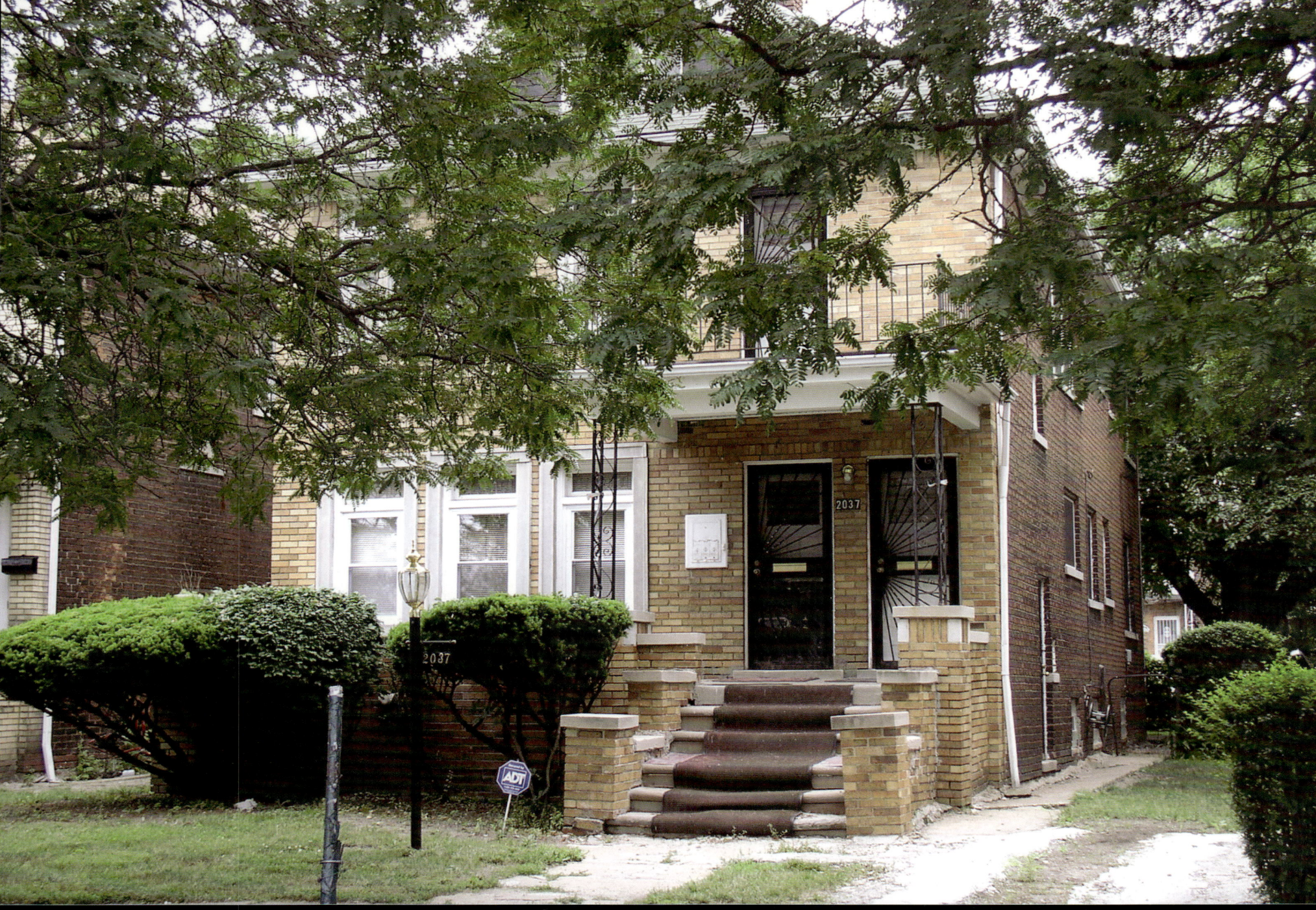

2037 West Grand

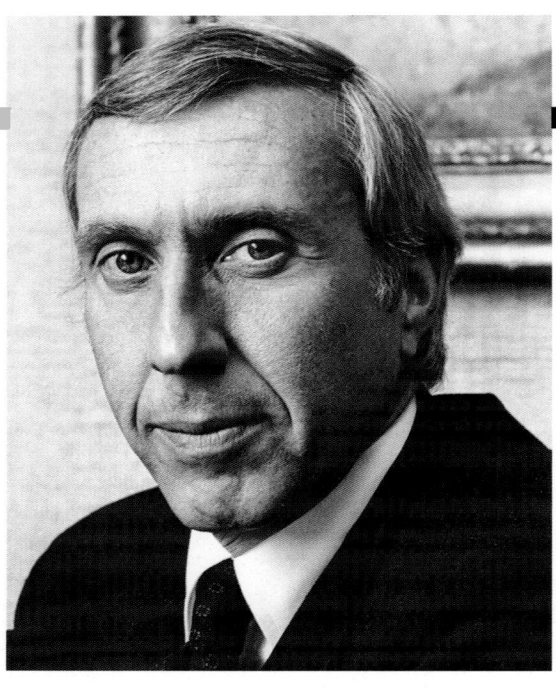

Ivan Boesky

Born on March 6th, 1937 in Detroit, Ivan is best known for the Wall Street insider trading scandal in the 1980s in which he was convicted and received a three-and-a-half year sentence and a $100 million fine. He grew up in Detroit, graduated from Mumford High School, and went on to earn a law degree from the Detroit College of Law.

In 1986 Boesky gave a speech at the University of California where he said, "I think greed is healthy." That speech inspired the "Greed is Good" speech that character, Gordon Gekko, gave in the 1987 movie, *Wall Street*. Ivan's Detroit home is located in the prestigious Palmer Park neighborhood.

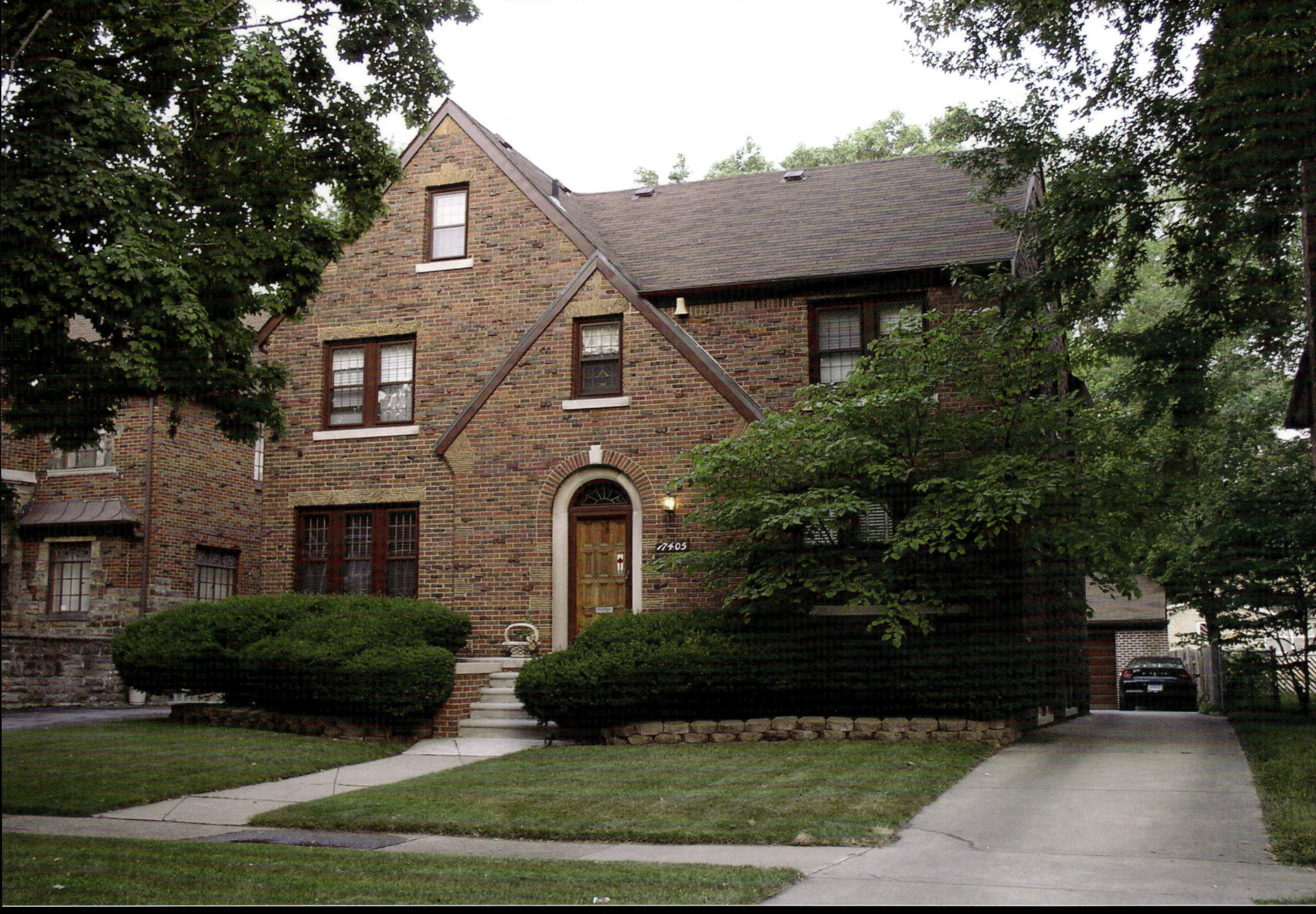

17405 Fairfield

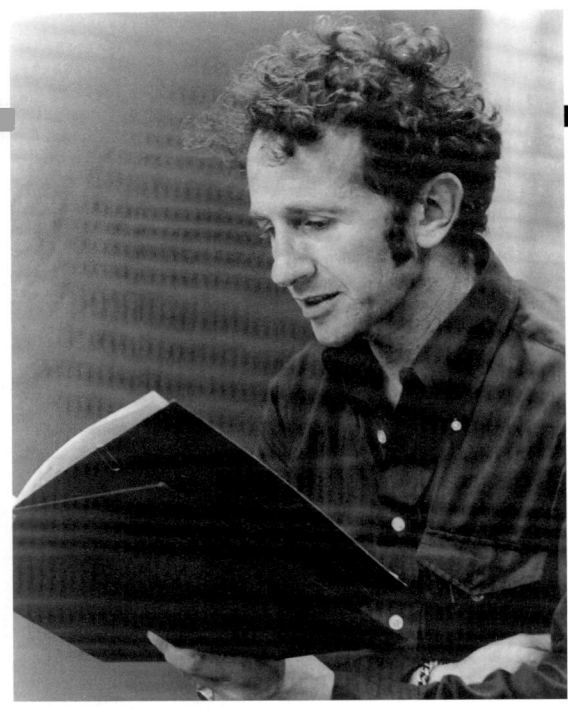

Philip Levine

Pulitzer award-wining poet Harry Levine was born in 1928 in Detroit to Russian-Jewish immigrants, Harry and Esther Levine. Philip spent most of his childhood fighting anti-Semitism due to the fact that Detroit was home to a large Catholic population and Father Coughlin, a fanatical anti-Semite Catholic priest who broadcasted on the radio every Sunday.

Philip attended Wayne State University during the evenings and worked in the local auto plants during the day. The pictured home on Santa Rosa is where he lived when he began to write poetry, it is located a few blocks northwest of the Seven Mile - Livernois intersection.

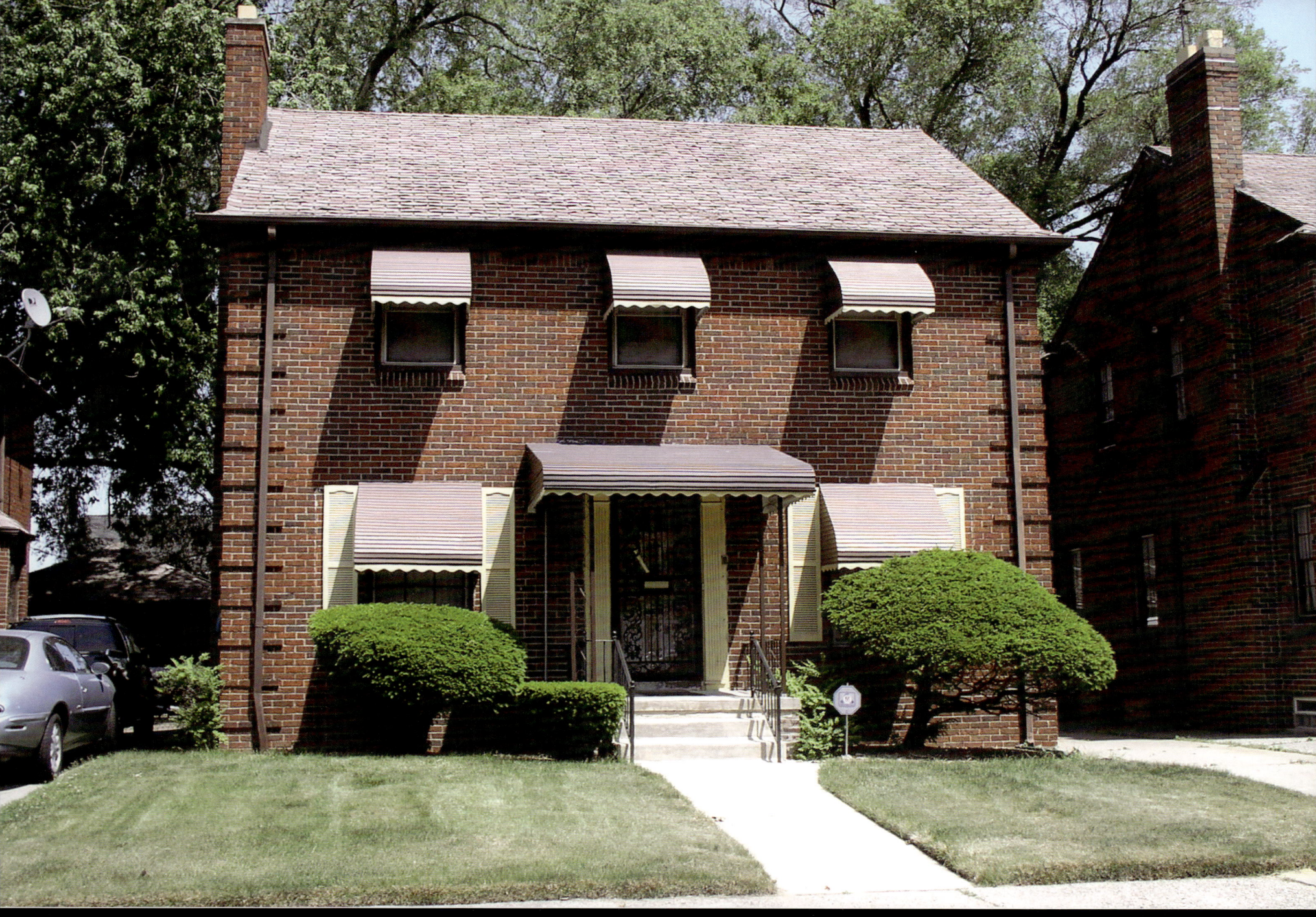

19360 Santa Rosa

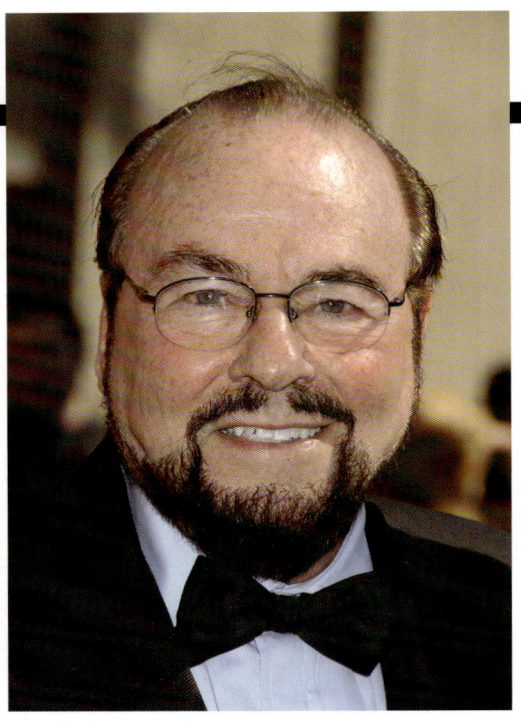

James Lipton

James was born on September 19th, 1926 in Detroit to Betty and Lawrence Lipton, who divorced while James was very young. He is a writer, poet and host of *Inside the Actors Studio* on the Bravo network. In the early 1940s, James played the Lone Ranger's nephew on the Detroit original radio show.

James has appeared on *The Simpsons*, where he played himself, and his show has been parodied on several different programs including *The Howard Stern Show, The Dave Chappelle Show,* and *Saturday Night Live*. James and his mother lived with his grandparents, Abraham and Rose Weinberg in the pictured home during his early childhood. The home is located in the heart of Detroit, just a couple blocks east of Woodward Avenue.

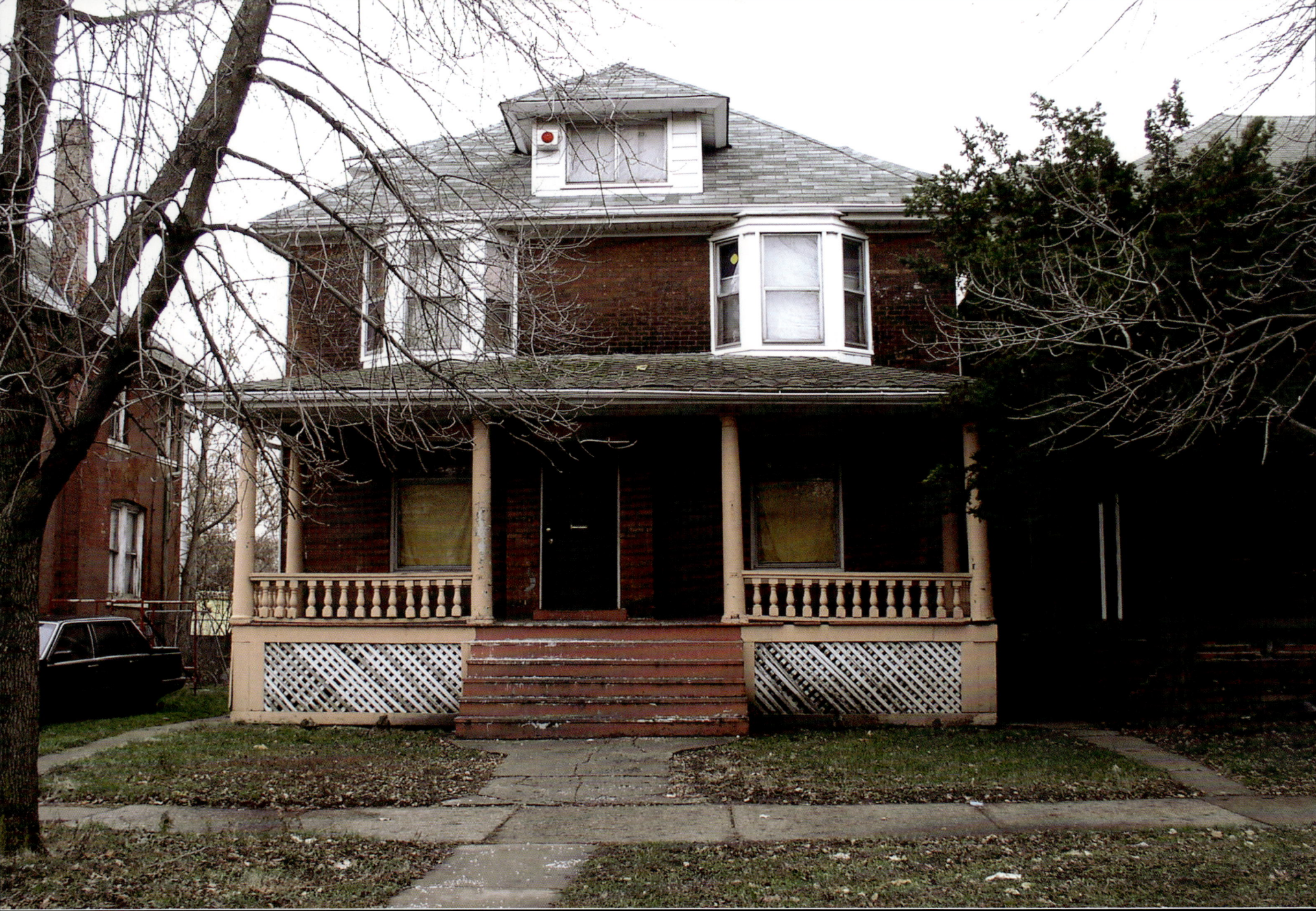

280 Hague

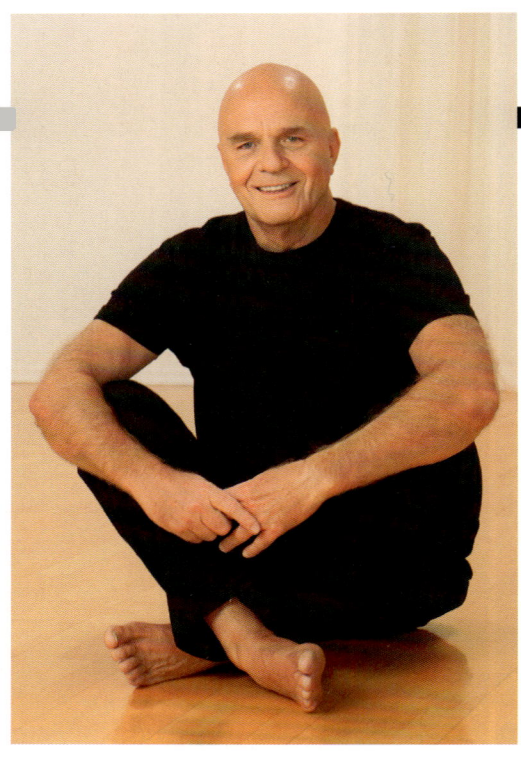

Dr. Wayne Dyer

Dr. Wayne Dyer was born on May 10th, 1940 to Melvin Lyle and Hazel Irene Dyer in Detroit. His father abandoned the family at an early age and Wayne spent the first ten years of his life in local foster homes because his mother could not afford to raise him. She eventually re-married and got back custody of Wayne. He lived in this duplex on Moross while he attended Denby High School.

After graduating from high school, Wayne went on to Wayne State University, he jokes now that the school was named after him. He earned a doctorate in counseling and psychology. Dr. Dyer is a world known self-help advocate, author and speaker. His home is located just a couple blocks west of I-94 on the north side of Moross.

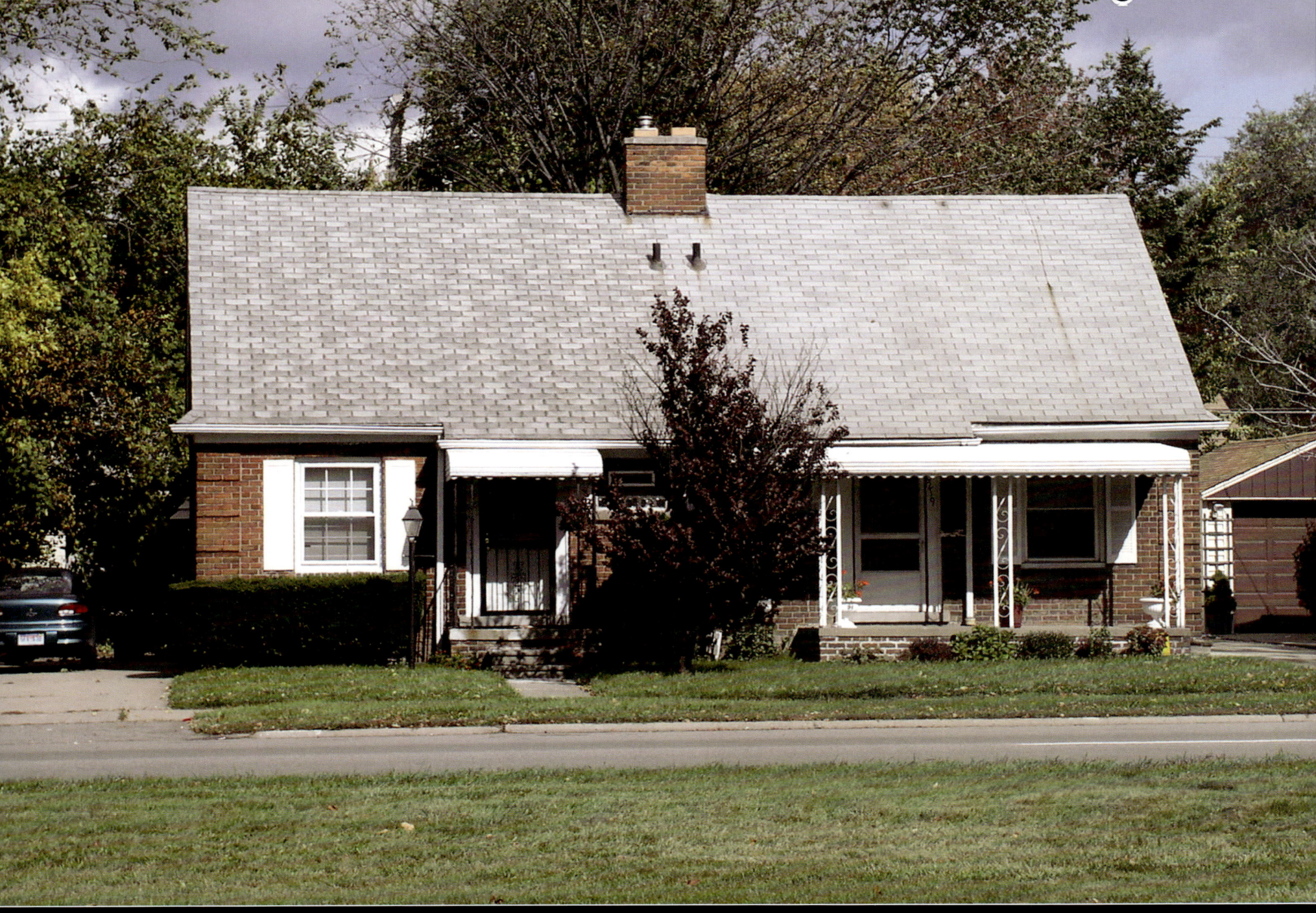

20217 Moross

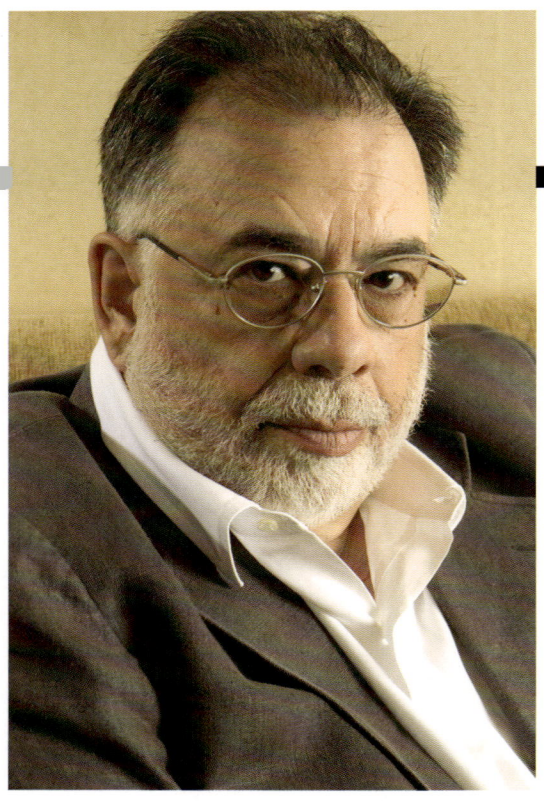

Francis Ford Coppola

Francis was born on April 7th, 1939 in Detroit to composer and musician Carmine Coppola and his wife Italia. He did not live long in Detroit and grew up primarily in Queens, New York. While in film school at UCLA, he worked for another native Detroiter, film producer and director Roger Corman, who as a young child lived at 11641 N. Martindale in Detroit, his home is no longer standing.

Francis has directed and produced some of the biggest movies ever made including Academy Award Best Pictures *The God Father* in 1972 and *The God Father II* in 1974. In 1988, he released *Tucker*, a Man and his Dreams, about an aspiring automaker, Preston Tucker, from Ypsilanti, Michigan. Coppola's father, Carmine, was an investor in the real-life Tucker Company. Francis lived in the pictured home on Kentucky in 1940; it is located just north of Six Mile Road and east of Wyoming.

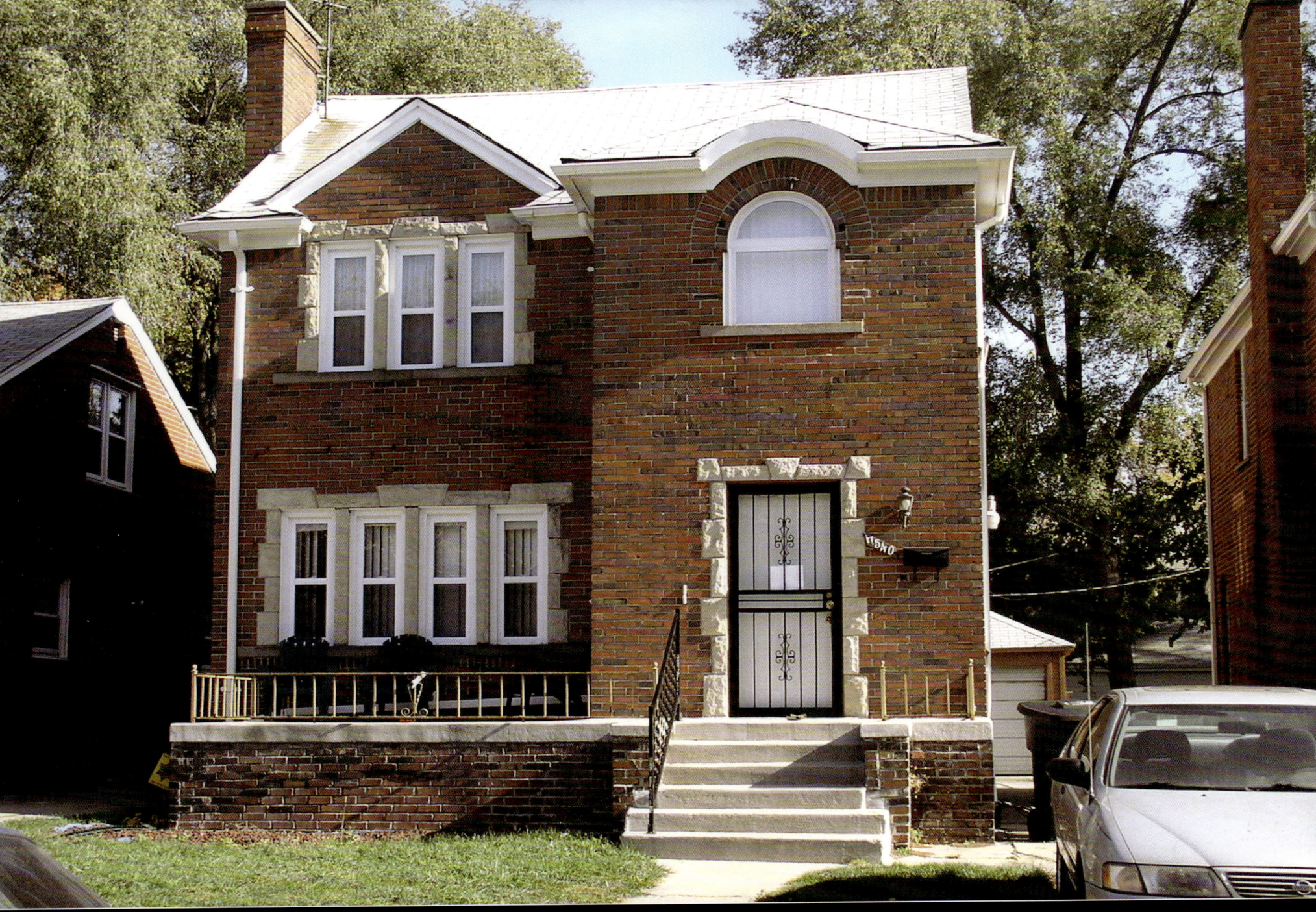

17540 Kentucky

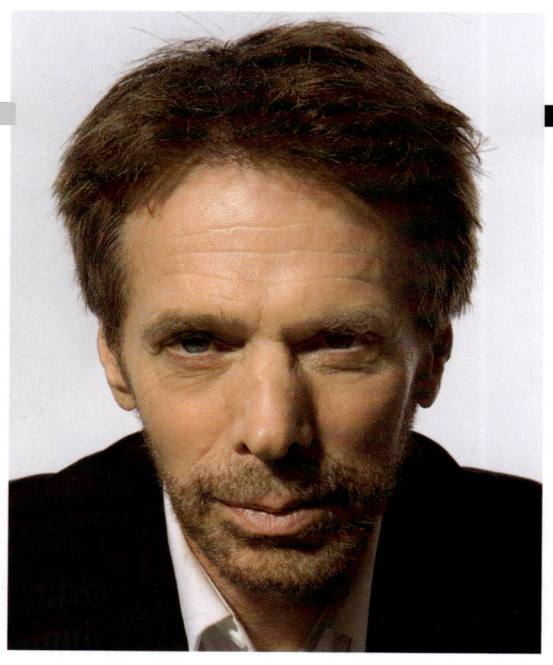

Jerry Bruckheimer

Born Jerome Bruckheimer on September 21st, 1945 in Detroit, the son of Ludwig and Anna Bruckheimer, who were both immigrants from Germany. He grew up living in the pictured home on Ardmore, located in the northwest area of Detroit. His love of movies started when his parents would take him to the local cinemas as a youth. He has produced several blockbuster movies, including *Beverly Hills Cop, Top Gun, and Remember the Titans.*

Jerry also produces the television series, *CSI (Las Vegas, New York, and Miami)* and the reality show *The Amazing Race.* His home is located just east of the Lodge Freeway and south of Eight Mile Road in the northwest area of Detroit. In Jerry's movie *Beverly Hills Cop*, Eddie Murphy's character, Axel Foley, a Detroit Cop, donned a Mumford High School Athletic tee-shirt, which is Jerry's alma mater.

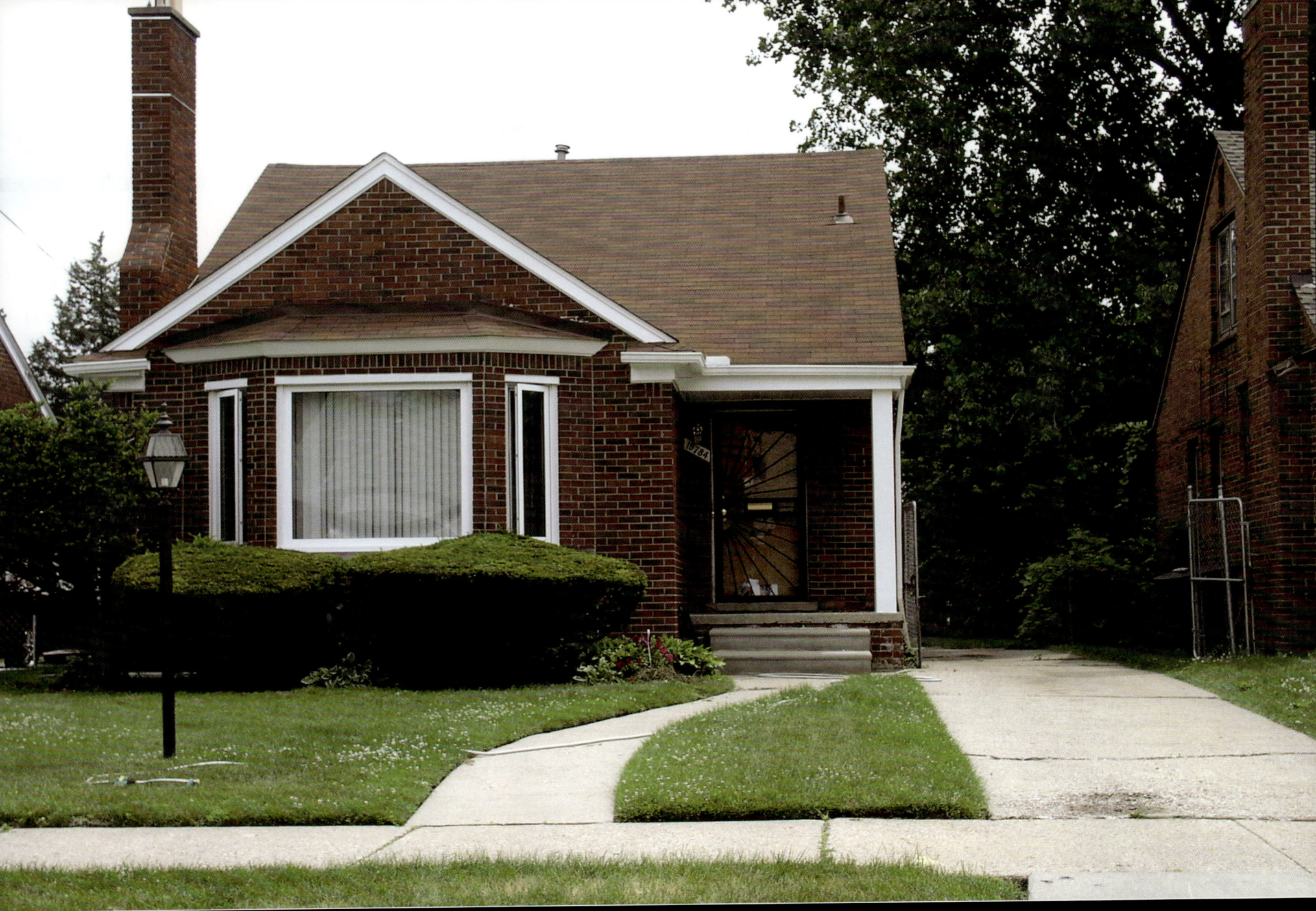

19784 Ardmore

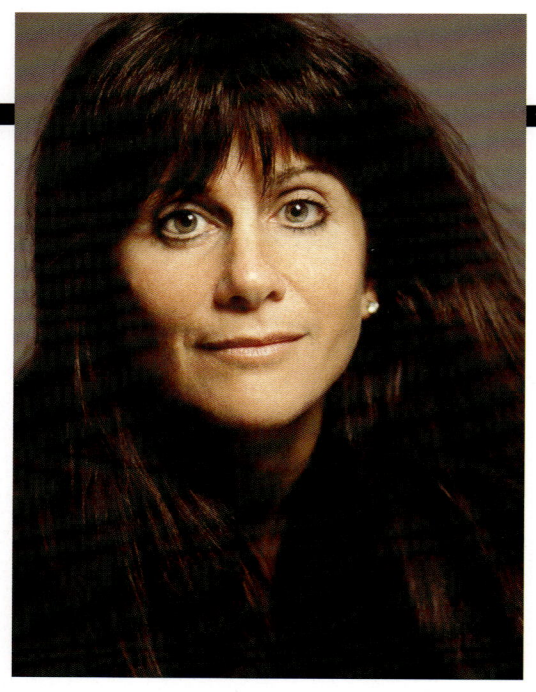

Lynn Goldsmith

Lynn was born on February 11th, 1948 to Shakespeare and Edythe in Detroit. Multi-talented, she is best known as a celebrity portrait photographer and her work has been featured in several national magazines including, *Newsweek, People, and Rolling Stone;* to name a few. While growing up in Detroit, Lynn was a childhood friend of Gilda Radner, who lived just east of her in the Palmer Park area. She moved to Florida, but after graduating high school, she retuned to attend the University of Michigan, where she graduated magna cum laude.

In 1971 Lynn became the youngest person to ever be a member of the Directors Guild of America. Lynn's portraits of Rock and Roll inductees like Bob Dylan, Sid Vicious, and the Beatles have been on display at the Rock and Roll Hall of Fame in Cleveland, Ohio. Lynn's home is located just north of Seven Mile Road and east of Outer Drive.

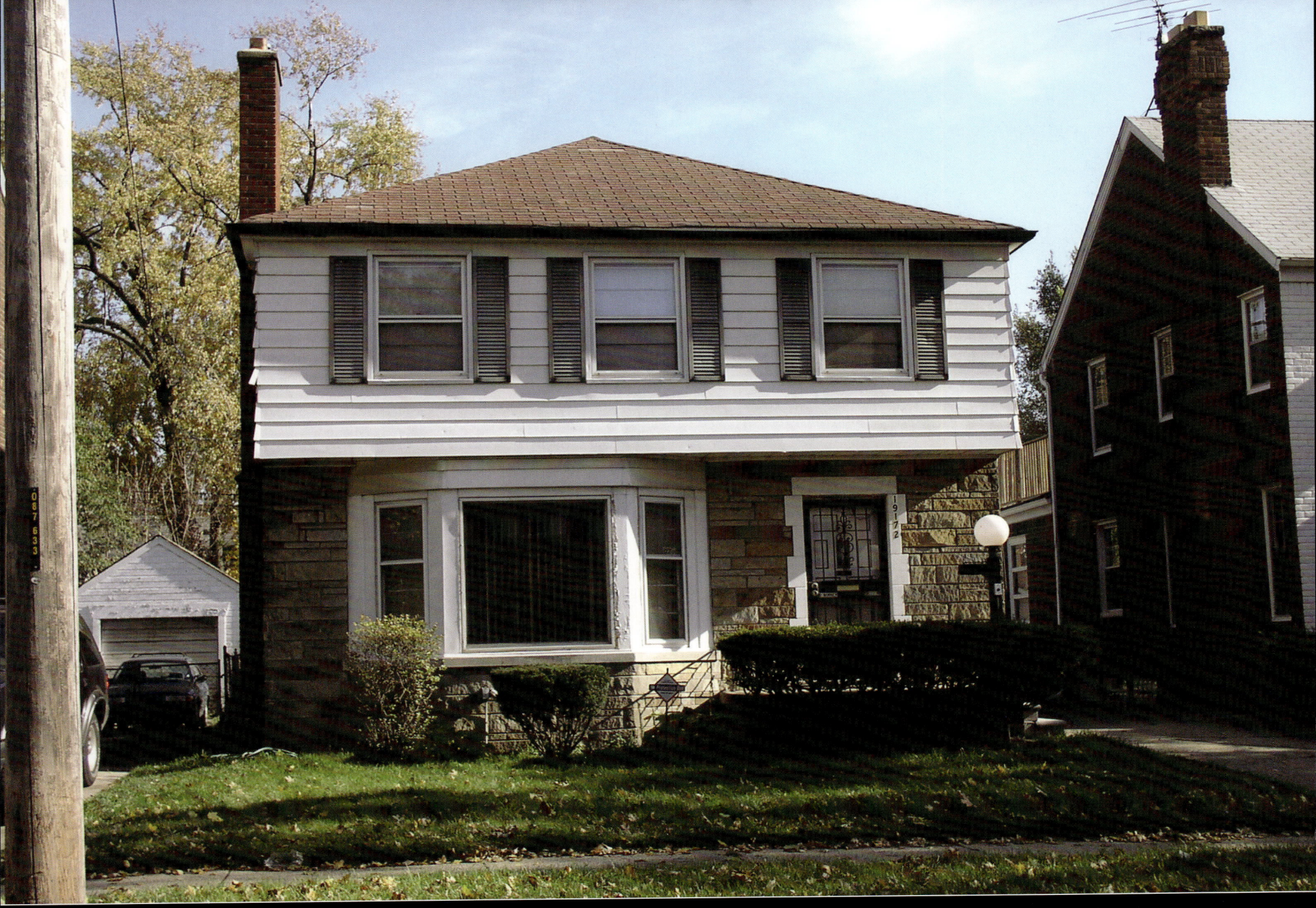

19172 Steel

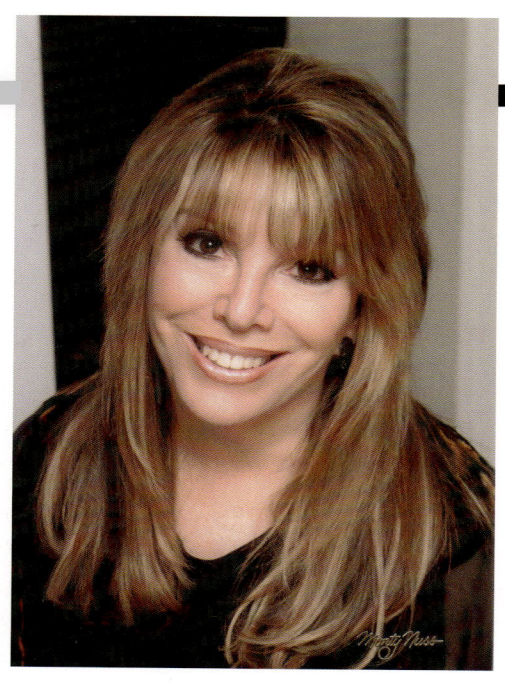

Jackie Kallen

Jackie was born Jackie Kaplan in Detroit in 1946. After graduating from Detroit's Mumford High School in 1964, she started a career in show-business journalism and interviewed many celebrities including the Rolling Stones and Elvis Presley. Kallen became fascinated with boxing after covering Detroit's Thomas "The Hit Man" Hearns and became Hearn's publicist for ten years.

In 1988, Kallen became a boxing manager, something she still does today, living in the Los Angeles area. The movie, *Against the Ropes*, starring Meg Ryan was inspired by Kallen's life and career; she was also a consultant on the reality television show *The Contender*. Jackie's home is located in northwest Detroit; her mother picked a light-colored brick so it would stand out from all the dark brick homes on the street.

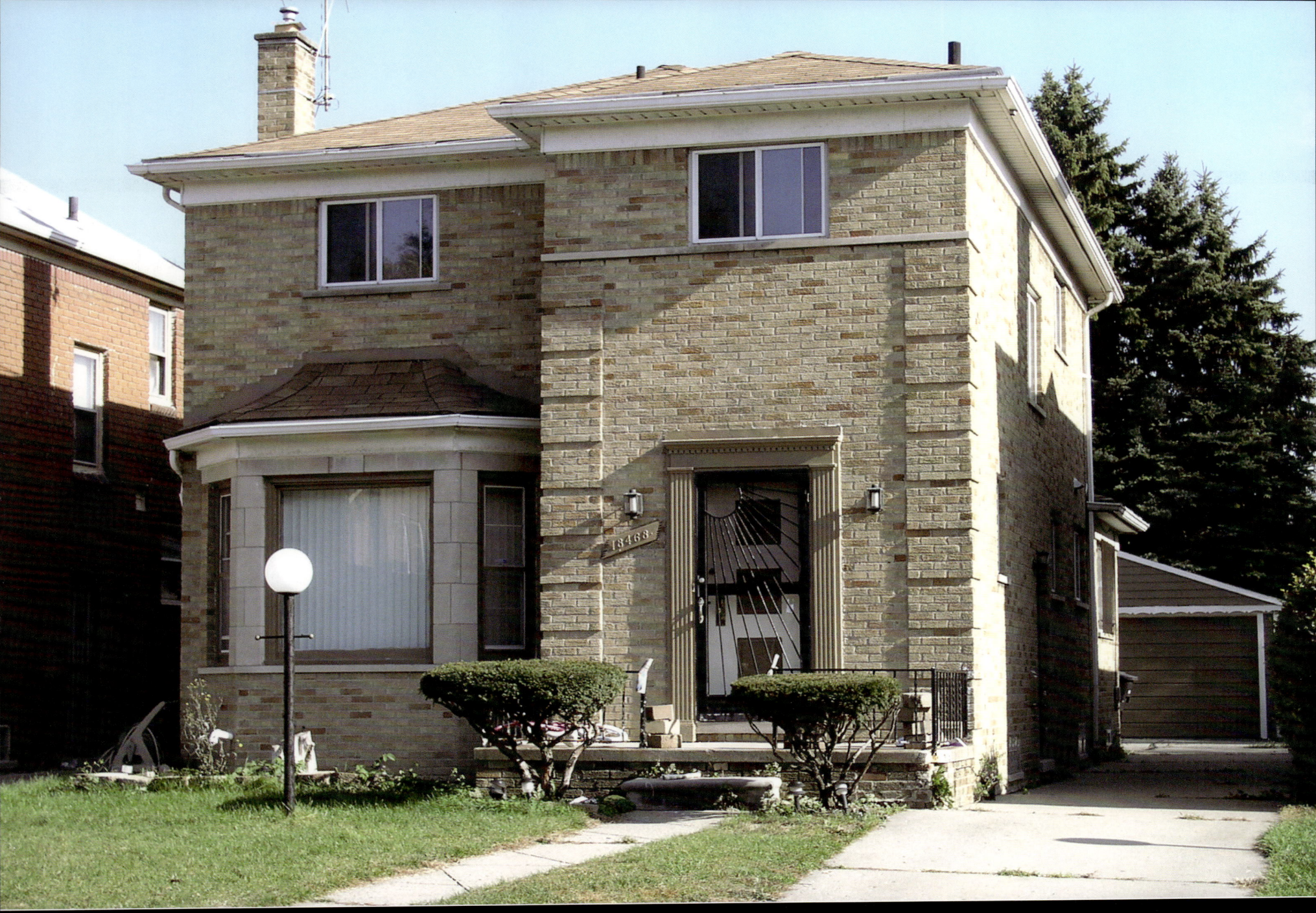

18468 Hartwell

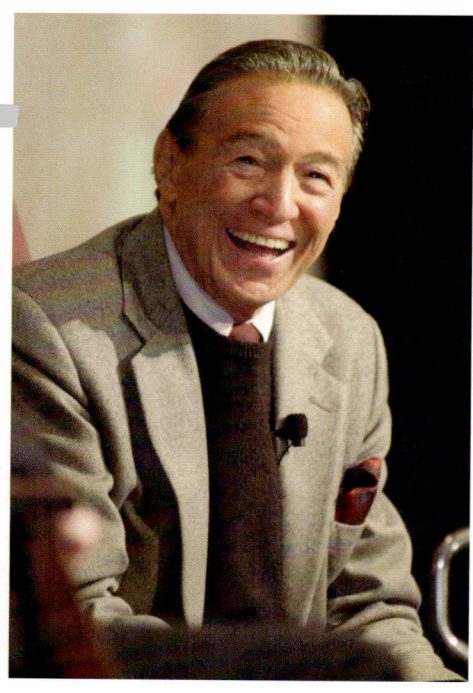

Mike Wallace

Mike was born Myron Leon Wallace on May 9th, 1918 to Frank and Zina Wallace in Massachusetts. After graduating from high school, Mike was off to the University of Michigan due to the support from his uncle who worked in the school's economics department. After college, Mike's career started in Grand Rapids, Michigan and then in 1940, he came to Detroit to work as a newscaster for WXYZ radio. Mike lived in apartment 203 on 2nd Boulevard, just south of Wayne State University.

He joined the Navy in 1943 and served in World War II, after the war he worked for CBS radio as a staff announcer. Mike hosted two night time interview programs but is most well known for his work on CBS's *60 Minutes*. Mike was on 60 Minutes for 37 years, starting in 1968 and ending with his recent retirement from the program in 2006, although he still contributes periodically to the show.

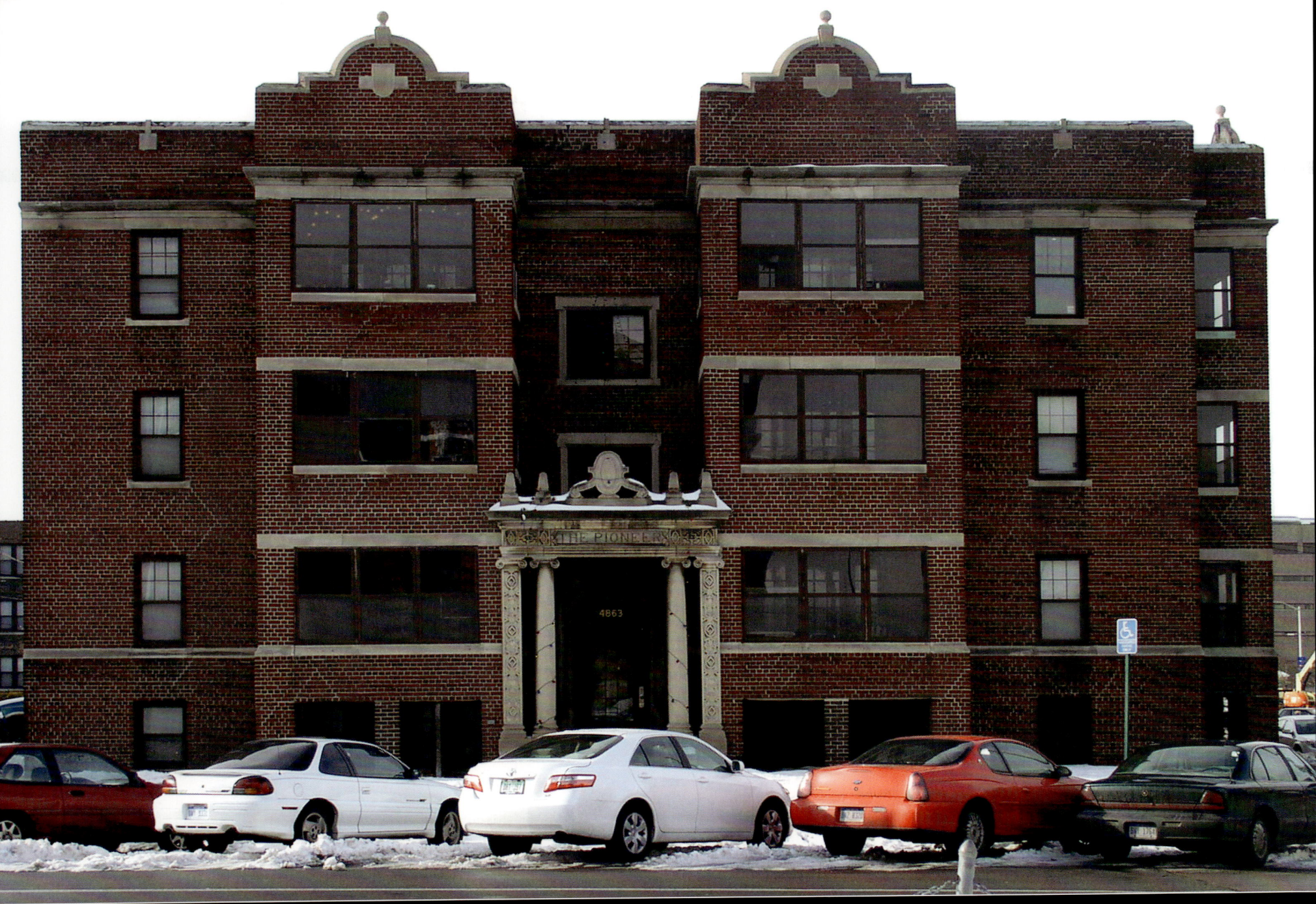

4863 Second Blvd.

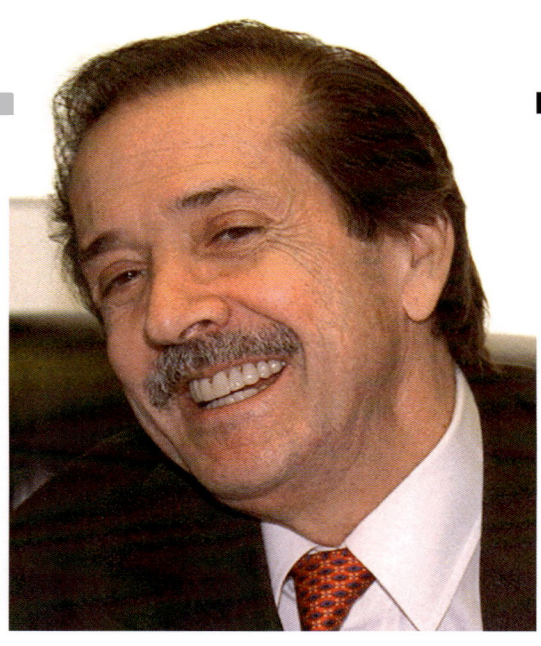

Sonny Bono

Sonny was born Salvatore Phillip Bono on February 16th, 1935 in Detroit. He lived at the pictured home on the city's east side for only a year before his family moved to 11406 Camden Street, that house is no longer standing. Sonny lived in Detroit for about seven years until his family moved out west in 1942.

Sonny is best known for being married to Cher and forming the entertainment duo, Sonny & Cher. Sonny wrote and produced the couple's biggest hits including *I Got You Babe*. The duo act ended when the two divorced and went their separate ways in 1975. Sonny eventually became a U.S. Senate Representatives for California but tragically died on January 5th, 1998 from a head injury, suffered in a skiing accident.

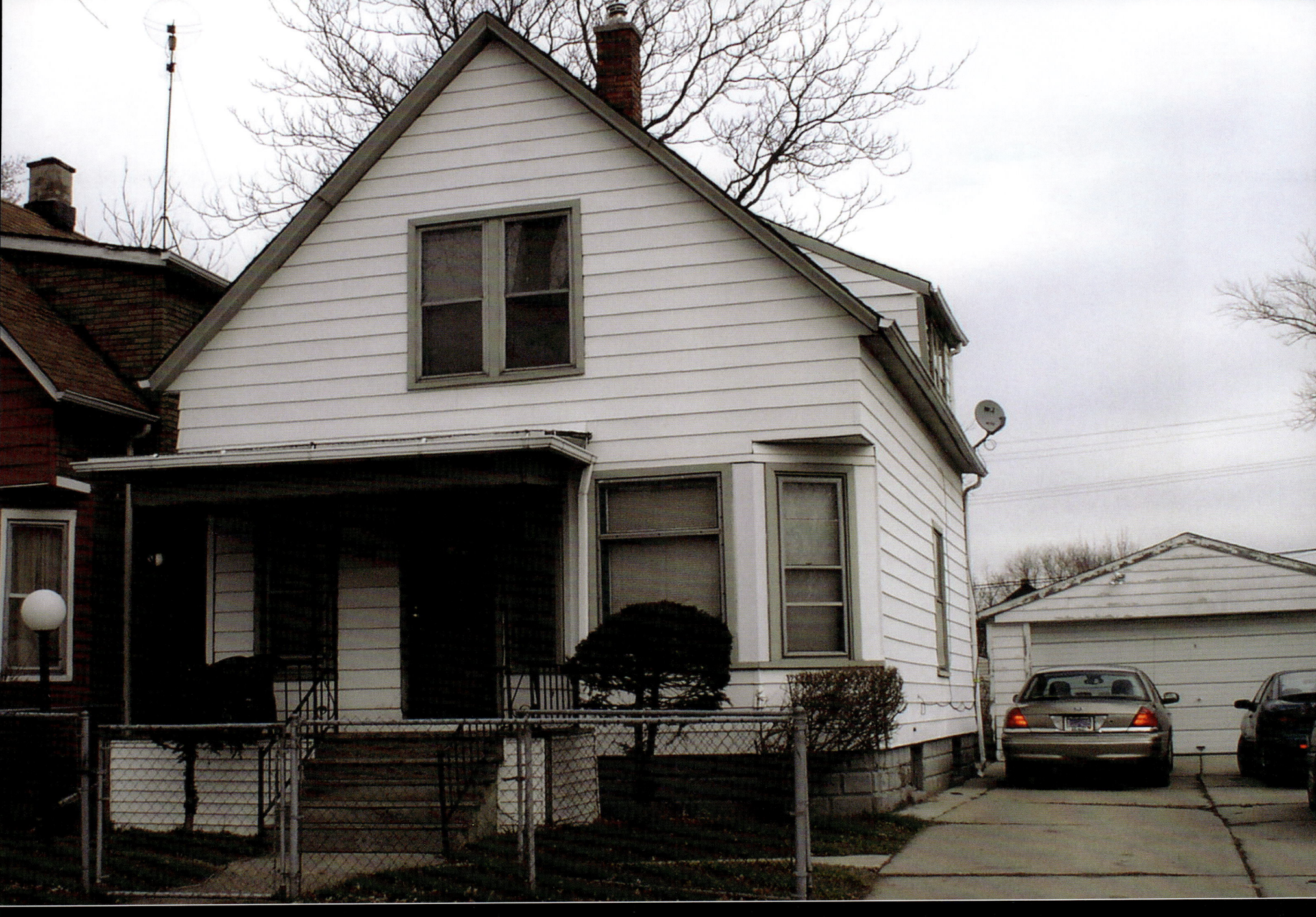

5380 Holcomb

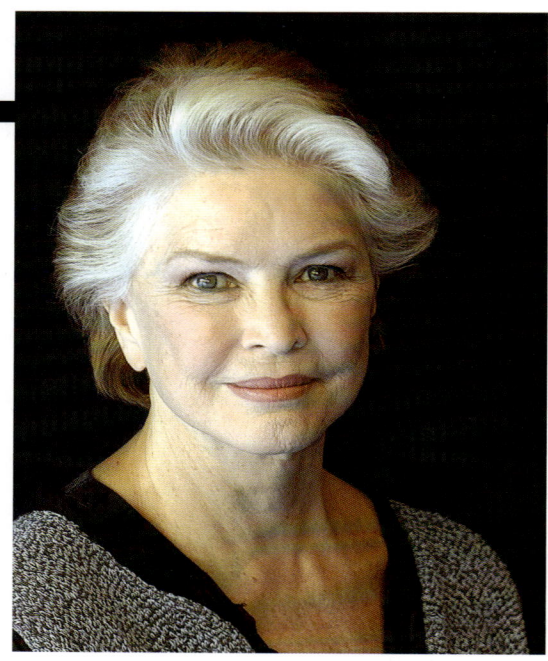

Ellen Burstyn

Ellen was born Edna Rae Gillooly on December 7th, 1932 in Detroit. Edna graduated from Cass Technical High School, after which she went to Texas to model and then on to New York as a showgirl on *The Jackie Gleason Show*. She later took some time off to study acting at the Actors Studio, with Lee Strasberg, which subsequently led to an award-winning acting career.

Her breakthrough role was in the 1971 movie, *The Last Picture Show*, for which she was nominated for an Academy Award for Best Supporting Actress. Ellen would later win the Best Actress award for her performance in *Alice Doesn't Live Here Anymore*. For most of her childhood, Ellen lived in the upper flat at the pictured 3271 Hazelwood. At age fourteen, she moved next door when her mother and husband purchased the home at 3277 Hazelwood. These homes are located on the west side of Detroit, just north of West Grand Boulevard and east of Dexter.

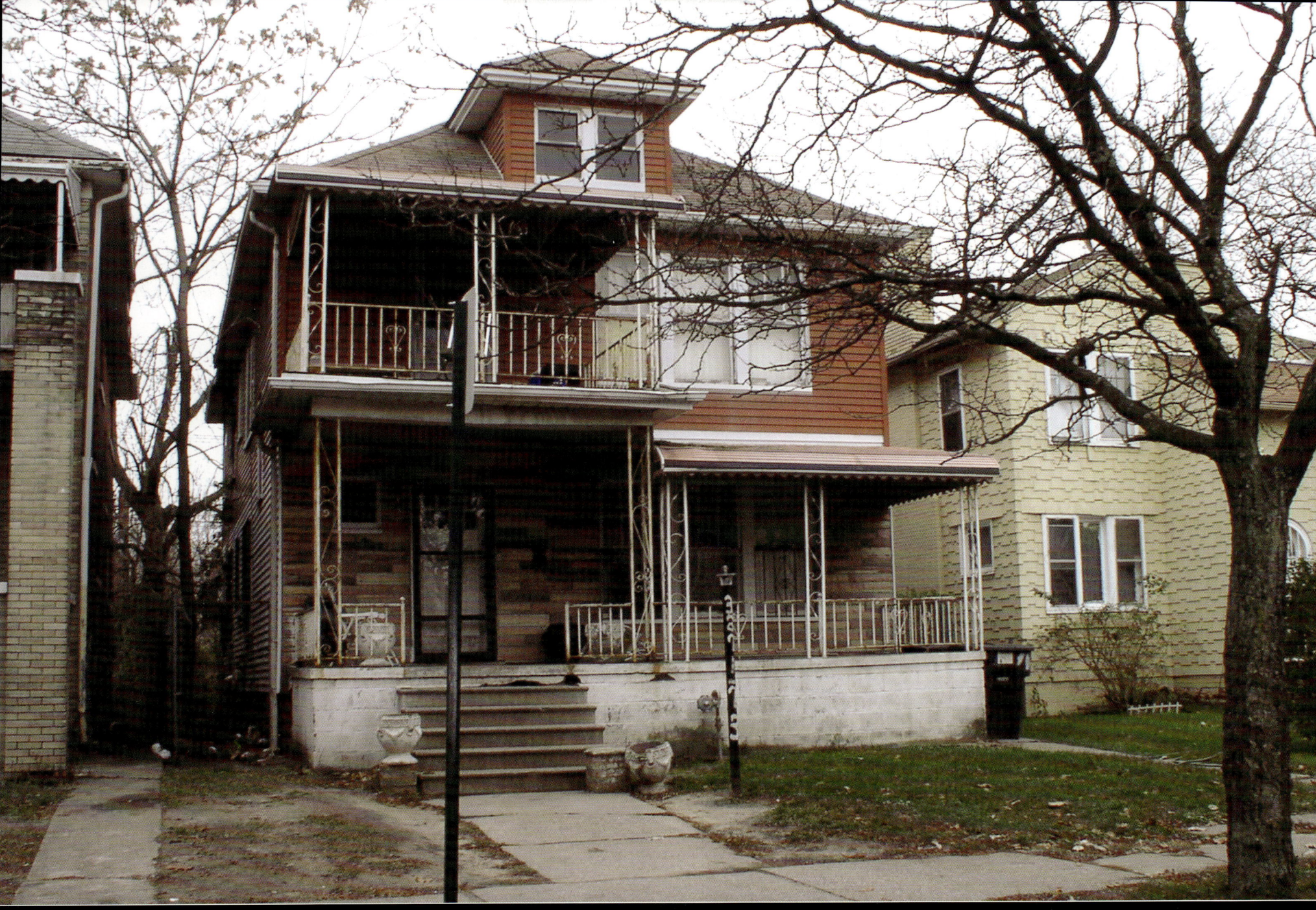

3271 Hazelwood

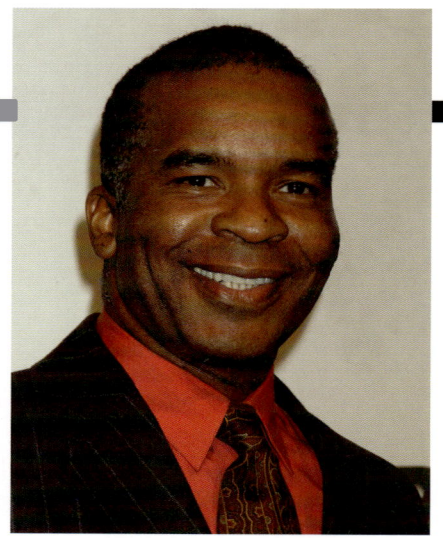

David Allen Grier

David Allen Grier was born to William H. and Aretas Grier on June 30th, 1955 in Detroit. After graduating from Cass Technical High School in Detroit, David earned a Bachelor's Degree from the University of Michigan and a Master of Fine Arts degree from Yale. He became a star in the Emmy Award-winning sketch comedy show *In Living Color* and has been in several movies including *Boomerang*, *Jumanji*, and *Streamers*. His home is located on the city's west side between the Lodge Freeway and Linwood Avenue.

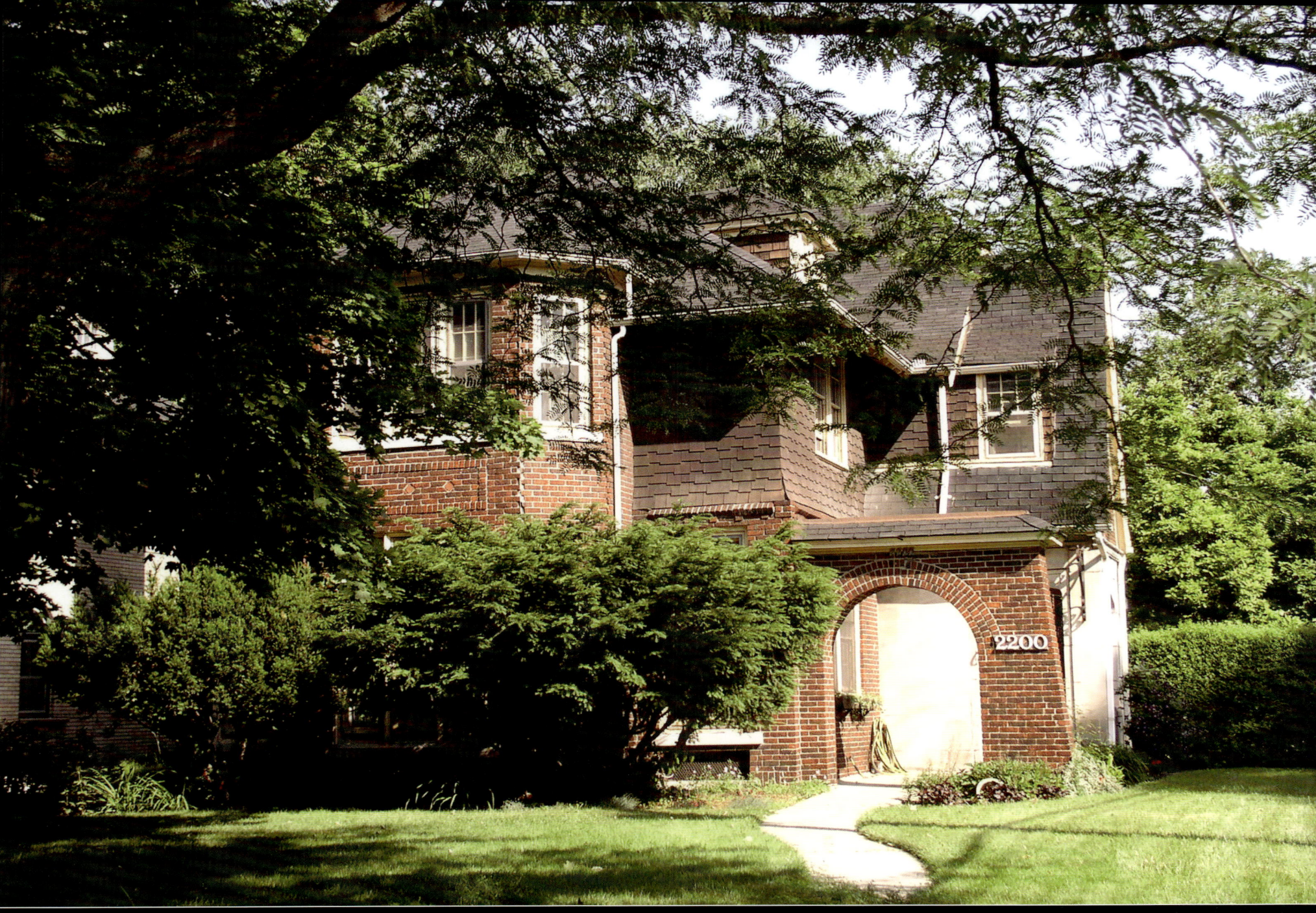

2200 West Boston

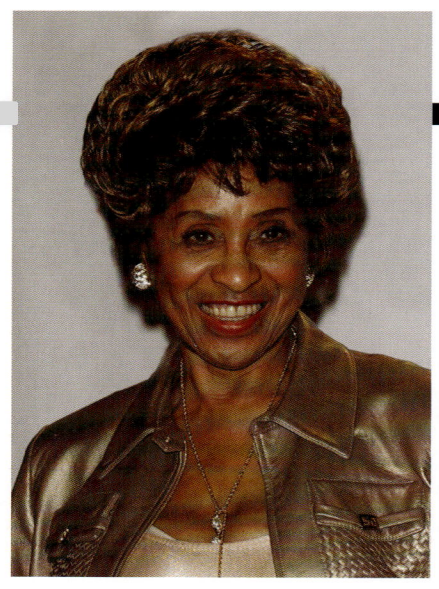

Marla Gibbs

Best known as Florence, the maid, on the television series, *The Jeffersons,* Marla was born Margaret on June 14th, 1931 in Chicago. Marla moved to Detroit, where she worked as a switchboard operator at the legendary Gotham Hotel, located at John R and Orchestra Place. Her first acting experience came on the local *People's Court* television show.

Marla was working for United Airlines when she was transferred from Detroit to Los Angeles, in 1971. She lived at the pictured residence on Clements Street in the late 1960s before moving to California. The house is located two blocks north of Davison and east of Livernois.

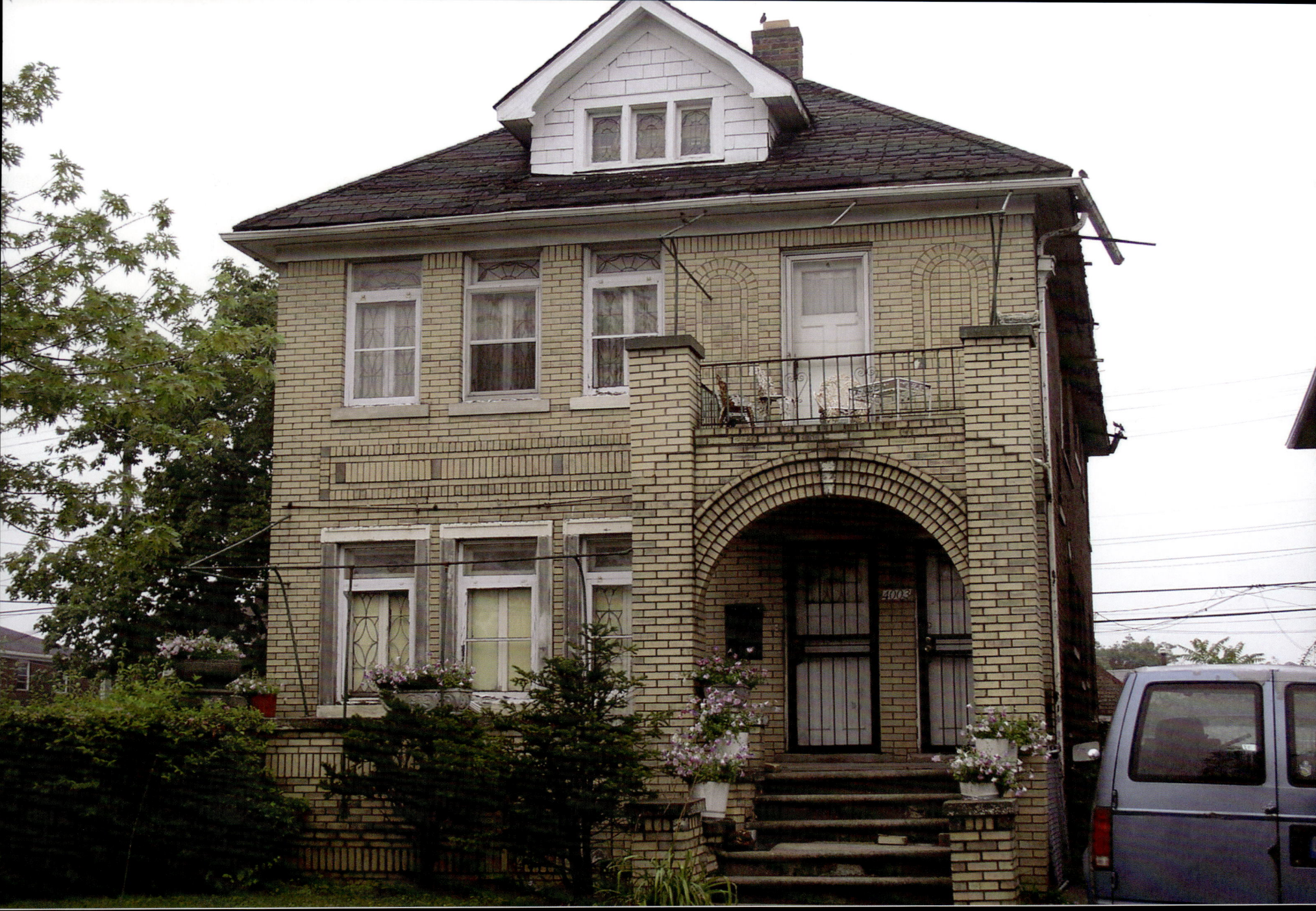

4003 Clements

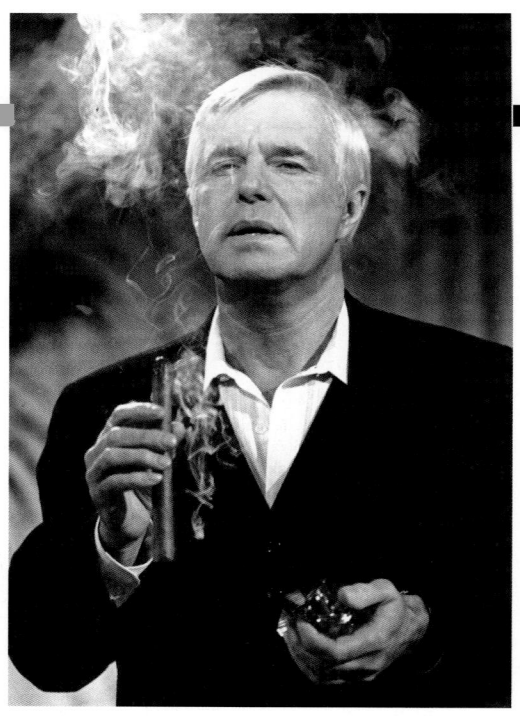

George Peppard

Born to parents George and Vernelle on October 1st, 1929 in Detroit. George Jr. spent his early childhood in Detroit but graduated from Dearborn High School. He is best known for his role as Col. John "Hannibal" Smith on the television show, *The A-Team*. He became jealous of "Mr. T's" stardom on the show and would only communicate with Mr. T through cast members. George was 65 when he passed away on May 8th 1994. George's home is located just a few blocks west of Woodward in the heart of Detroit.

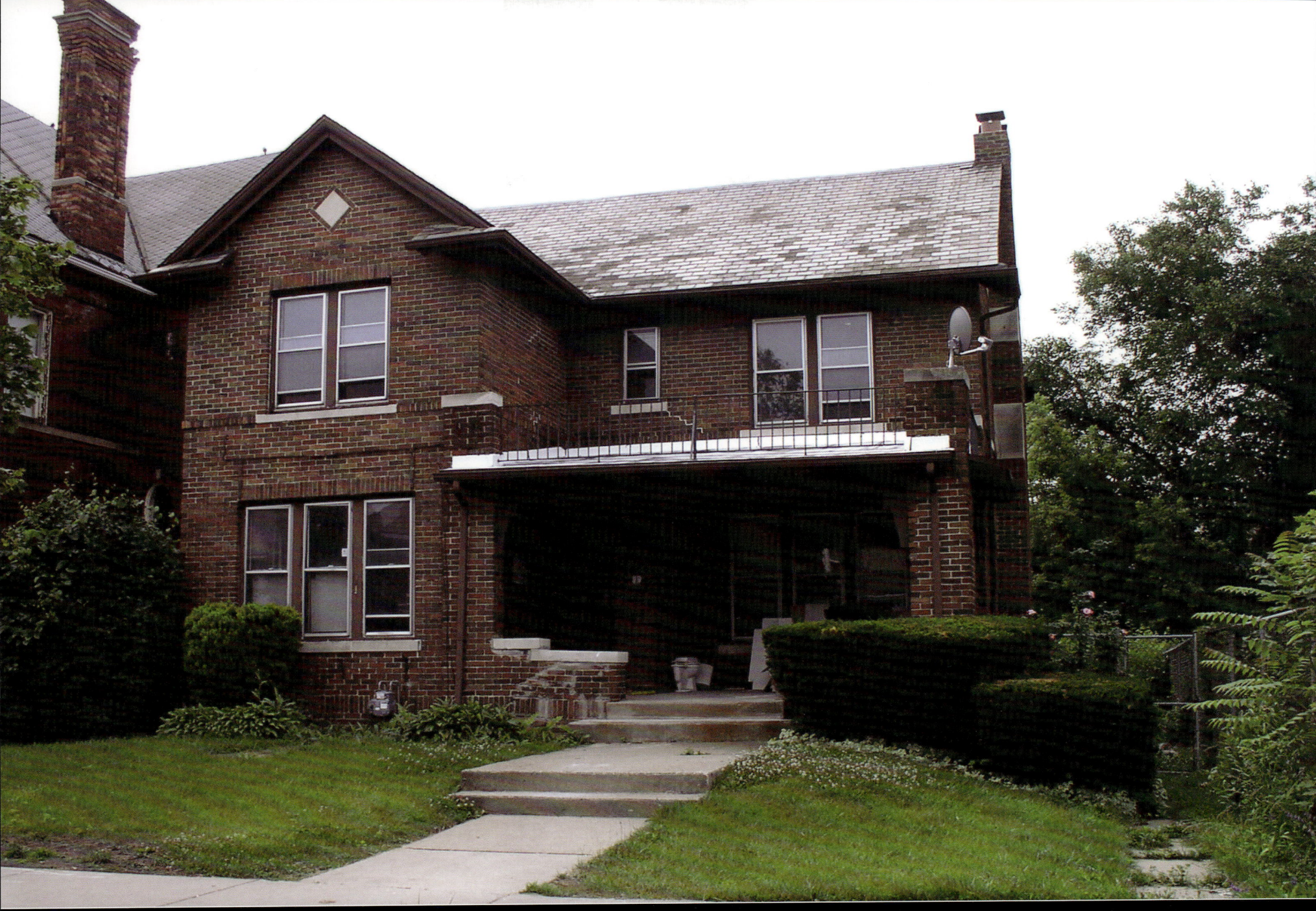

99 Burlingame

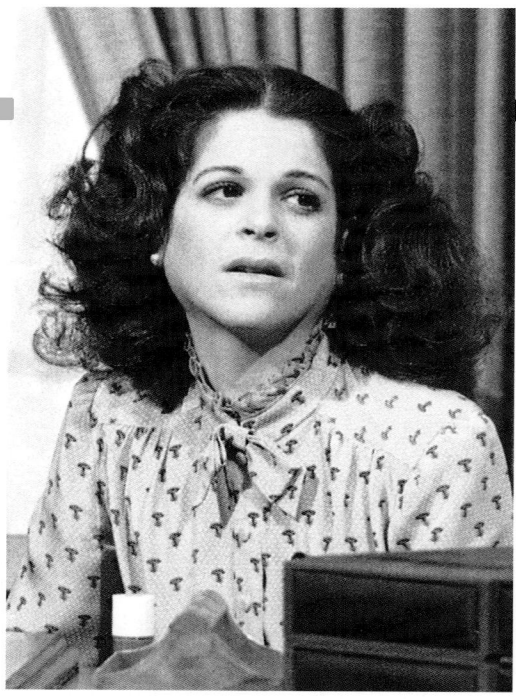

Gilda Radner

Gilda was born on June 28th, 1946 to Herman and Henrietta Radner in Detroit. Gilda's mother did not like the cold Detroit winters so the family split time between Detroit and Florida. Gilda grew up in Detroit but attended University Liggett School in Grosse Pointe and went on to study drama at the University of Michigan.

Gilda is best known for her five years as part of the original cast of *Saturday Night Live* and her most famous character, Roseanne Roseannadanna. Gilda died of ovarian cancer at age of 42. Her legacy lives on through Gilda's Club, an organization started by her husband, Gene Wilder, and others to provide cancer patients a place to go for information and support. The Gilda's Club Metro Detroit is located at 3517 Rochester Road in Royal Oak. Gilda's pictured home is located in the southern portion of the Palmer Park neighborhood.

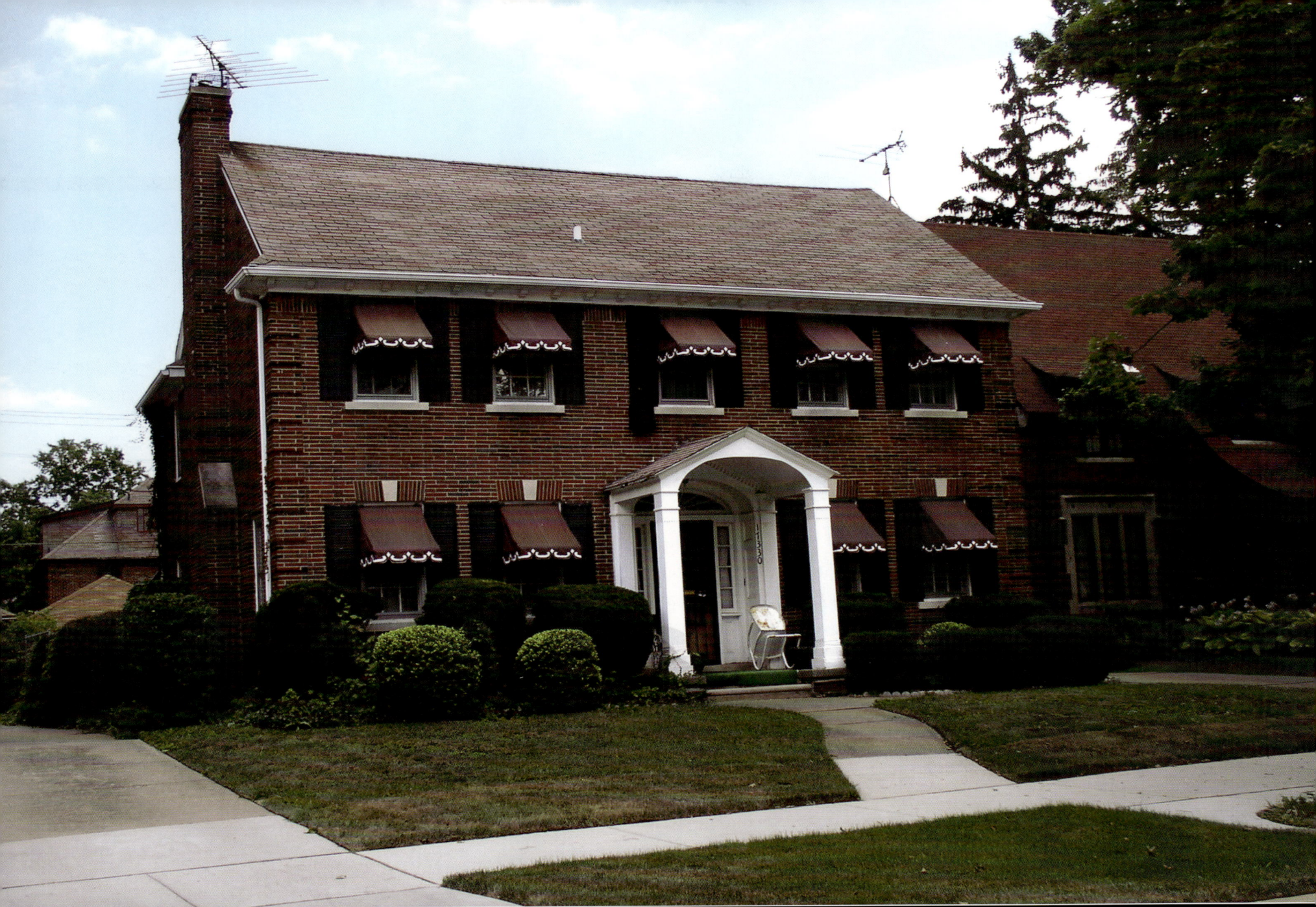

17330 Wildemere

George C. Scott

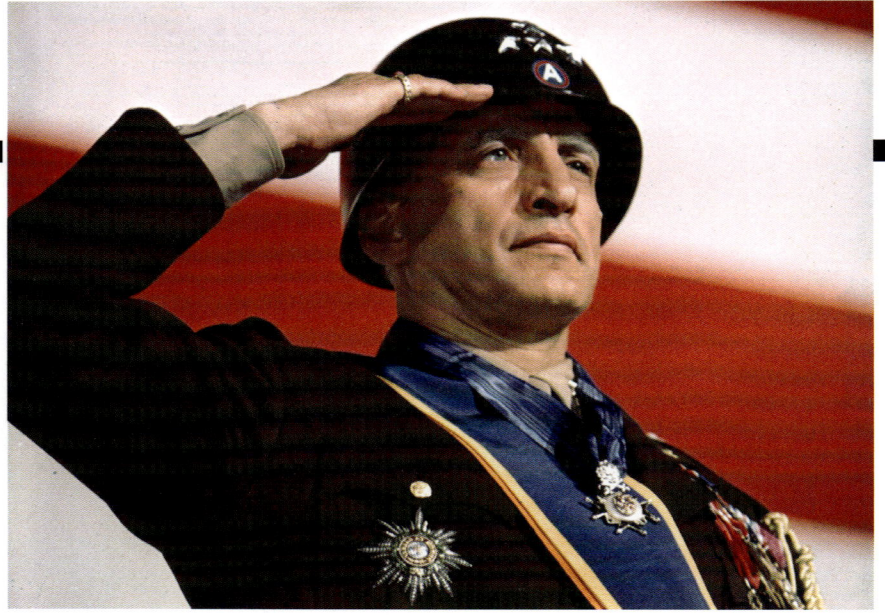

George C. was born on October 18th, 1927 in Wise, West Virginia; his father moved the family to Pontiac, Michigan in the early 1930s and then to Detroit. His mother died just before he was eight, and he was raised by his sister Helen, stepmother Betty, and father George Dewey Scott, who was an auto executive. He lived at the residence on Pennington in the early 1940s and graduated from Redford High School in Detroit.

He is best known for his performance as General George S. Patton, Jr. in the Academy award-winning movie, *Patton*. Scott created a stir when he did not attend the 1970 Academy Award ceremony and retuned his Oscar because he did not feel he was in competition with other actors. The house is located on the west side of the Palmer Park neighborhood, just a few houses south of Seven Mile Road.

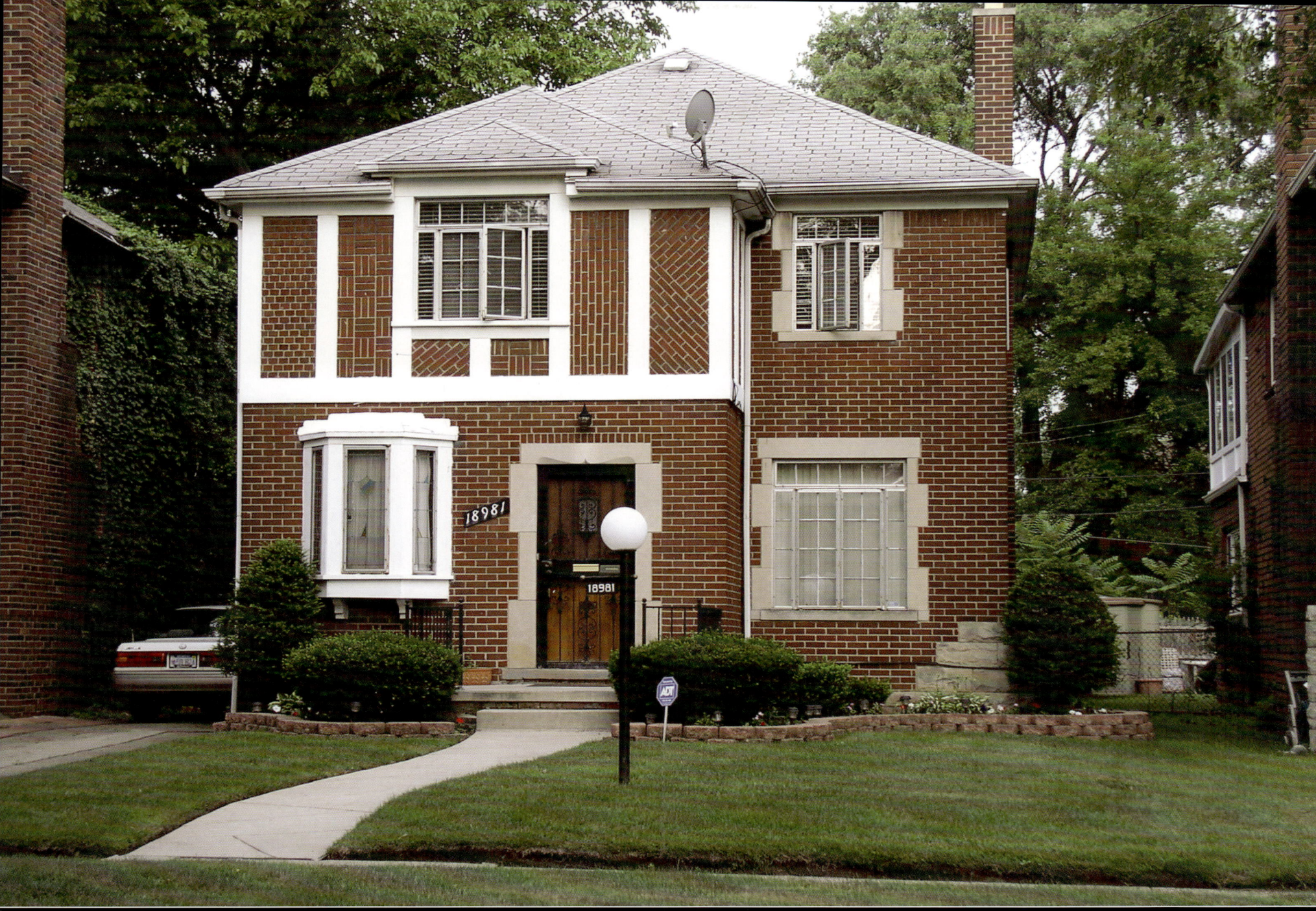

18981 Pennington

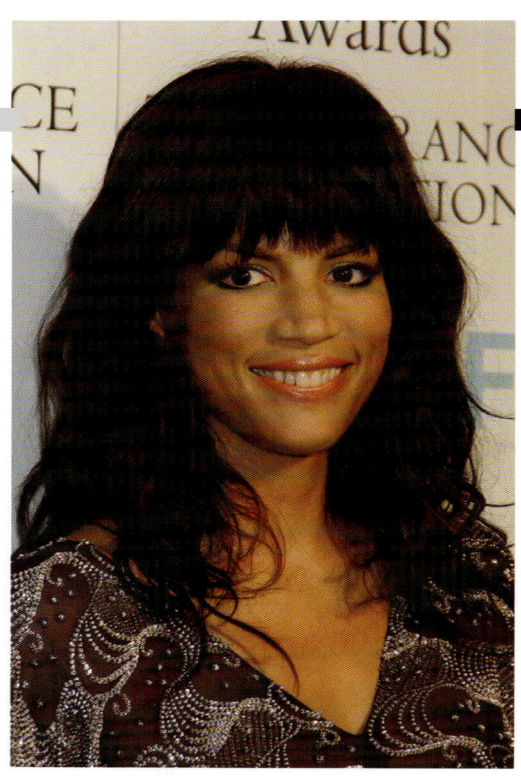

Veronica Webb

Veronica was born on February 23rd, 1965 to parents Doug and Marion Webb in Detroit. After graduating for the Waldorf School in Detroit in 1983, Veronica moved to New York to attend college and pursue a modeling career. She became the first black supermodel to score a major cosmetics campaign in 1992 with Revlon. She has also had roles in several movies including the 1991 movie, *Jungle Fever* and the 1992 critically acclaimed, *Malcolm X*.

Webb is involved in several charities including LIFEBeat and the RPM Nautical Foundation, and is the co-host of the *Tim Gunn's Guide to Style* on the Bravo network. Her home is located a few blocks west of the historic Indian Village neighborhood on the city's east side.

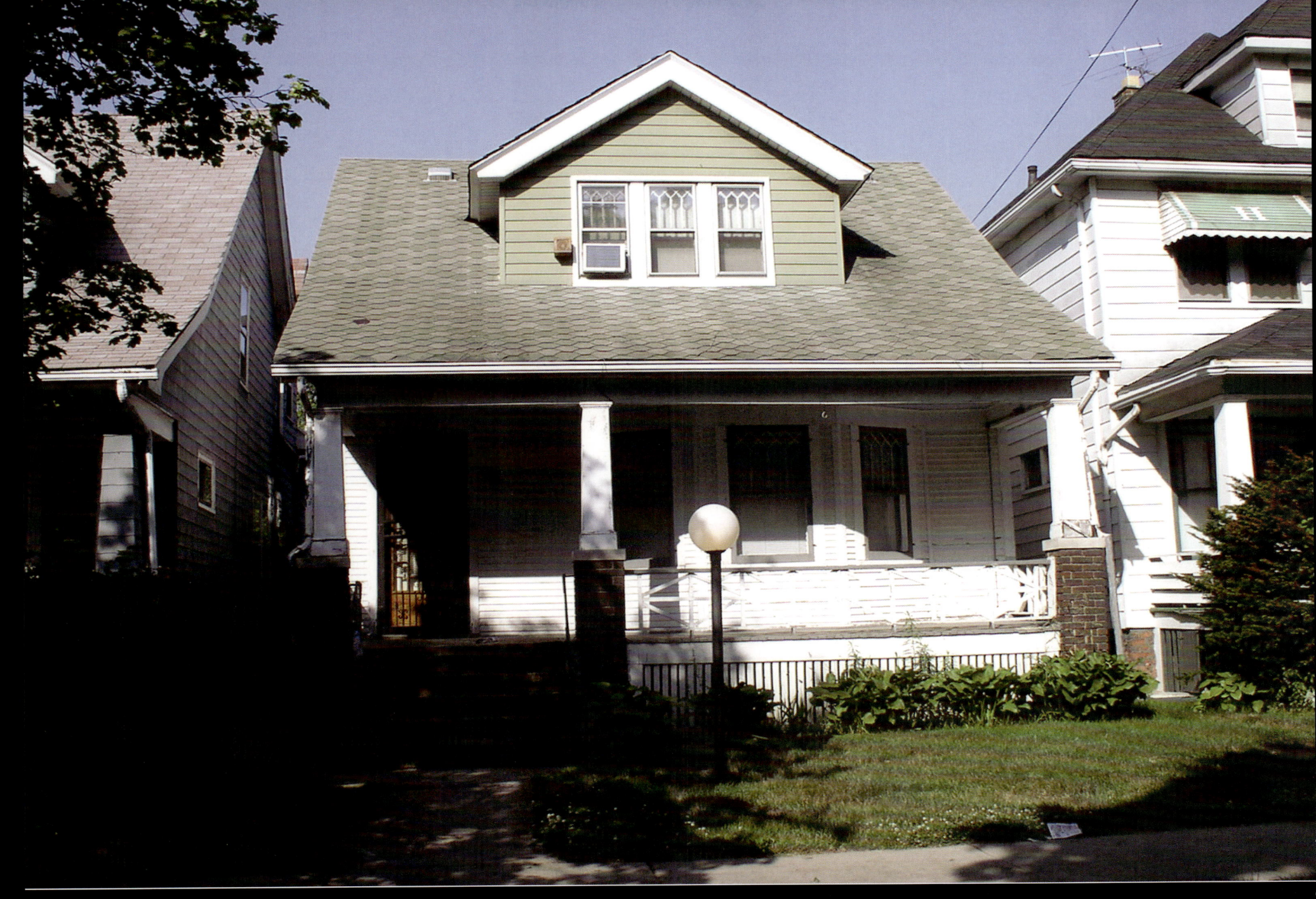

4187 Burns

1. Archer, Dennis
2. Ballard, Florence
3. Bettis Jerome
4. Boesky, Ivan
5. Bono, Sonny
6. Bruckheimer, Jerry
7. Burstyn, Ellen
8. Cobb, Ty
9. Coppola, Francis Ford
10. DeBusschere, Dave
11. DeLorean, John
12. Dodge, John
13. Dyer, Wayne
14. Eliot, Sonny
15. Ford, Henry
16. Franklin, Aretha
17. Franklin, Melvin
18. Gaye, Marvin
19. Gibbs, Marla
20. Glanville, Jerry
21. Goldsmith, Lynn
22. Gordy Jr., Berry
23. Grier, David Allen
24. Haywood, Spencer
25. Hoffa, Jimmy
26. Illitch, Mike & Marion
27. Kallen, Jackie
28. Karmanos, Peter
29. Kasem, Casey
30. Kelser, Greg
31. Kendricks, Eddie
32. Knight, Gladys
33. Kresge, Sebastian
34. Leflore, Ron
35. Levin, Carl
36. Levine, Phillip
37. Lindbergh, Charles
38. Lipton, James
39. Malcom X
40. Mathers, Marshall
41. Mitchelson, Marvin
42. Mohummad, Elijah
43. Morgan, Harry
44. Nugent, Ted
45. Parker Jr. Ray
46. Mrs. Parks
47. Parsons, Benny
48. Peppard, George
49. Radner, Gilda
50. Reeves, Martha
51. Reuther, Walter P.
52. Robinson, Smokey
53. Ross, Diana
54. Ruffin, David
55. Scott, George C.
56. Selleck, Tom
57. Shabazz, Betty
58. Skerritt, Tom
59. Starr, Edwin
60. Tanana, Frank
61. Thomas, Danny
62. Tomjanovich, Rudy
63. Tomlin, Lilly
64. Wagner, Robert
65. Wallace, Mike
66. Webb, Veronica
67. Webber, Chris
68. White, Jack
69. Williams, Otis
70. Williams, Paul
71. Wilson, Jackie
72. Wilson, Mary
73. Wonder, Stevie

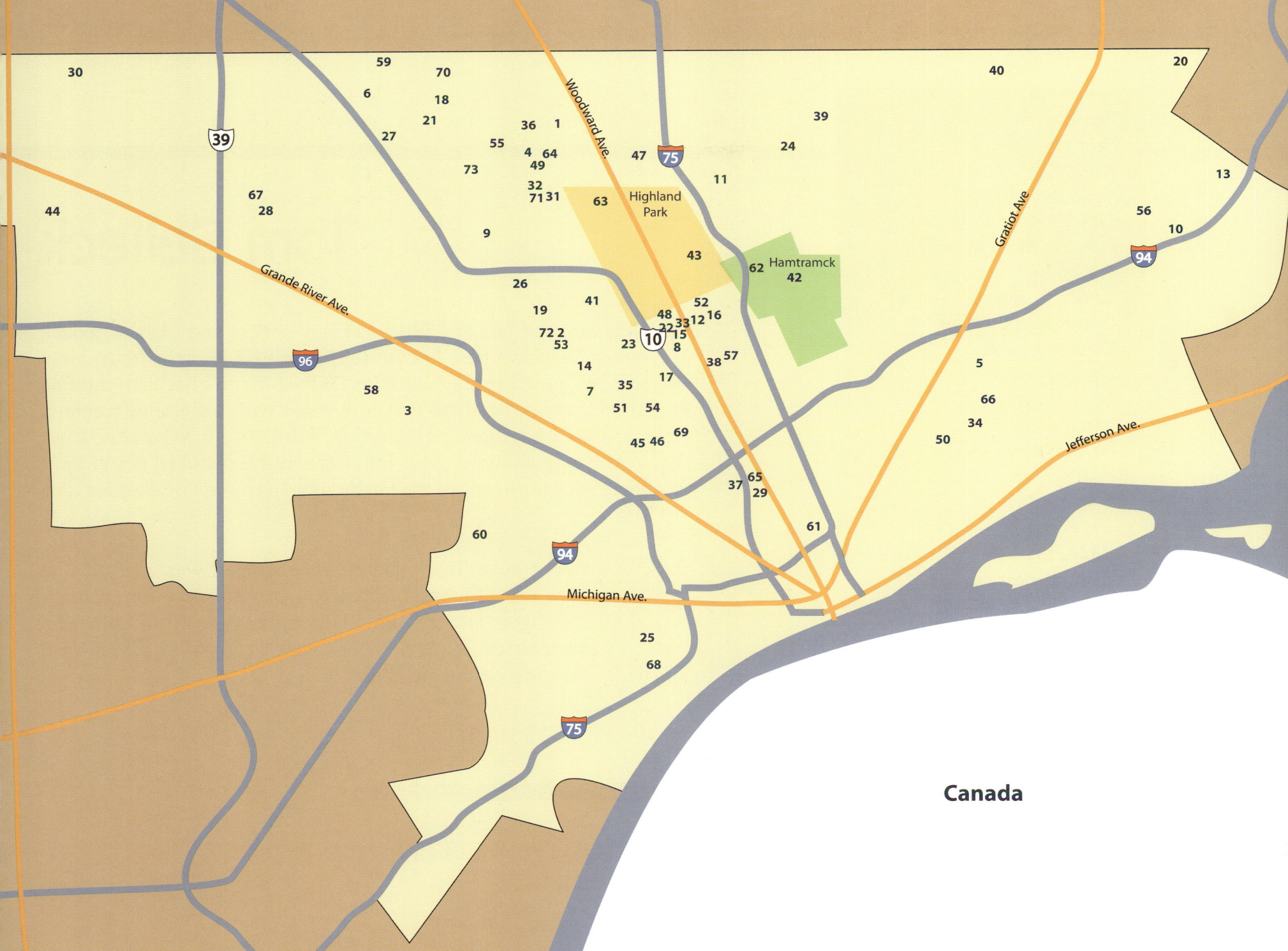

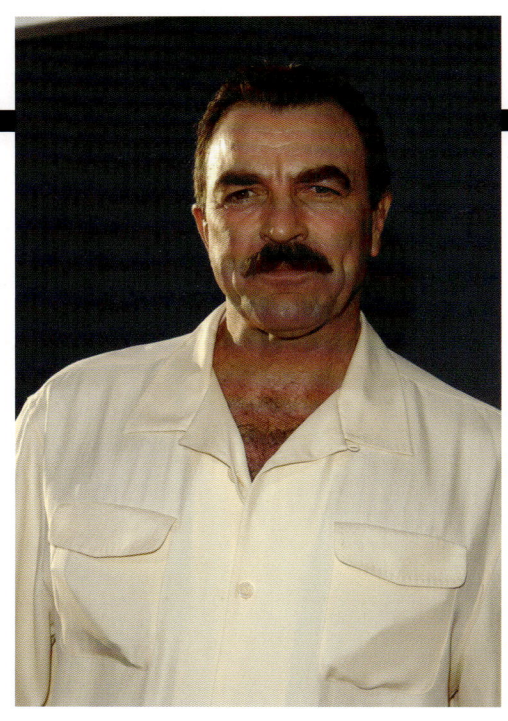

Tom Selleck

Tom was born on January 29th, 1945 to Robert and Martha Selleck in Detroit. Selleck is best known for his role as Thomas Magnum in *Magnum, P.I.*, who proudly wore his Detroit Tiger's hat with the Old English D. Selleck lived his first few years with his grandparents in Detroit while his father was fighting in World War II. When his father returned home after the war, Tom lived in the pictured home for a brief period of time before the family moved to the Los Angeles area in 1949.

Tom remained a huge Tigers fan after he moved west because, at the time, there wasn't a baseball team in Los Angeles. Tom actually played for the Tigers in a spring training game against the Cincinnati Reds as a pinch hitter. Tom's home is located across the street from Wayne Elementary on the city's east side.

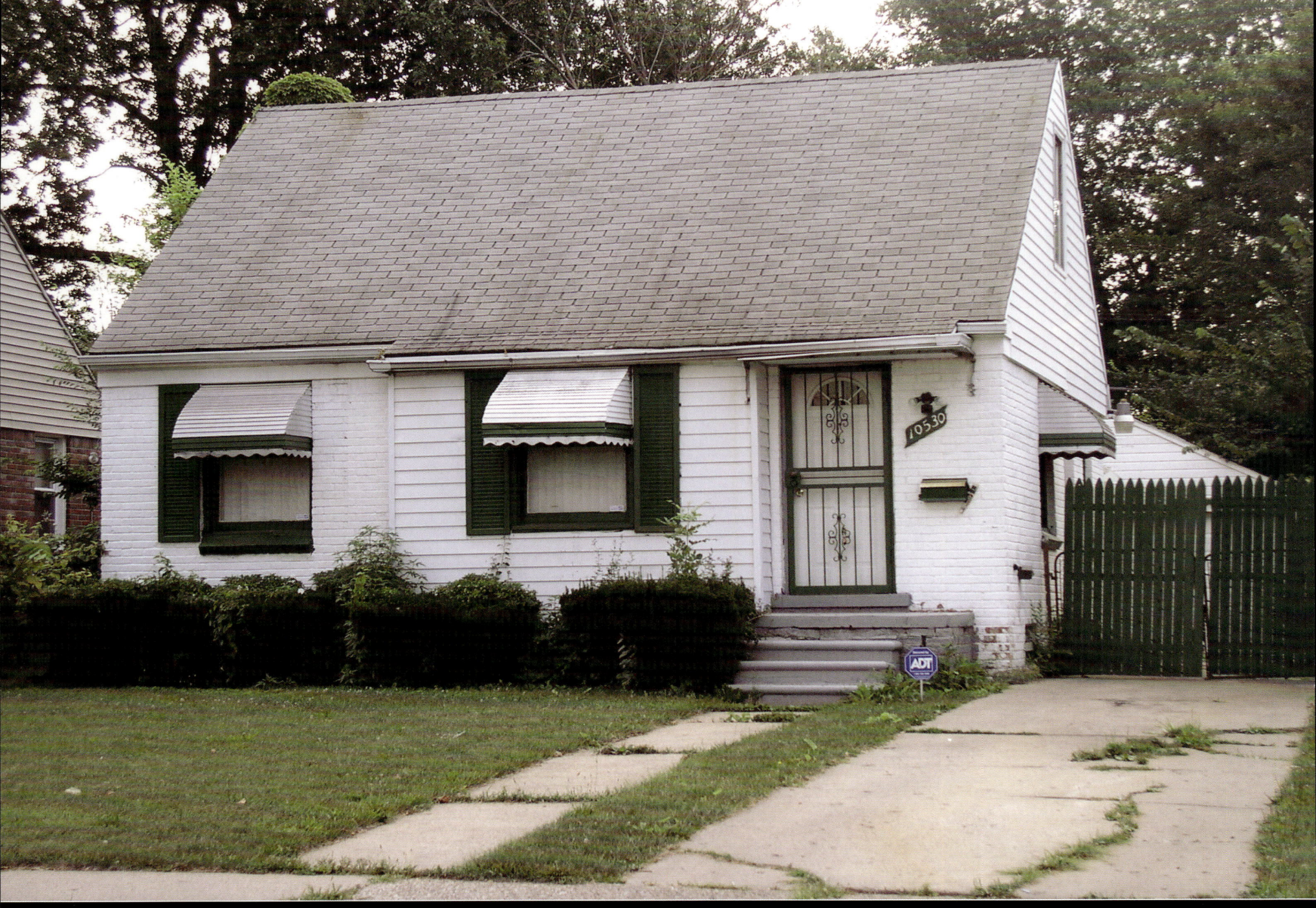

10530 Lakepointe

Lilly Tomlin

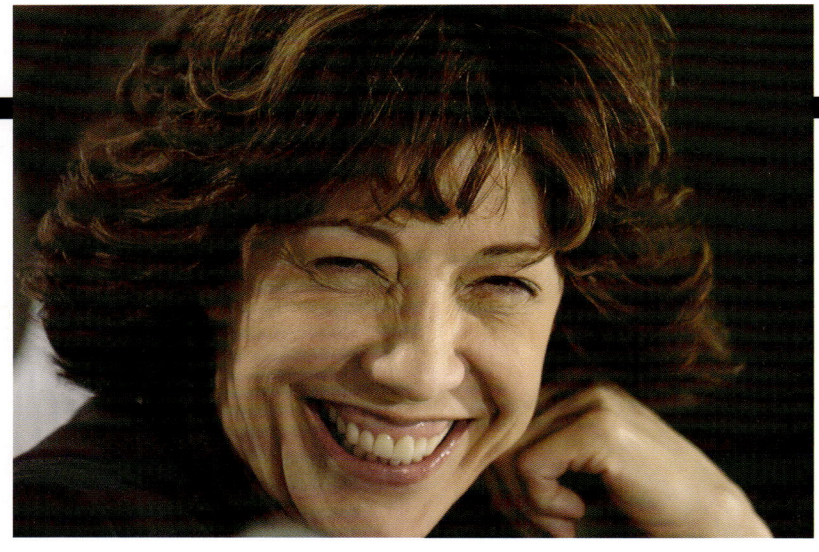

Born Mary Jean Tomlin on September 1st, 1939, to parents Guy and Lillie Mae Tomlin in Detroit. Lilly graduated from Cass Technical High School in Detroit and attended Wayne State, where she became interested in acting. She performed stand-up comedy in Detroit and later in New York City. In 1969, she joined the sketch comedy show, *Laugh In*. Tomlin's biggest movie role was in the 1981 smash, *9 to 5*, and has appeared in several movies and TV shows since.

During her childhood, Lilly lived in an apartment building at 8917 Byron and then later moved to 9765 N. Martindale. She moved with her family to the pictured home on Louise in Highland Park when both Lilly and her brother, Richard, were actors at the Unstable Coffeehouse Theatre in Detroit.

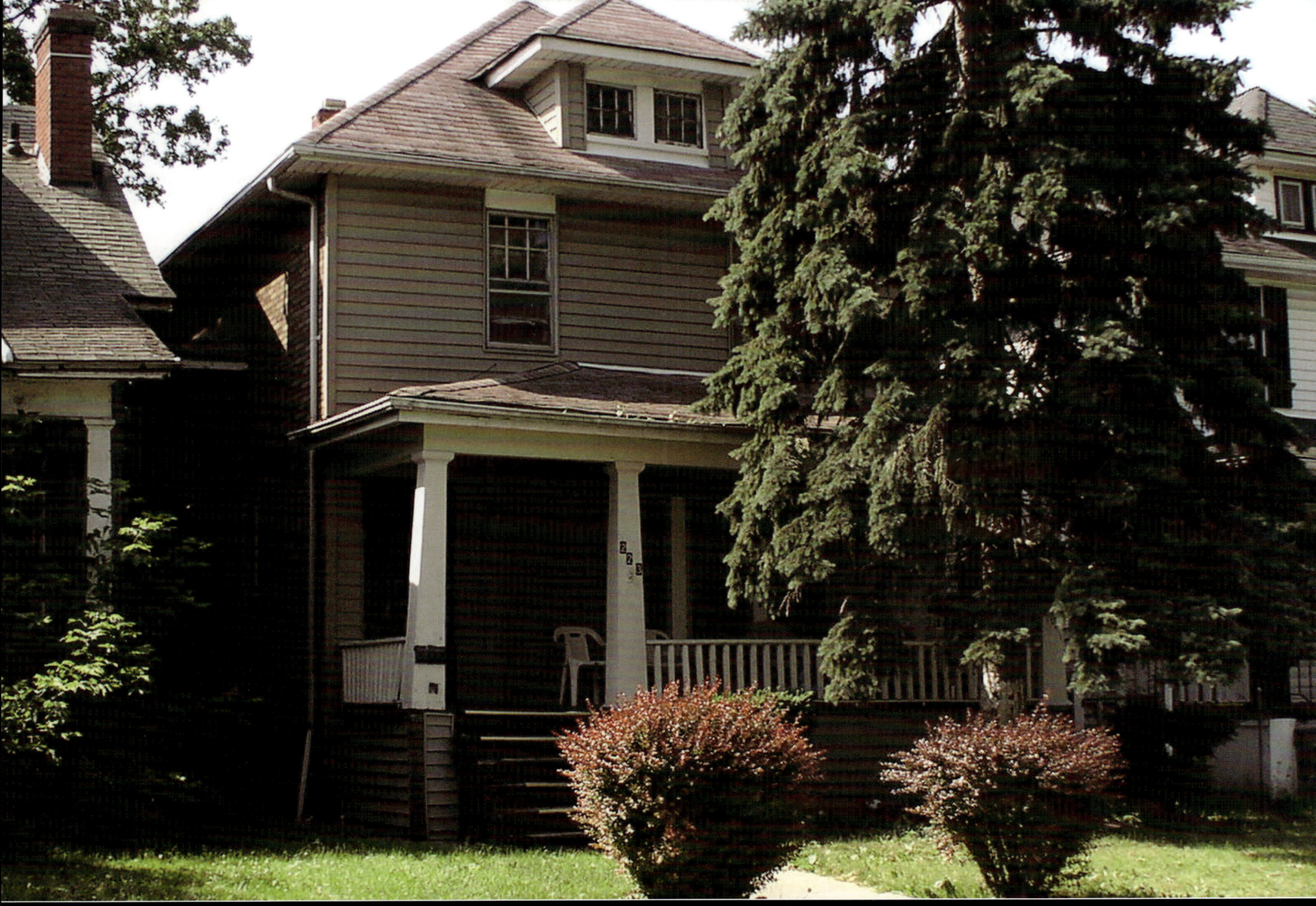

223 Louise

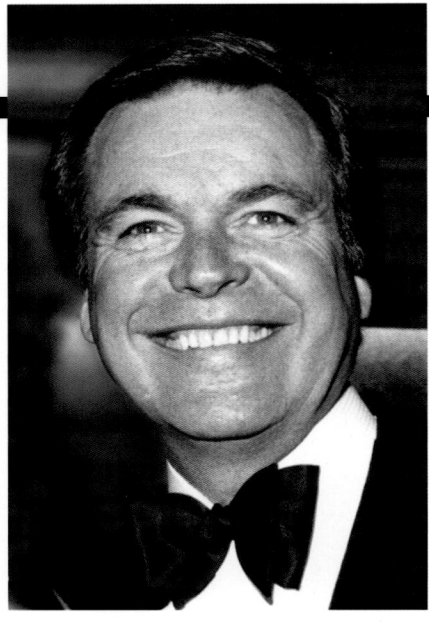

Robert Wagner

Robert John Wagner Jr., nicknamed R.J., was born to parents Robert and Hazel Wagner on February 10th, 1930 in Detroit. While in Detroit, he lived on Fairway Drive, which backed up to the Palmer Park Golf Course. Robert first lived at 17500 Fairway Drive and then in 1935 moved two houses down to the pictured home at 17140 Fairway.

Robert was married twice to actress Natalie Woods, who tragically drowned on the couple's boat in 1981. He has more movie and television credits than I can possibly list, but one of his most recent memorable roles was as the assistant to Dr. Evil in the Austin Powers film, *The Spy Who Shagged Me*. Robert and his family left Detroit in the late 1930s and moved to the Los Angeles area.

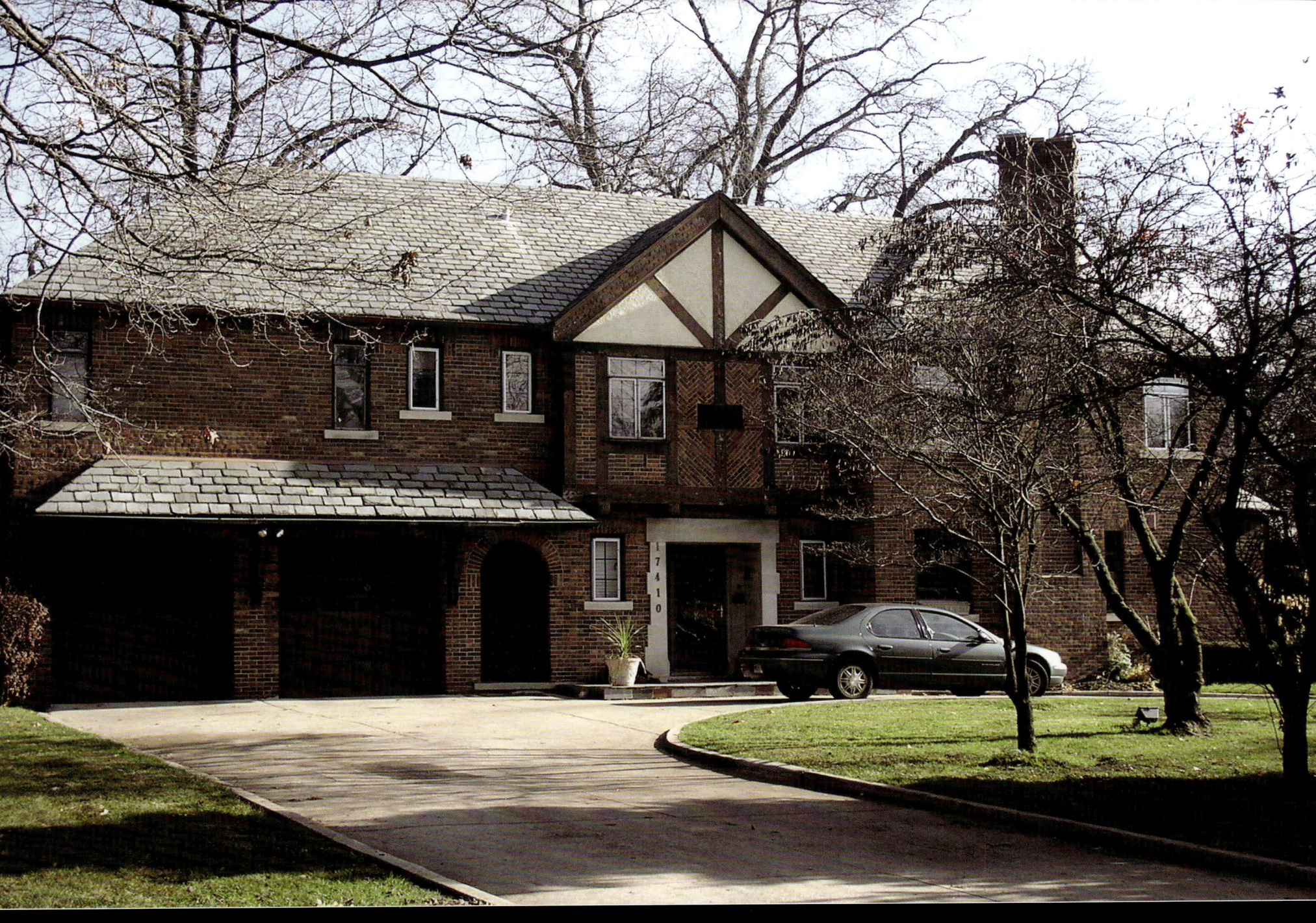

17410 Fairway

Tom Skerritt

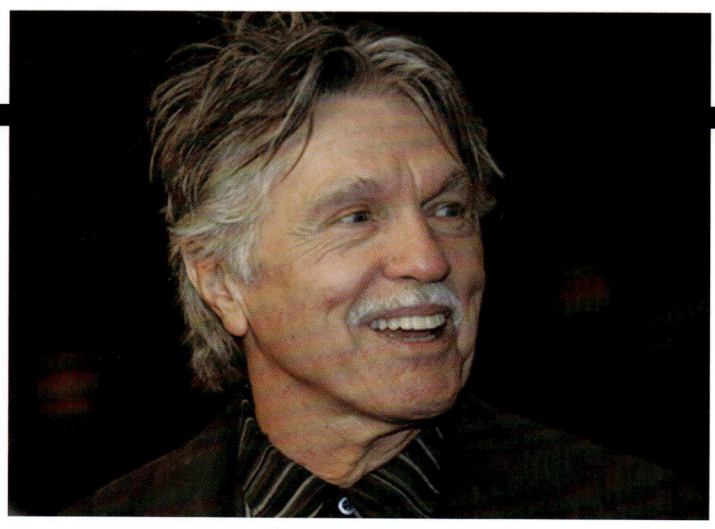

Thomas Alderton Skerritt was born on August 25th, 1933 in Detroit. He was raised in Detroit and graduated from MacKenzie High School in 1951 and started acting while attending Wayne State University in Detroit. Tom moved to Los Angeles and was discovered in a UCLA production of *The Rainmaker.* Tom is best known for his roles in the movies, *Top Gun, Alien,* and *A River Runs through It*; along with the TV series, *Picket Fences.* Tom's home is located just east of Schaefer and north of Plymouth Road, actress Ellen Burstyn lived around the corner from Tom at 11724 Ward when both were about six years old.

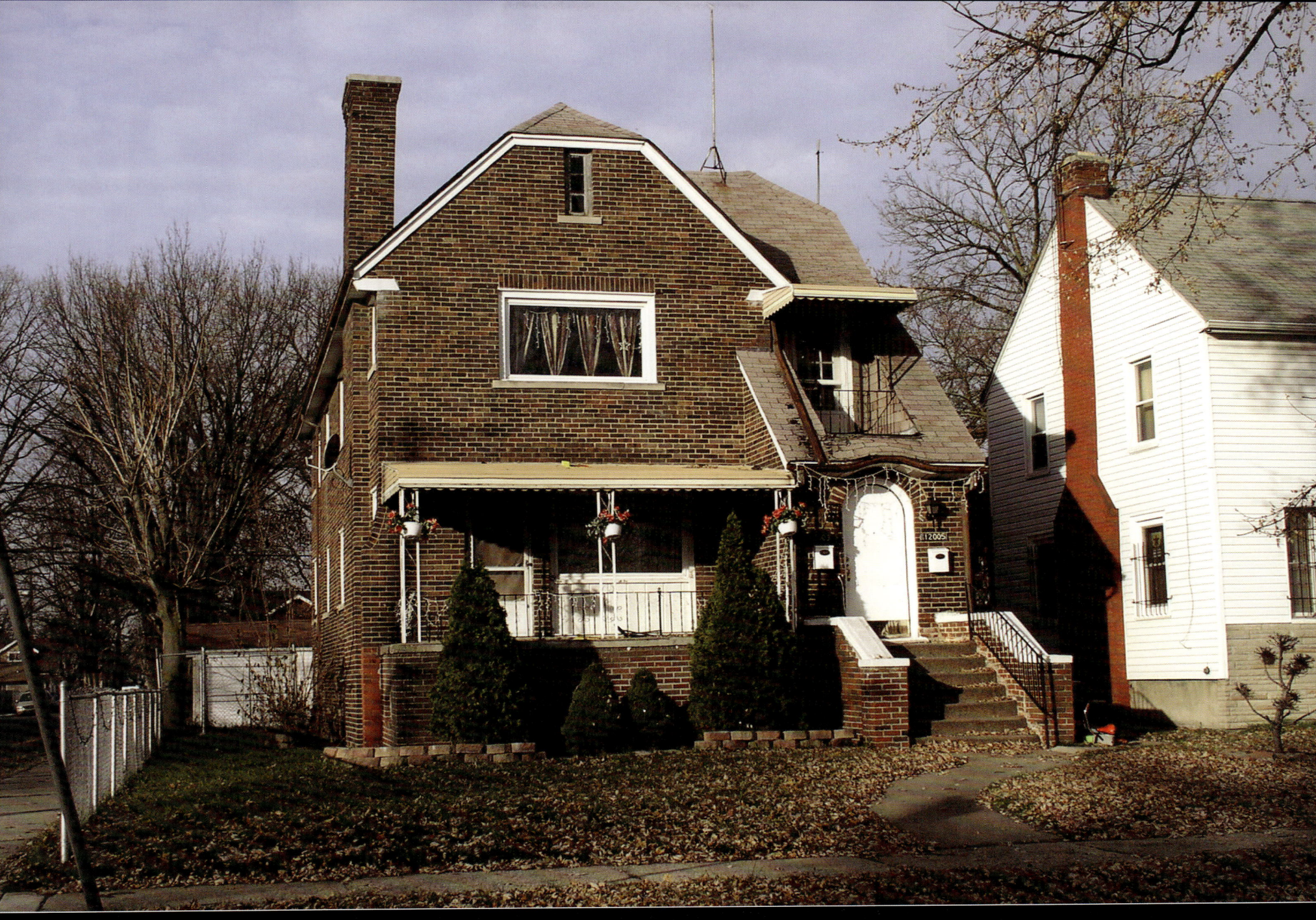

12003 Cheyenne

Danny Thomas

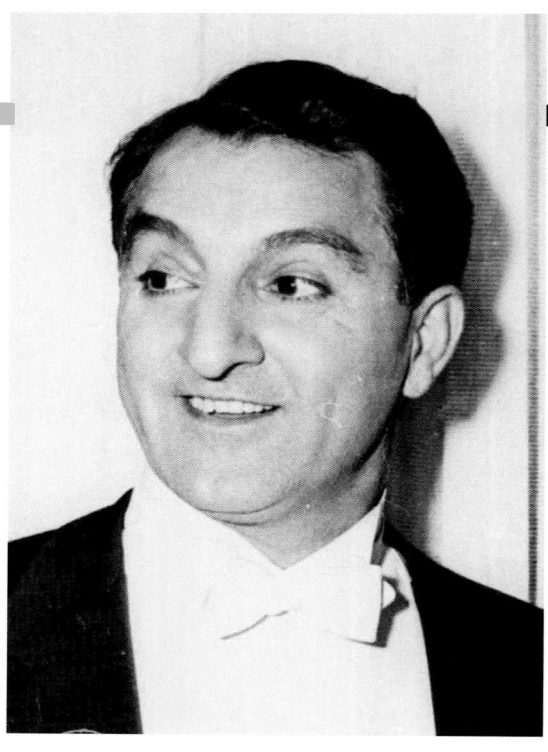

Danny was born Amos Muzyad Yahkoob in Deerfield, Michigan on January 6th, 1941. Danny saved enough money to move to Detroit in the early 1930s, performing as Amos Jacobs. One if his first jobs in Detroit was a singer on the Detroit radio show *The Happy Hour Club*. On the program was a young lady by the name of Rose Marie Mantell, who would become his wife. In 1936, they lived at the pictured home located just east of Woodward and north of I-94 & Comerica Park.

Danny hit the big screen in the early 1950s, starring in *I'll See You in My Dreams* and *The Jazz Singer*. Later he starred on the television show *Make Room for Daddy*, which later became the *Danny Thomas Show*. In 1962, Danny founded the St. Jude Children's Hospital, which has treated thousands of children cancer patients. In 2004, he won the Bob Hope Humanitarian Award for his work with St. Jude's. Danny died of a heart attack in 1991.

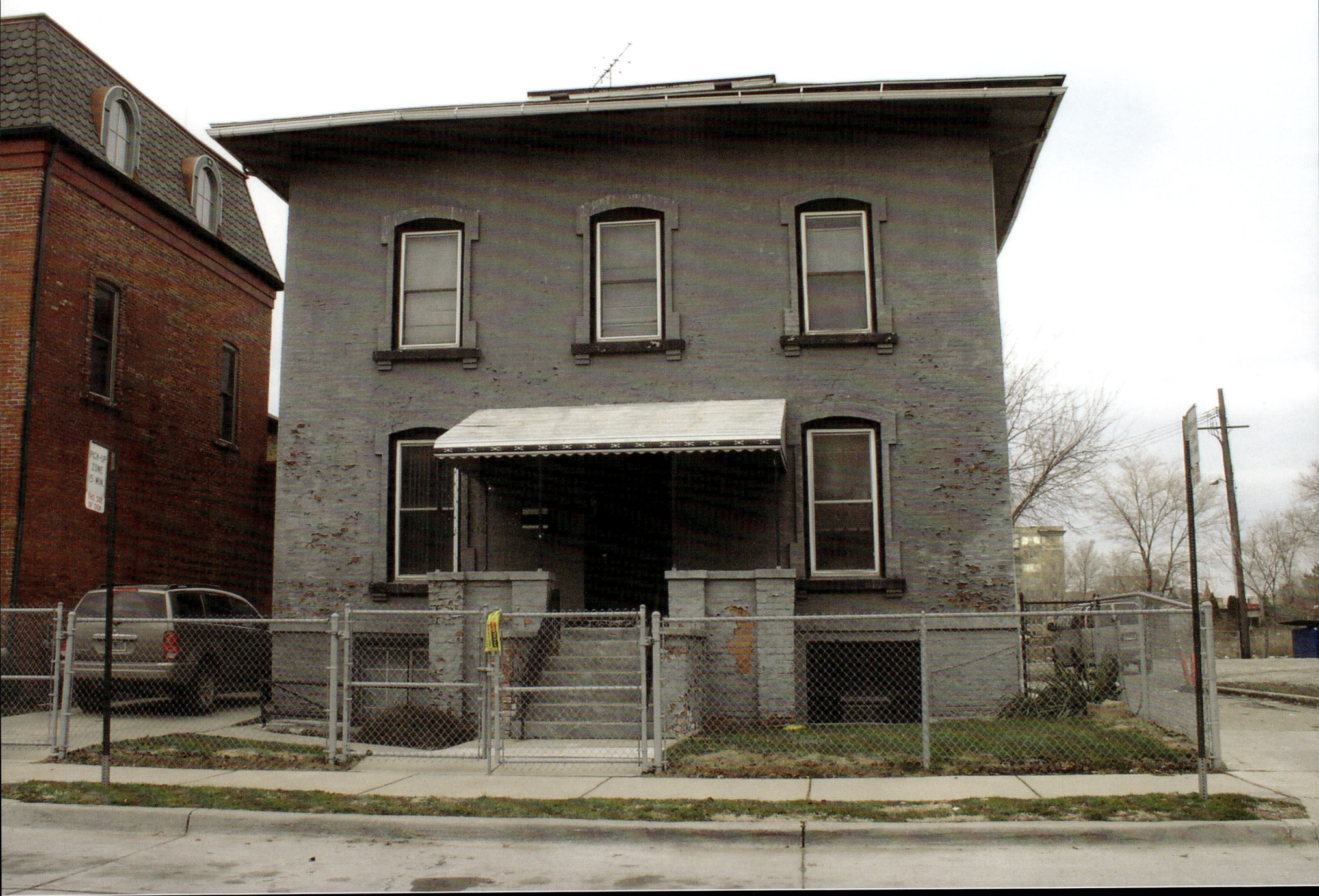

93 Adelaide

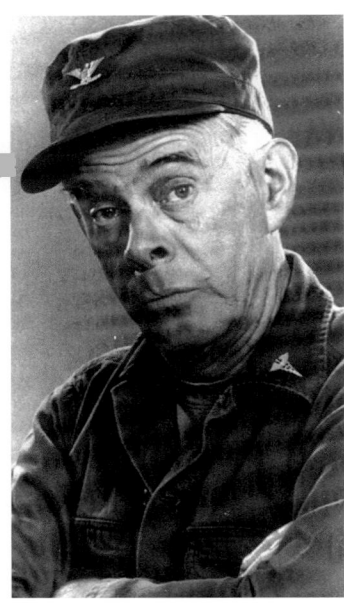

Harry Morgan

Born Henry Bratsberg to Henry & Hannah on April 10th, 1915. Harry lived in Highland Park, a separate city located within the borders of Detroit, for about 7 years before moving to Muskegon, Michigan. He went on to Chicago to study law but instead found a passion for theatre. He is best remembered for his roles as Bill Gannon in Dragnet and Colonel Sherman T. Potter in the TV smash hit series, M.A.S.H.

In September 1915, Henry L. Bratsberg is listed as a boarder in the pictured Rhode Island street home, but Harry's father's middle initial was "A". There was not a listing for a Henry A. Bratsberg that year; researching city directories after 1915 I found multiple listings for Henry A. Bratsberg. In fact, one listing, 166 E. Buena Vista, is right around the corner from this pictured home. Henry A. Bratsberg lived there from 1916 to 1919, but the home is no longer standing. Henry L. Bratsberg is only listed in 1915; he is never listed again before or after 1915.

I strongly believe that Henry L. and Henry A. Bratsberg, are the same person, Harry Morgan's father because of the information stated above plus the fact that Henry L. and Henry A. Bratsberg are never listed in the same year. A Norwegian accent may have made an "L" sound like an "A" when he first arrived and was later corrected, I found similar occurrences while researching this book. Some of the city directories I used are over ninety years old; it is easy to understand how inaccuracies like this occurred in 1915 when Detroit was the one of the fastest growing cites in the Midwest. Keep this in mind when you research your ancestry.

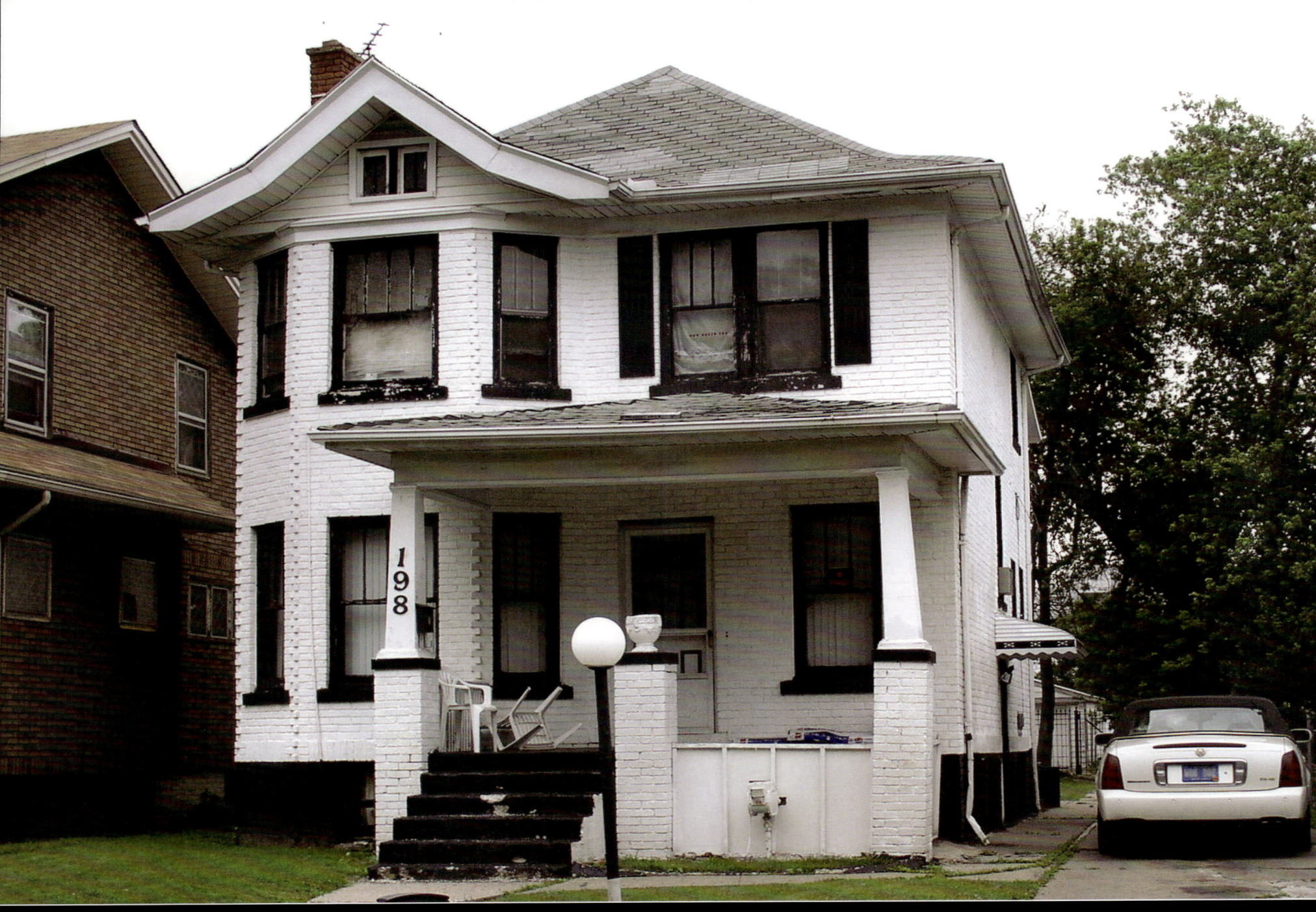

198 Rhode Island

Berry Gordy

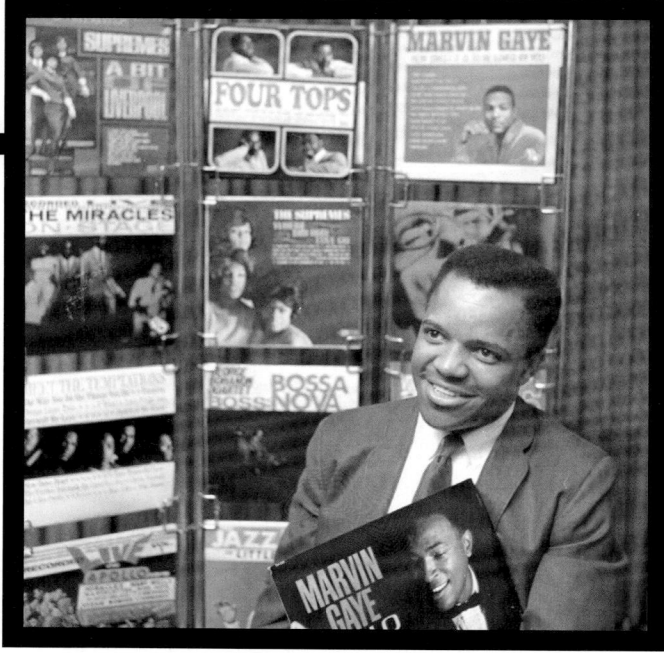

Motown founder Berry Gordy was born in November 28th, 1929 in Detroit, growing up on the city's west side at 5469 Roosevelt. Berry dropped out of high school and became a pro boxer until he was drafted into the Army in 1950. In 1959, Gordy borrowed money from his parents and started Tamla Records, which he later incorporated into Motown Records.

In 1959, Berry purchased the residence at 2648 W. Grand Boulevard, that house became Hitsville USA and home to mega stars Smokey Robinson, The Supremes, The Temptations, Martha Reeves, Stevie Wonder, and Marvin Gaye. Berry moved the Motown operation to Los Angeles in the mid-1970s and sold the company to RCA for $61 million in 1988. Berry's home on Boston Boulevard is located in the Boston-Edison neighborhood just west of Woodward.

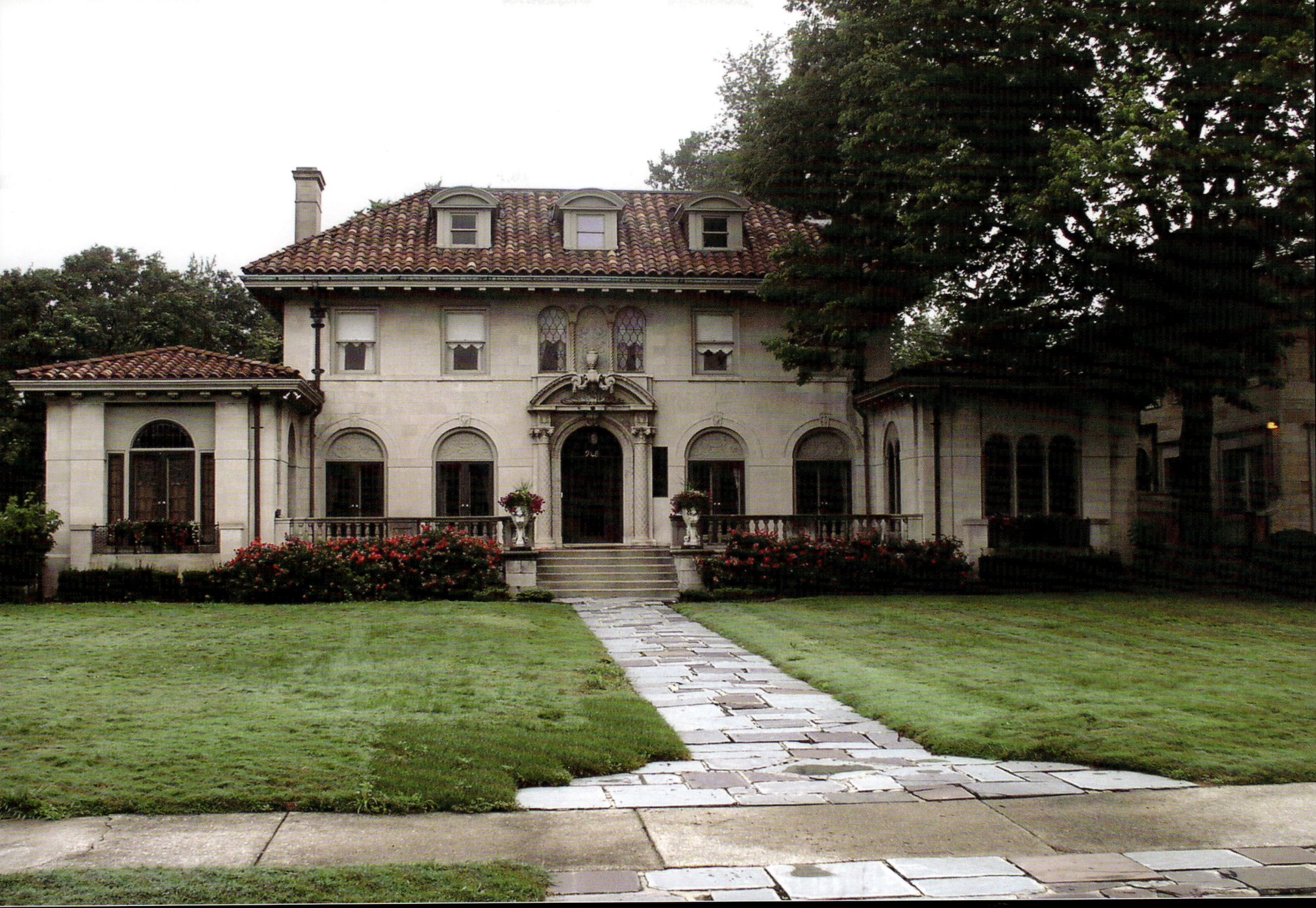

918 West Boston

Diana Ross

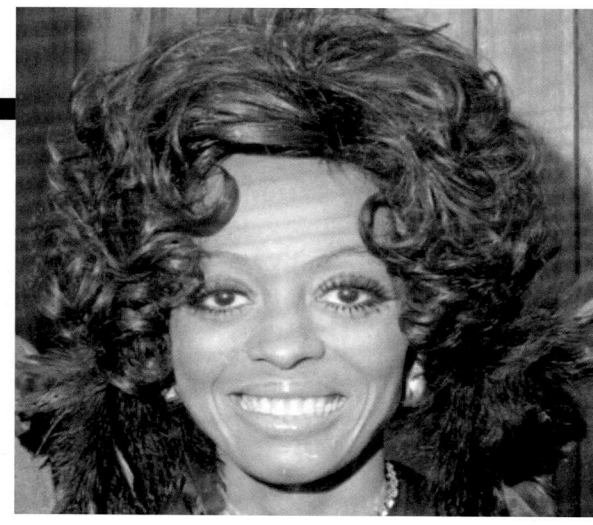

Born Diane Ross on March 26th, 1944 to Fred and Ernestine Ross in Detroit, she lived on Belmont, down the street from Smokey Robinson during her early teen years. Around 1960, her father moved the family from the home on Belmont to 2691 St. Antoine in the Brewster Projects before public housing held such a negative stigma. It was there where Mary Wilson and Florence Ballard recruited Diana into the Primettes, the three eventually became the Supremes. In 1965, Berry Gordy helped Diana buy this home on W. Buena Vista, located on the west side of Detroit, along with houses on the same street for fellow Supremes Florence Ballard and Mary Wilson. Ms. Ross is tied with Elvis Presley with 18 #1 hits, 12 as lead singer of the Supremes and 6 as a solo artist.

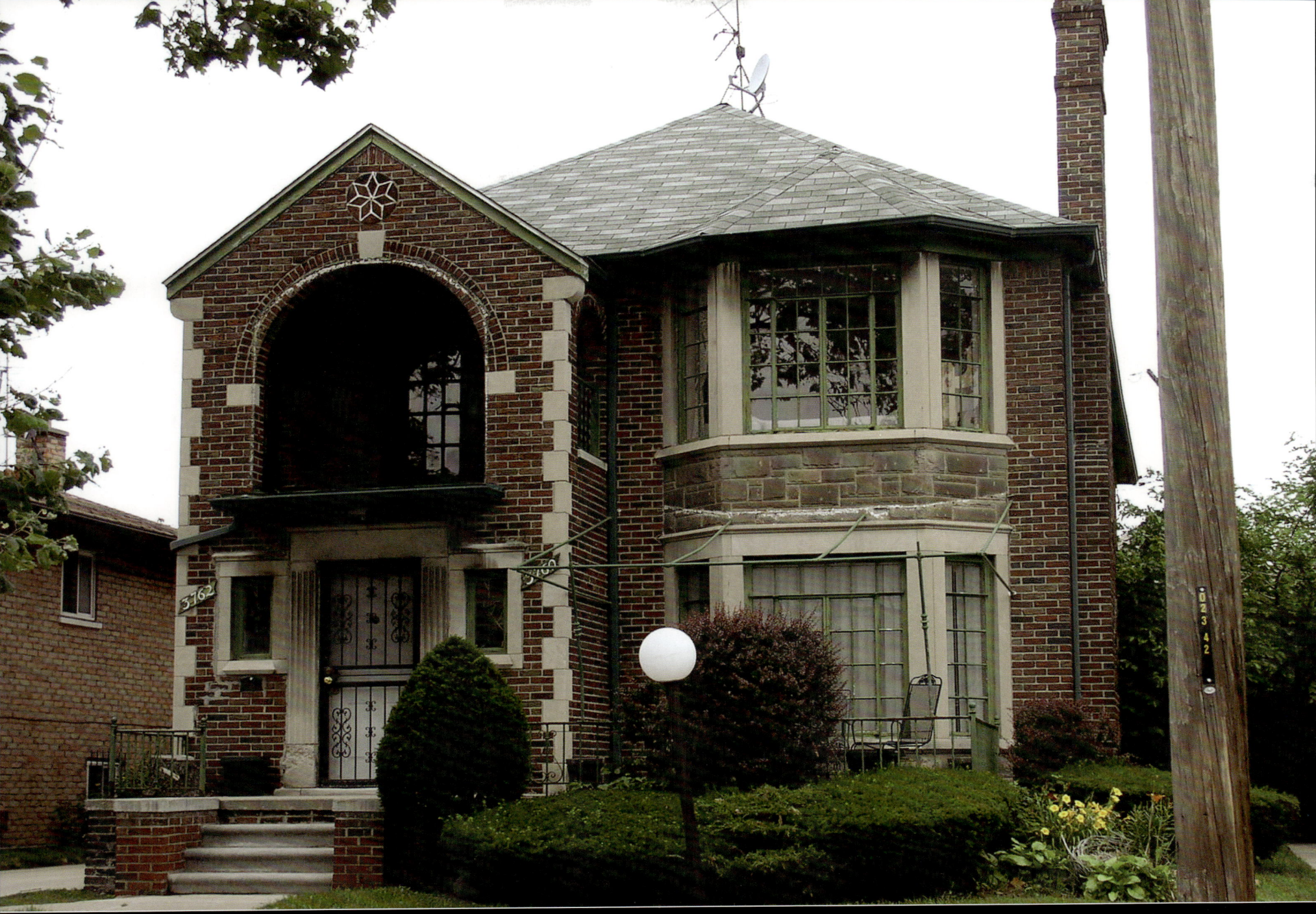

3762 W. Buena Vista

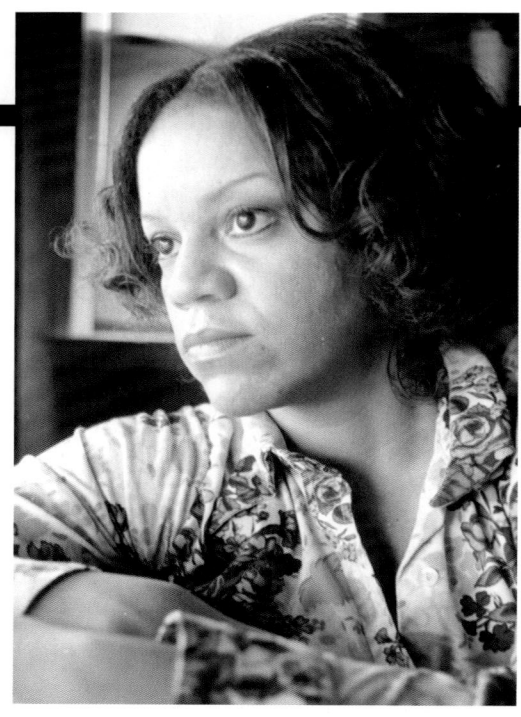

Florence Ballard

Born Florence Glenda Ballard on June 30th, 1943 in Rosetta, Mississippi, but moved to Detroit when she was ten years old. She is best known for being part of the award-winning Motown act, the Supremes, in which she was the original lead singer. She was replaced as lead by Diana Ross because Motown's leader Berry Gordy thought Ross's voice would better attract a white audience.

Florence left the group in 1967 and was replaced by Cindy Birdsong. In 1973, Florence's life hit rock bottom after her husband Thomas Chapman left her and their three children. Declining health ensued and Florence died from a blood clot in 1976; she was only 32 years old. This house is across the street from Diana Ross's W. Buena Vista home on the city's west side.

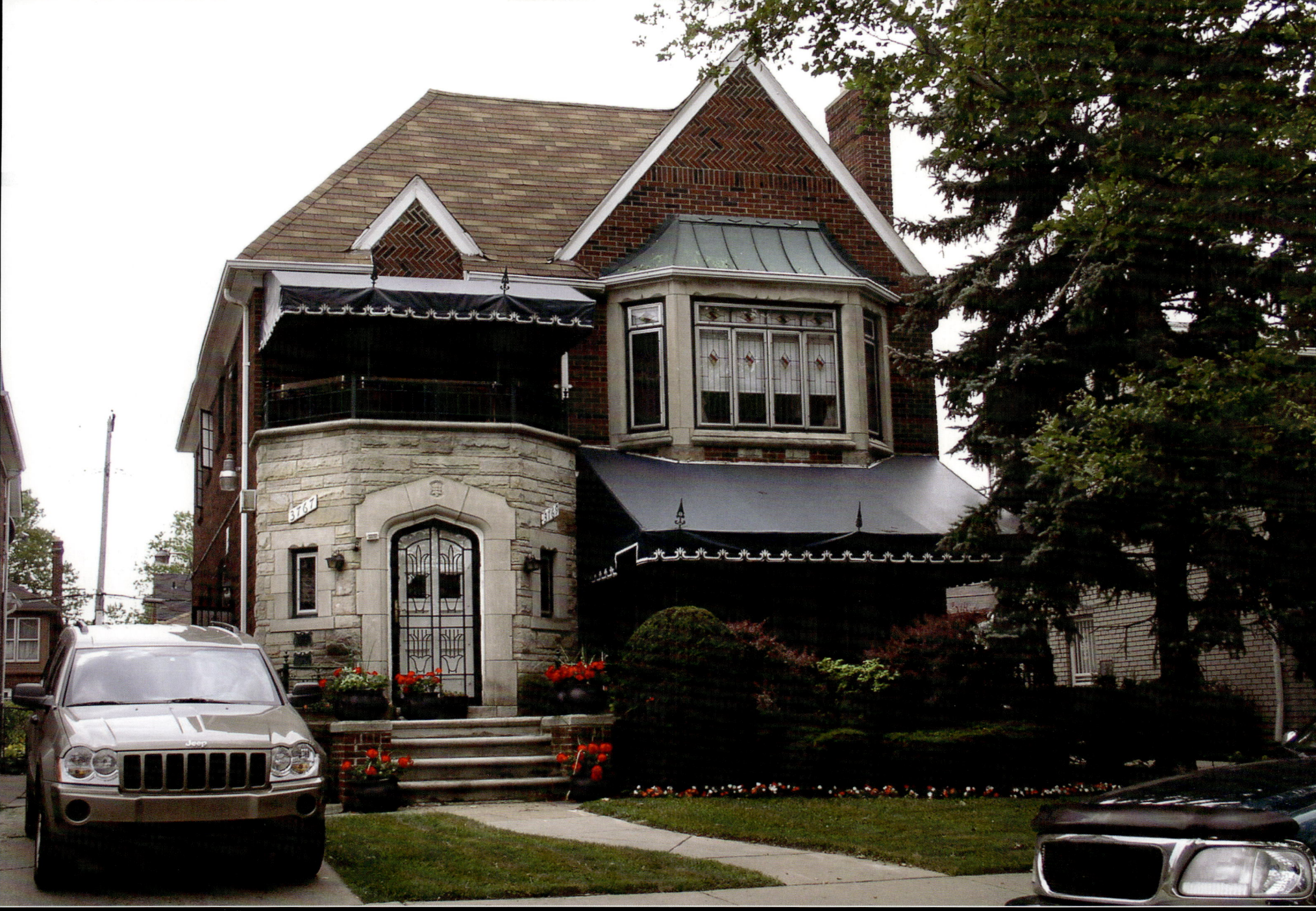

3767 W. Buena Vista

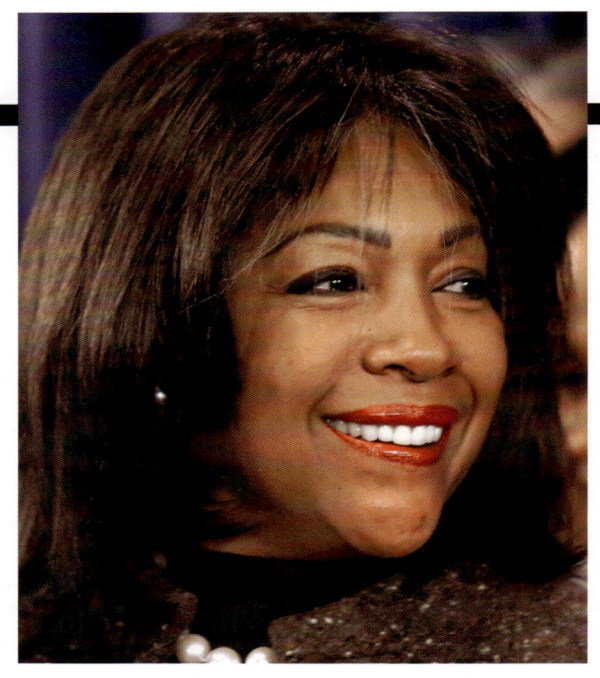

Mary Wilson

Supremes' Mary Wilson was born on March 6th, 1944 in Greenville, Mississippi. Mary was a junior high friend of Florence Ballard and together they started the group the Primettes. Mary then recruited new friend and fellow Brewster Project resident, Diane Ross. The three would eventually become the Supremes.

Mary wrote her autobiography called *Dreamgirl, My Life as a Supreme* in 1986. The name *Dreamgirls* was used for the Broadway musical based on the Supremes, which was recently made into a motion picture starring Beyonce Knowles, Jennifer Hudson, and Jamie Foxx. The pictured house is on W. Buena Vista, about a block down the street form Florence Ballard's and Diana Ross's W. Buena Vista homes.

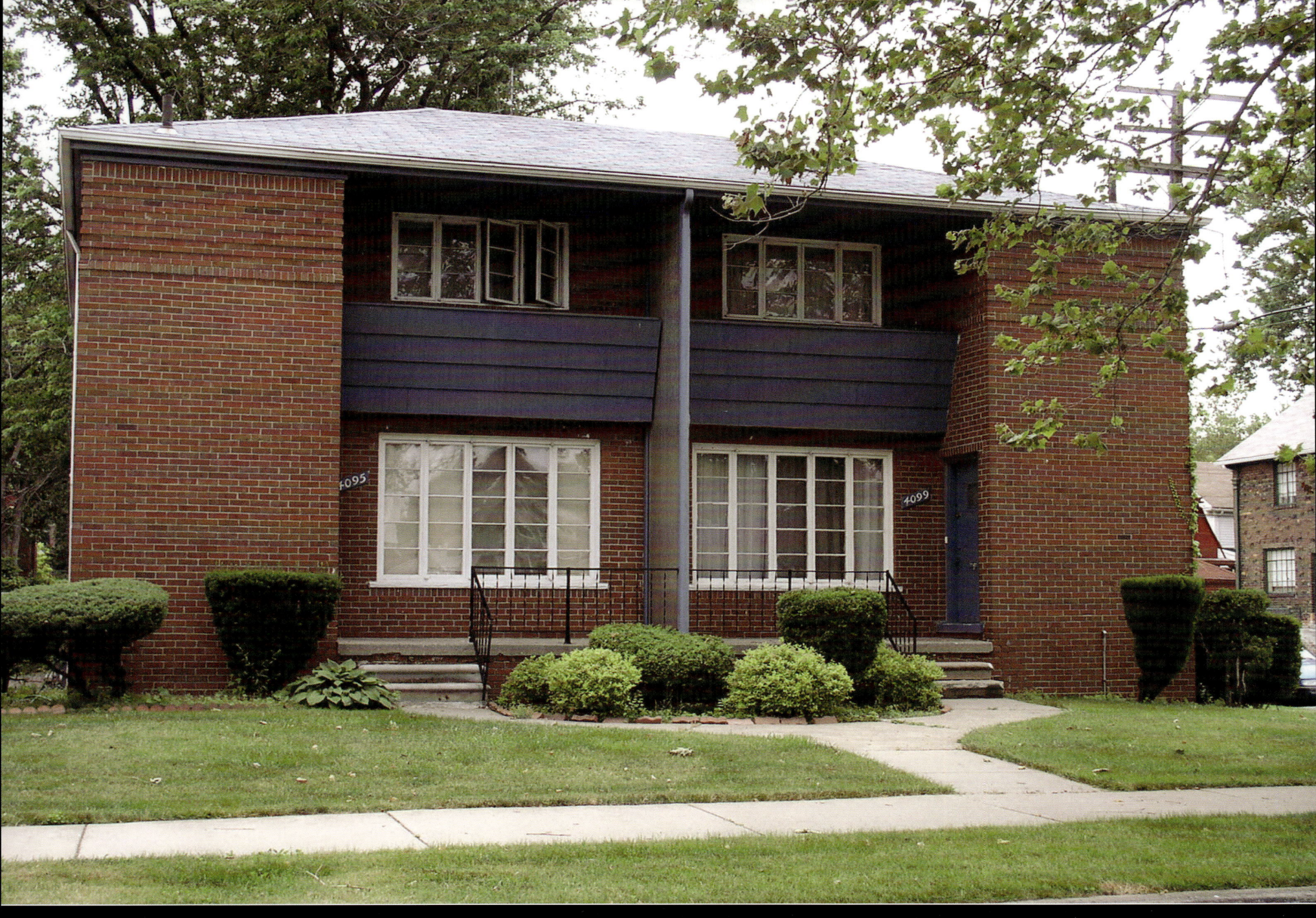

4099 W. Buena Vista

Temptations

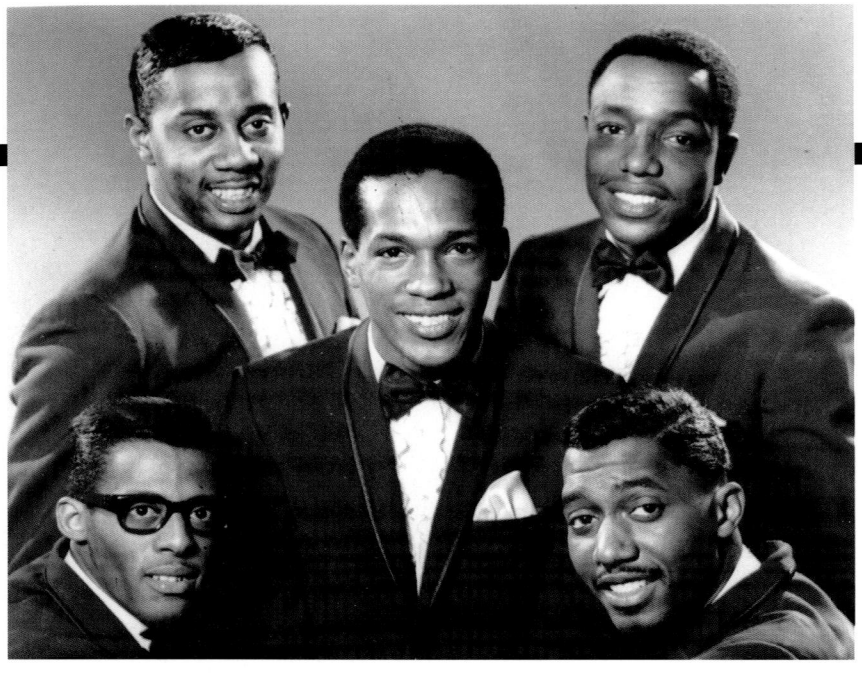

The Temptations consisted of Melvin Franklin(top left), Paul William(top right), Otis Williams(bottom right), David Ruffin(bottom left) and Eddie Kendricks(center). The band was a combination of two groups, Paul and Eddie were members of the Primes, they joined the three members of the Distants; Otis, Melvin, and Elbridge "Al" Bryant to form the Elgins in 1961. After they were signed to Miracle Records by Berry Gordy, Bryant was replaced by Motown Recording artist David Ruffin and the five would become the Temptations and have seven Top Ten singles and seven #1 singles on the R&B list.

The original members stayed together until 1968 when David Ruffin was forced out of the band. Later, Paul Williams left the group due to illness and Eddie Kendricks left to pursue a solo career. Melvin Franklin stayed in the band until his death in 1995, leaving Otis Williams as the only remaining original member of the Temptations who still tour today. Sadly, Otis is also the only living original Temptation as well. Eddie, Paul, and David all passed away before Melvin's death in 1995.

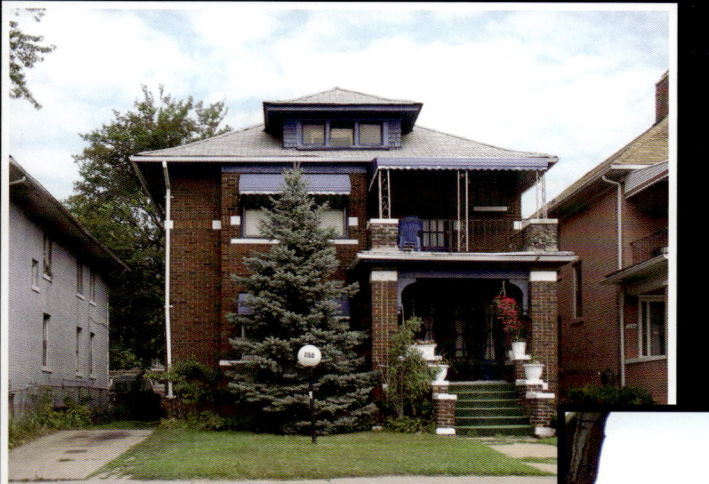

1160 Clairmount

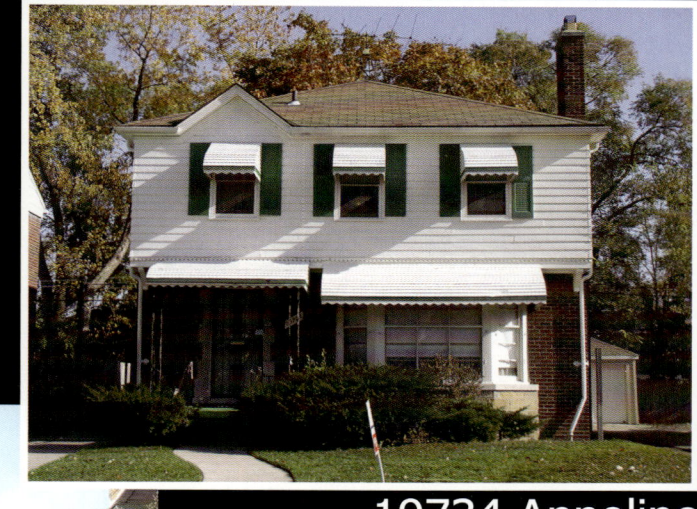

19734 Appoline

2211 Pingree

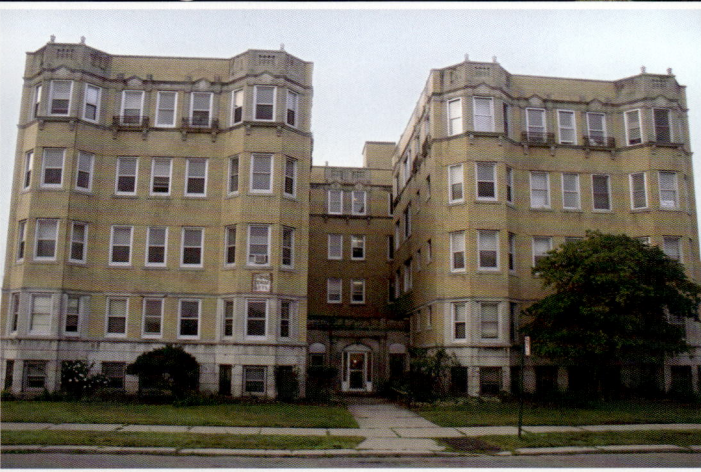

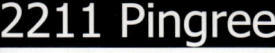

16531 Baylis

1979 Seward

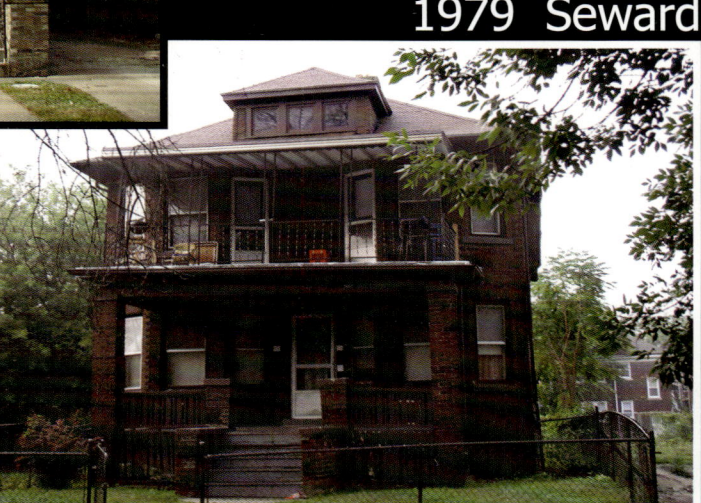

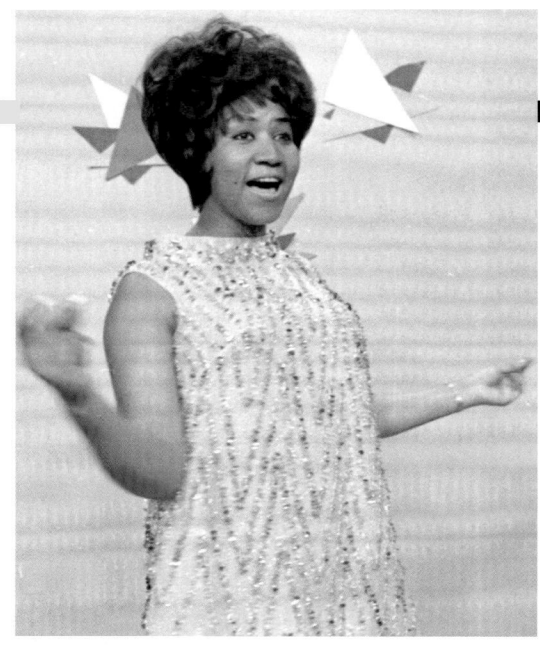

Aretha Franklin

The "Queen of Soul" was born on March 25th, 1942 in Memphis Tennessee, but grew up in Detroit after living for a short time in Buffalo, New York. She began her singing career in her father, Reverend C.L. Franklin's, Bethel Baptist Church.

In 1987, Aretha was the first woman inducted into the Rock and Roll Hall of Fame, her top hits include *Respect, Chain of Fools, and Think.* Aretha sang the National Anthem, along with Aaron Neville, at the Super Bowl XL, played at Ford Field in Detroit. Her home is located at East Boston Boulevard and Oakland Avenue.

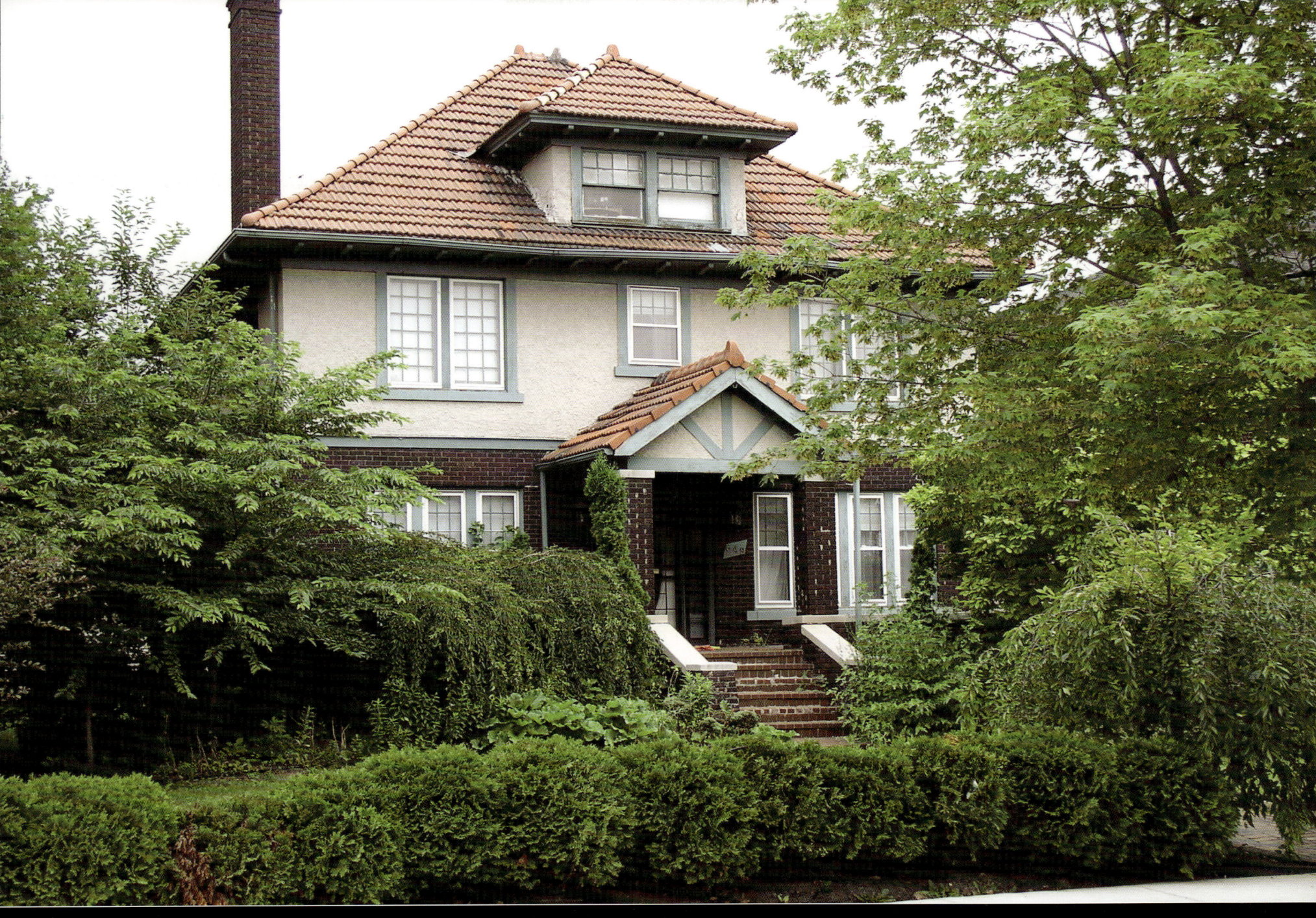

649 E. Boston

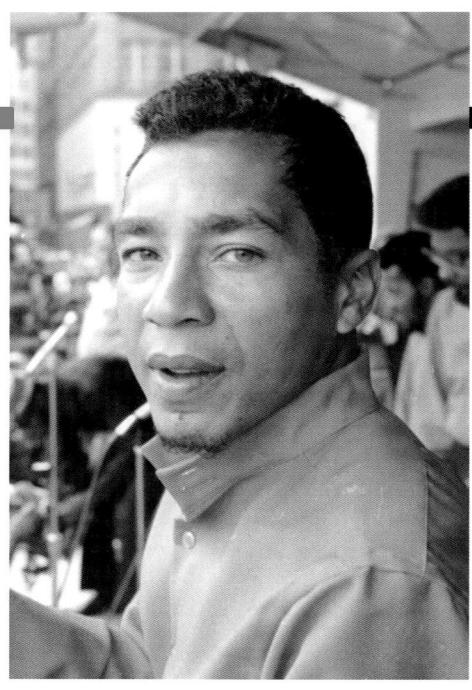

Smokey Robinson

William Robinson Jr. was born in Detroit on February 19th, 1940. Smokey lived with his sister, Geraldine Burston on Belmont Street after his mother passed away. Diana Ross lived a couple of houses down from him and Aretha Franklin lived around the corner, now that was a neighborhood full of talent! While Smokey attended Detroit Northern High School he formed the group The Matadors, which would become The Miracles.

He met and became friends with Berry Gordy and it was Smokey who suggested that Gordy start his own record label. Smokey later lived at 2750 Sturtevant, Apt. 101, with his ex-wife and Miracles member, Claudette Rodgers. Smokey is still very active today with a recent guest appearance on the 6th season of *American Idol* and his own line of food products.

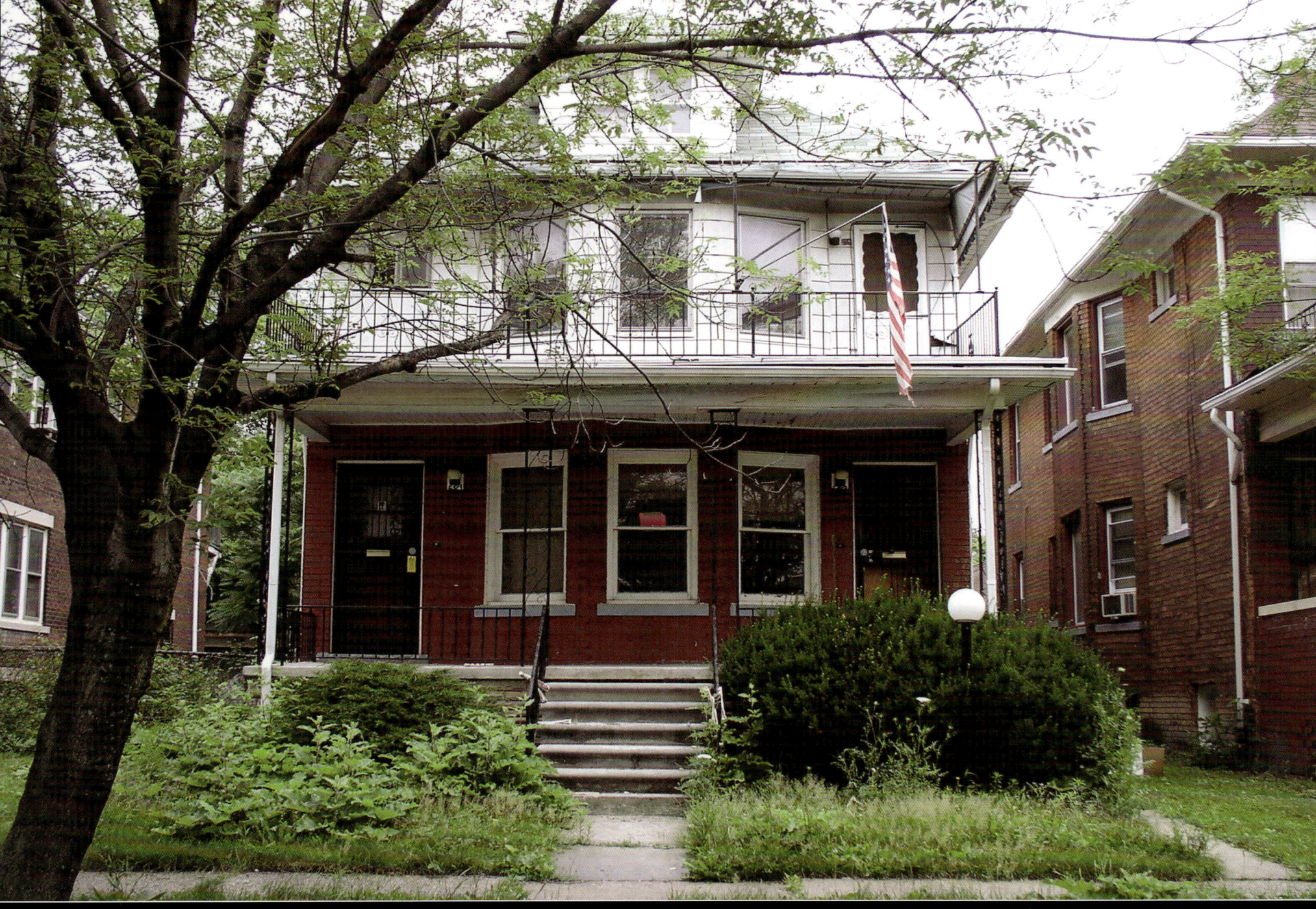

581 Belmont

Martha Reeves

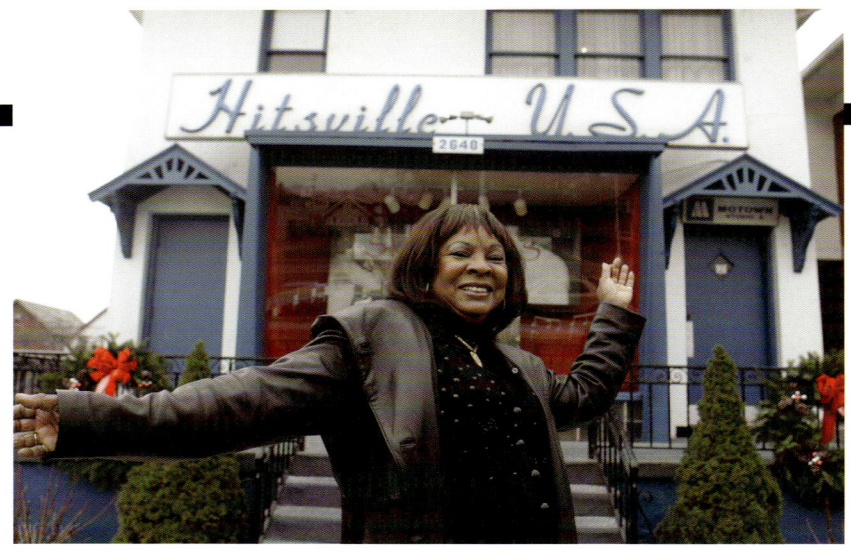

Rock and Roll Hall of Fame inductee, Martha Reeves, was born on July 18th, 1941 to Elijah and Ruby Reeves in Eufaula, Alabama. The family moved to Detroit shortly afterwards. Martha graduated from Detroit's Northeastern High School in 1959 and began her Motown career as a receptionist and background singer. In 1962, she became the lead singer of Martha and the Vandellas. The group's name, "Vandellas" was a combination of Detroit's famous soul singer, Della Reese, and Van Dyke Road, which is a couple of blocks from her pictured home on Townsend Avenue. The Vandella's top hits included *Love is like a Heat Wave, Dancing in the Streets*, and *Nowhere to Run*. Martha is currently a Detroit City Councilwoman.

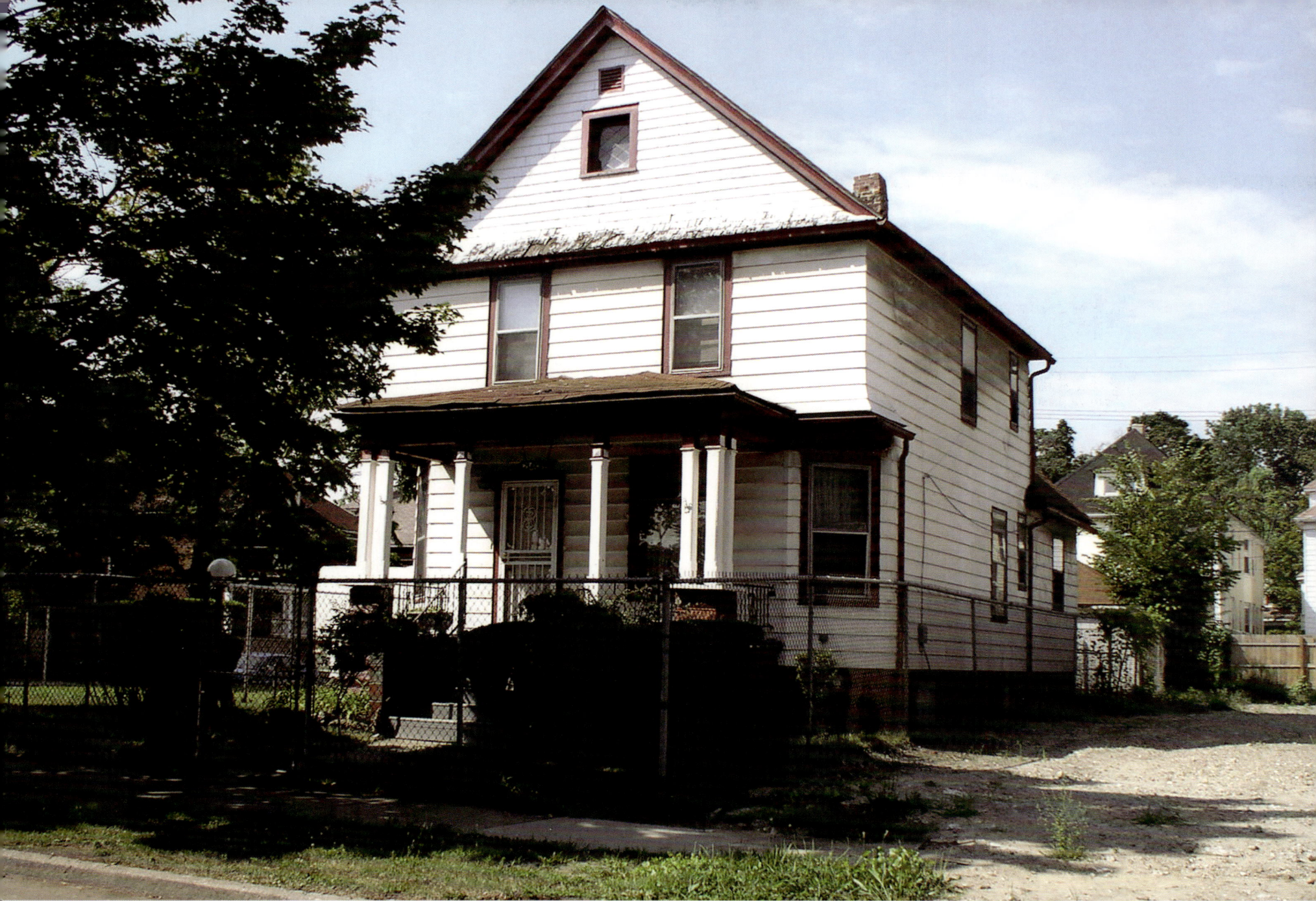

2409 Townsend

Marvin Gaye

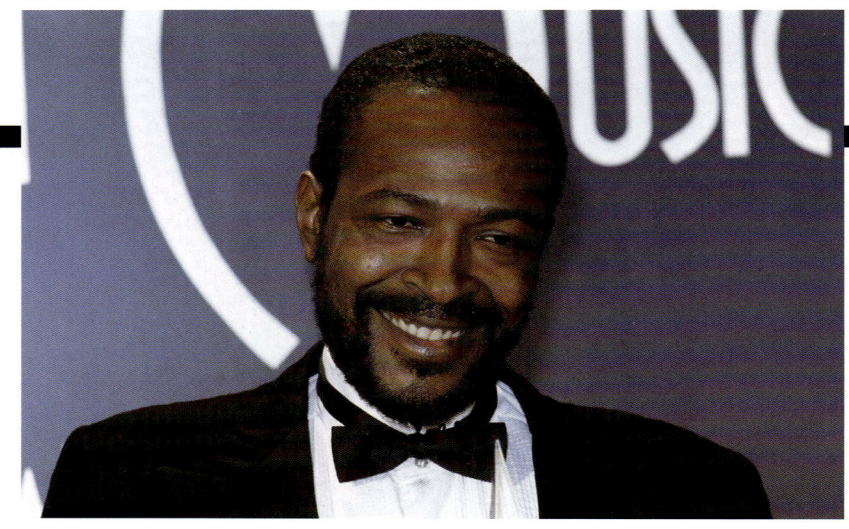

Born Marvin Pentz Gay Jr. on April 2nd, 1939 in Washington D.C. He added the "e" to his last name before he came to Detroit in 1960. Marvin started his career at Motown as a drummer and backup singer before starting a solo career that would produce hits *Let's Get it On, What's Going On, and Heard it through the Grapevine*. Marvin and his wife, Anna, sister of Motown founder, Berry Gordy, lived in the pictured home on Appoline just north of Outer Drive on Detroit's west side in the late 1960s. Marvin was one of the last big Motown acts to leave Detroit after Motown moved its headquarters to Los Angeles. In 1970, he tried out to play for the Detroit Lions but was cut early in training camp. Tragically, Marvin was shot and killed by his father during an argument in 1984.

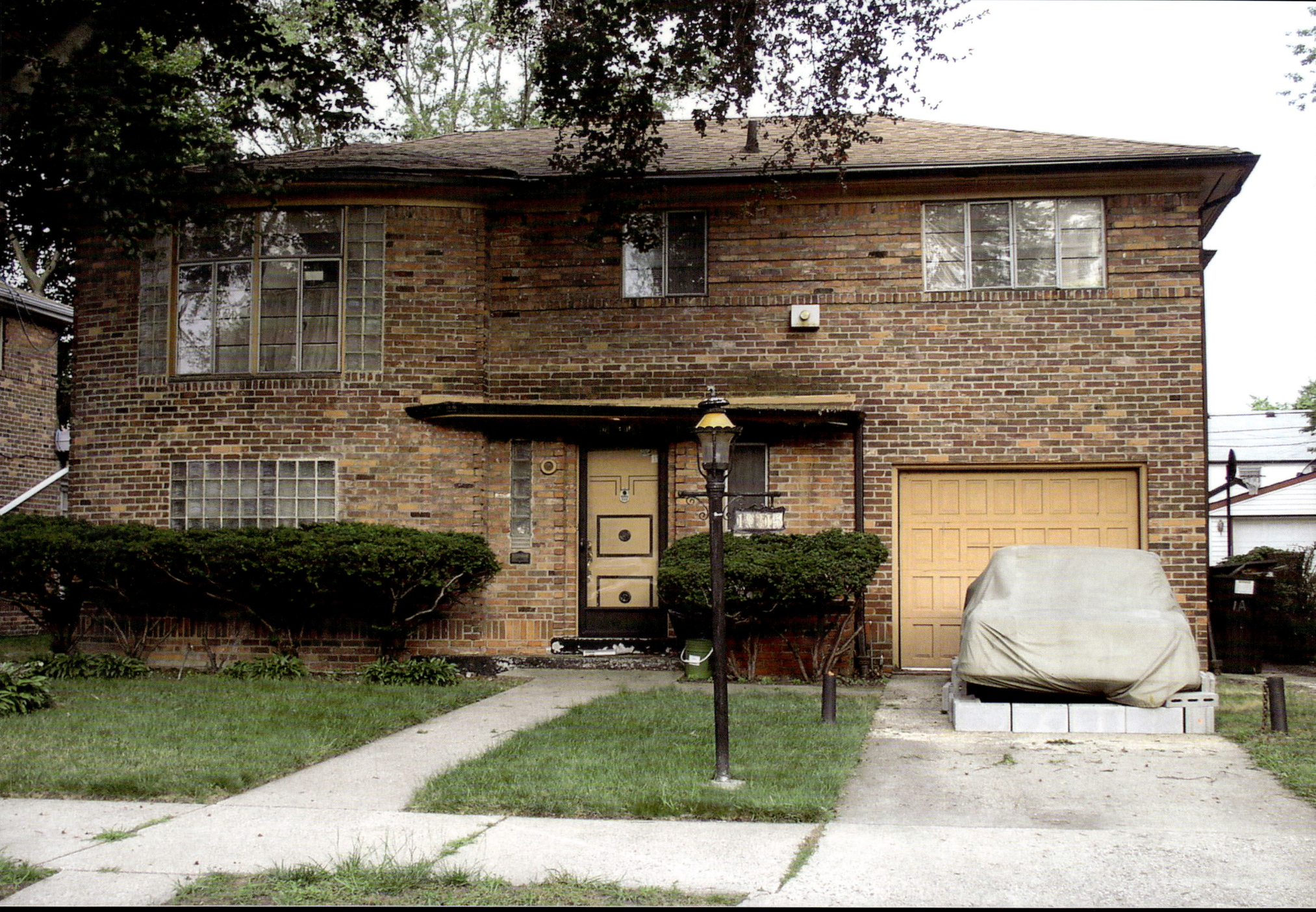

19315 Appoline

Gladys Knight

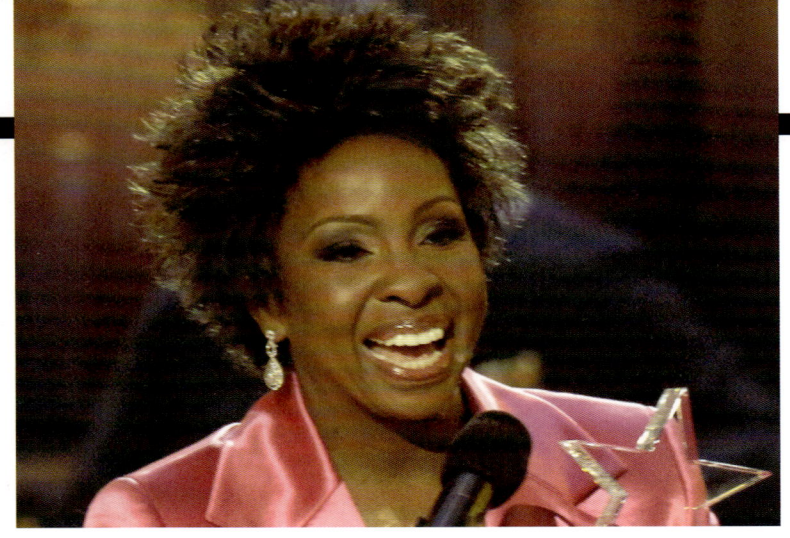

Singer and actress Gladys Maria Knight was born on May 28th, 1944 in Atlanta Georgia to Merald Knight and Sarah Elizabeth Woods. Gladys Knight and the Pips, which consisted of Gladys's brother, Merald, cousins Edward Patten and William Guest, joined Motown Records in 1966. One of their first hits was, *Heard it Through the Grapevine*, which went to #2 on the billboard charts. A year later, Marvin Gaye released the same song that went all the way to #1.

The band left Motown for Buddah Records in 1973 and recorded their best known and Grammy award-winning single *Midnight Train to Georgia*. Gladys Knight and the Pips were inducted into the Rock and Roll Hall of Fame in 1996. Gladys's home is located just south of McNichols Road.

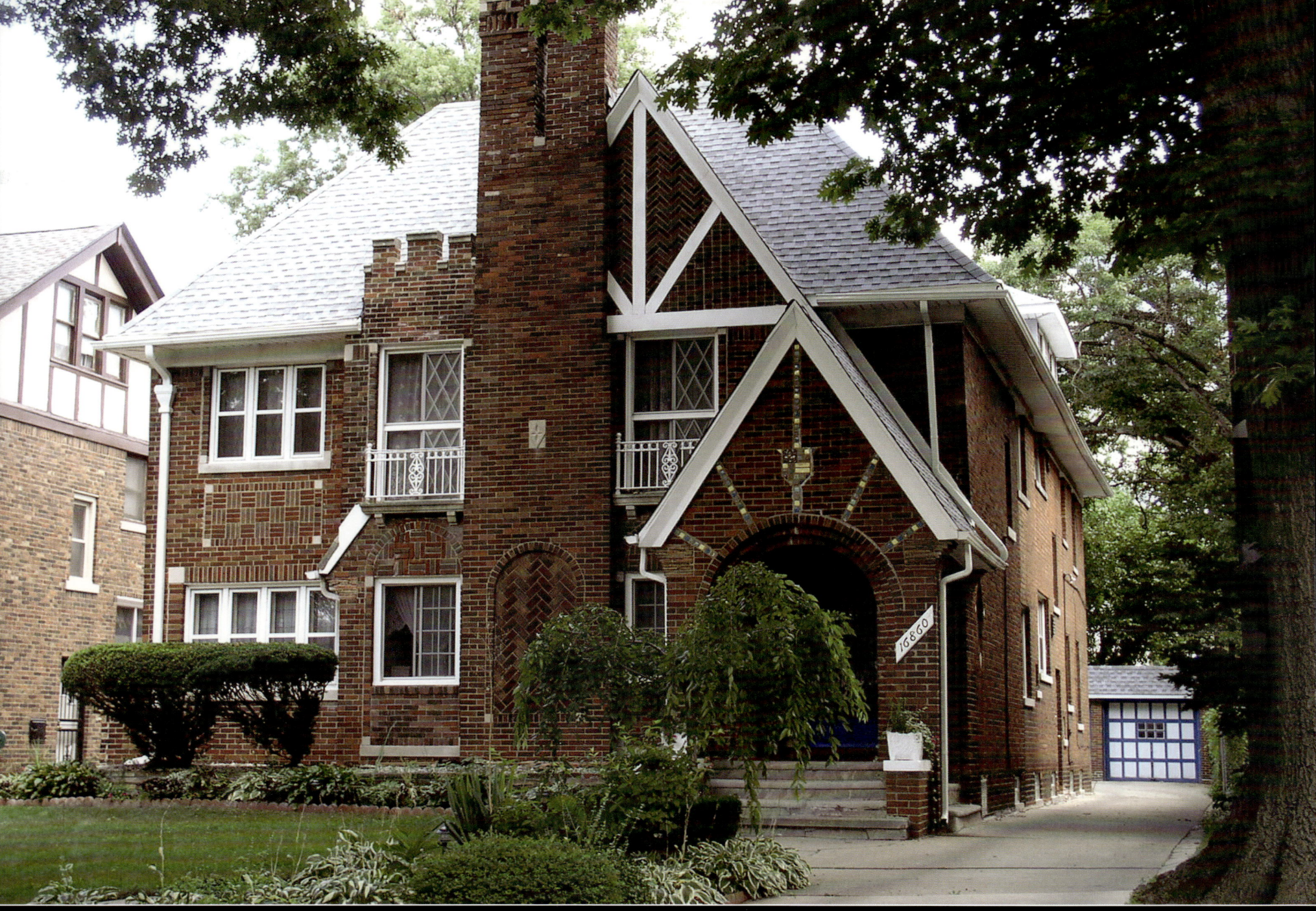

16860 La Salle

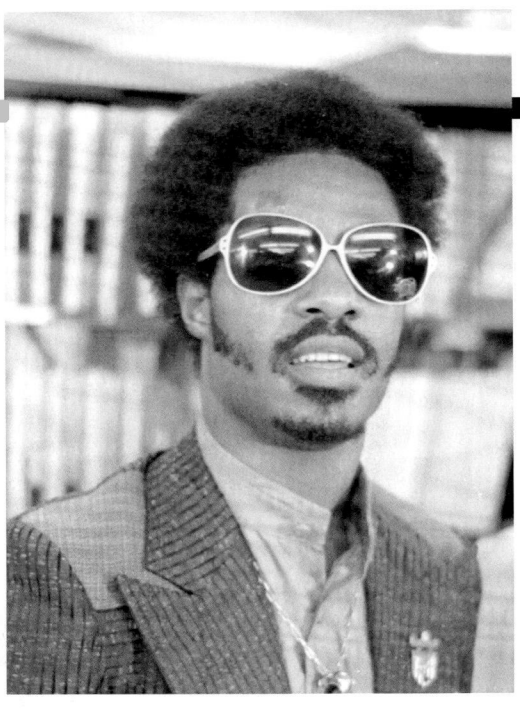

Stevie Wonder

Stevie Wonder is the stage name of Steveland Morris, who was born Steveland Junkins on May 13th, 1950 in Saginaw, Michigan. He was born premature, which caused his blindness. Stevie's mother LuLa Hardaway moved her family to Detroit's Brewster Projects from Saginaw in 1961. The family moved to 3347 Breckenridge, on the city's west side, where Stevie was noticed and later signed to Motown's Tamla Label in 1962.

Motown founder, Berry Gordy, helped move the family to the pictured home at 18074 Greenlawn, located between Seven Mile and West McNichols around 1965, because he wanted his stars to live in more desirable neighborhoods. Overall, Stevie has had 26 top-ten singles in both the United States and the U.K. and is a member of the Rock and Roll Hall of Fame.

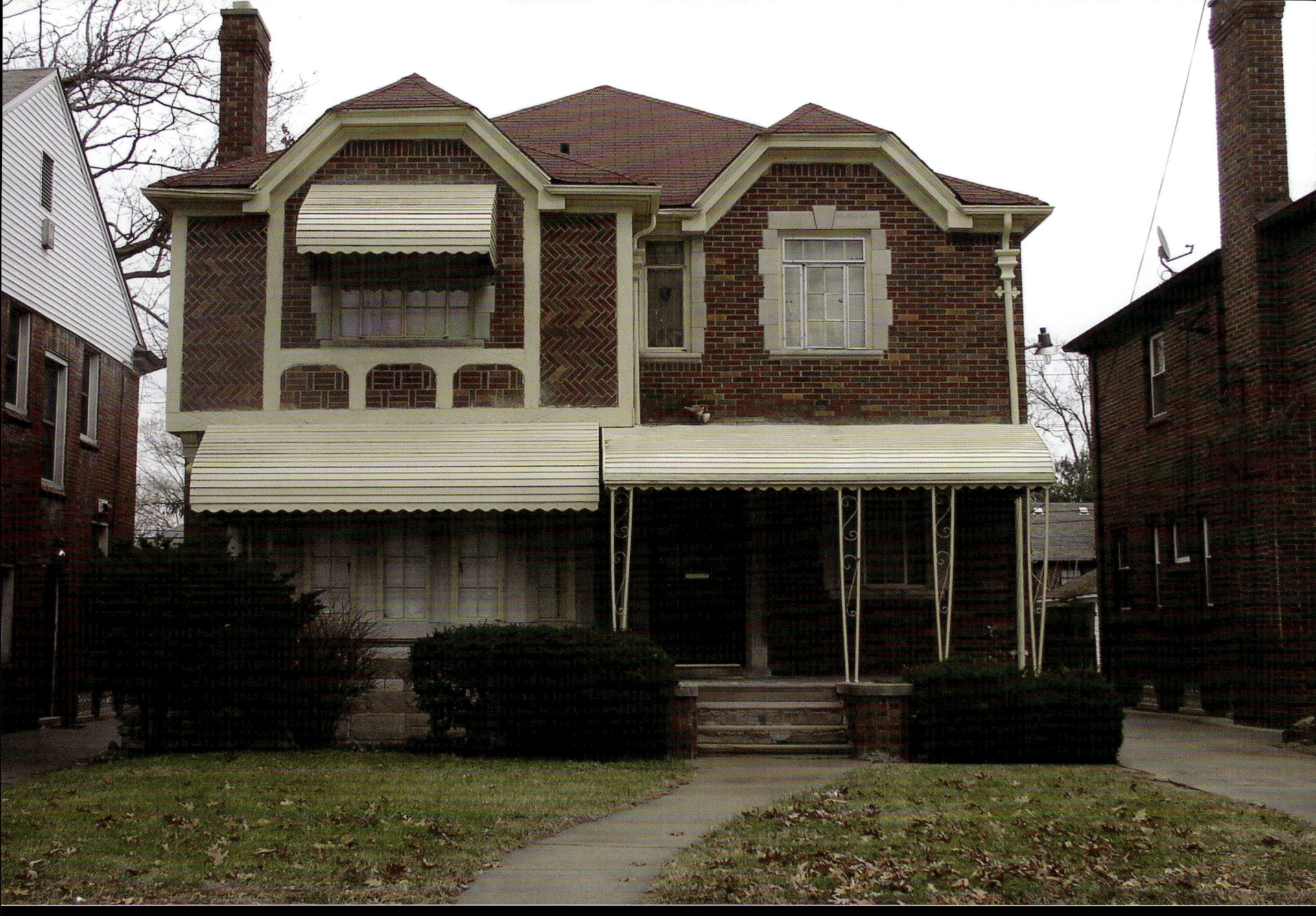

18074 Greenlawn

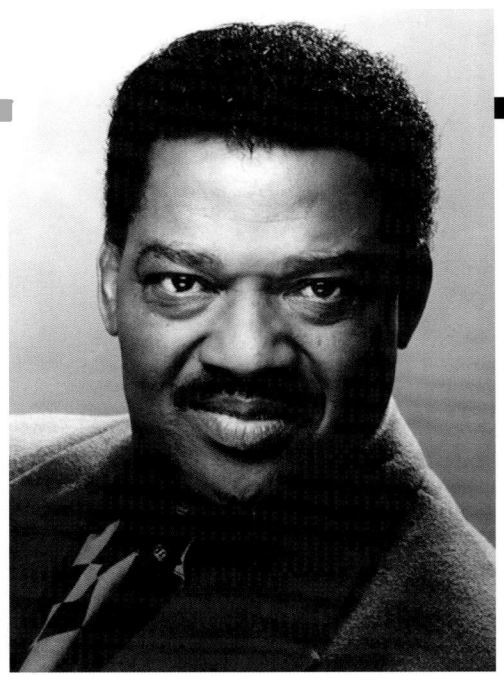

Edwin Starr

Born Charles Edwin Hatcher on January 21st, 1942 in Nashville, Tennessee. Edwin was raised in Cleveland, Ohio and moved to Detroit in the 1960s. He was first signed by Ric-Tic recording label before Motown Records bought out the label in 1968. In 1970, Edwin re-recorded the Temptations song *War*, which became an anthem for the anti-Vietnam War movement. In 1973, Edwin moved to England where he lived until 2003, when he died of a heart attack at the age of 61. Edwin and his wife Annette lived in the pictured home on Ardmore, just south of 8 Mile Road, in 1968.

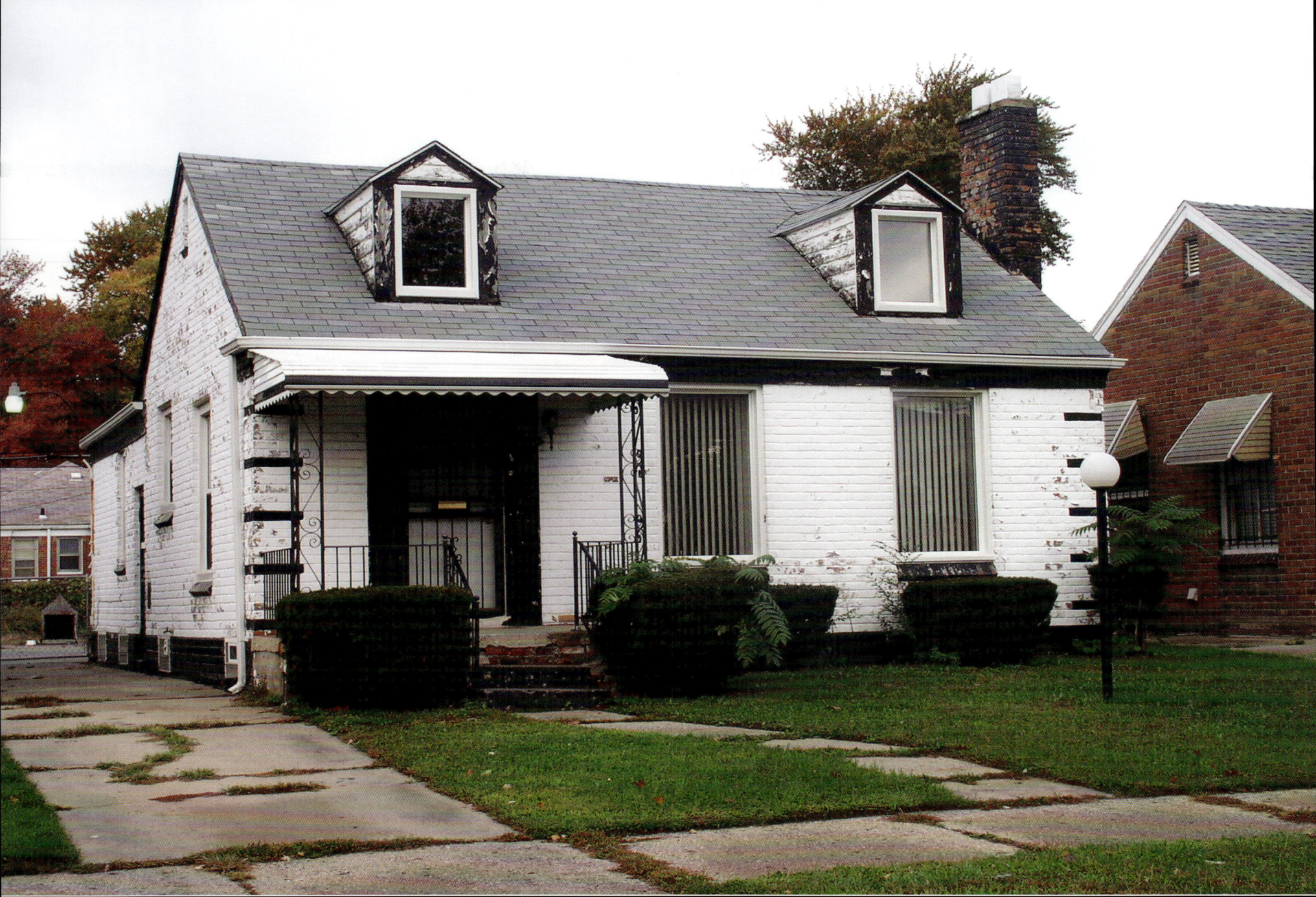

20511 Ardmore

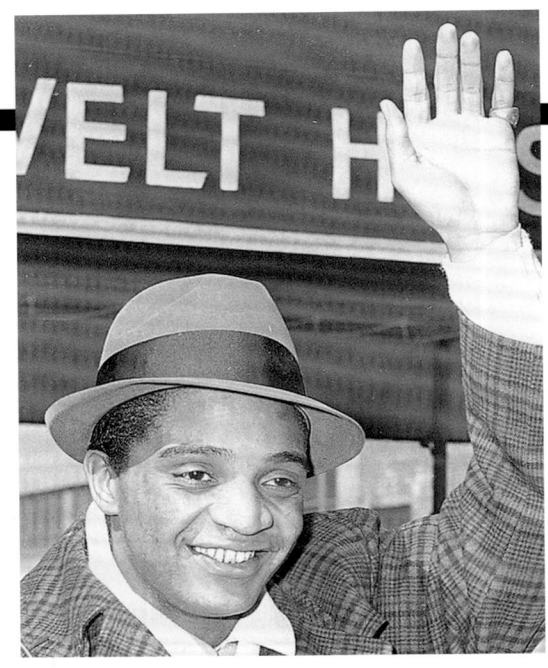

Jackie Wilson

Jack Leroy Wilson was born on June 9th, 1934 to Jack and Eliza Mae Wilson. Jackie had a wild childhood and married his first wife, Freda, at the age of 16. Early in his career, Jackie was in several vocal groups but is best known for his solo career with his first hit being *Reet Petite* in 1957, which was written by a young Berry Gordy.

Although married, Wilson was rumored to be quite the ladies' man and was shot by one of his lovers, Juanita Jones, in 1961. The record company described her as an obsessed fan and no charges where brought against Ms. Jones. In 1975, Wilson suffered a heart attack while performing; he stayed in a coma for nine years, until his death in 1984. The 1985 Commodores single, *Nightshift*, was in memory of Wilson and Marvin Gaye, who also died that year.

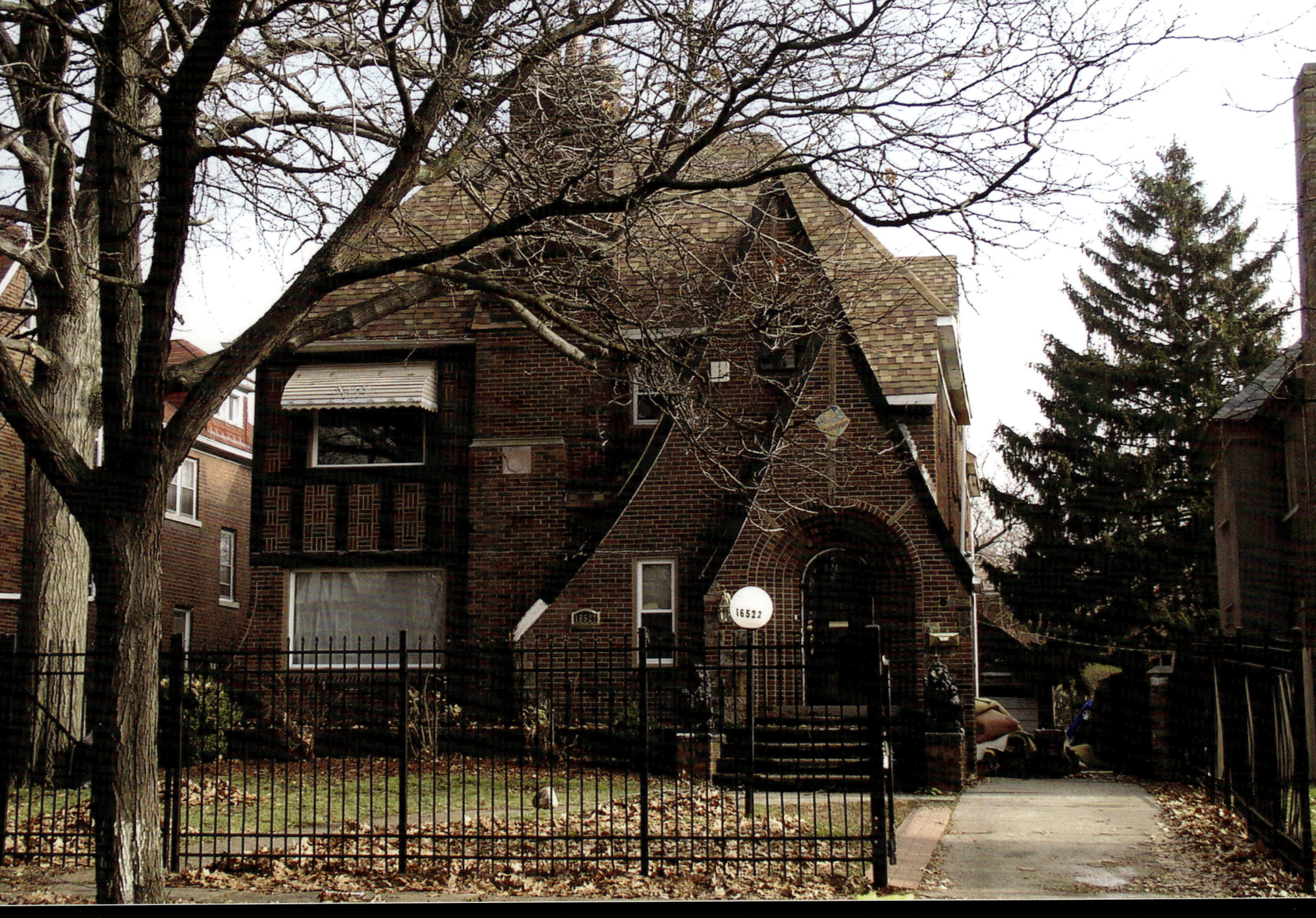

16522 La Salle

Ray Parker Jr.

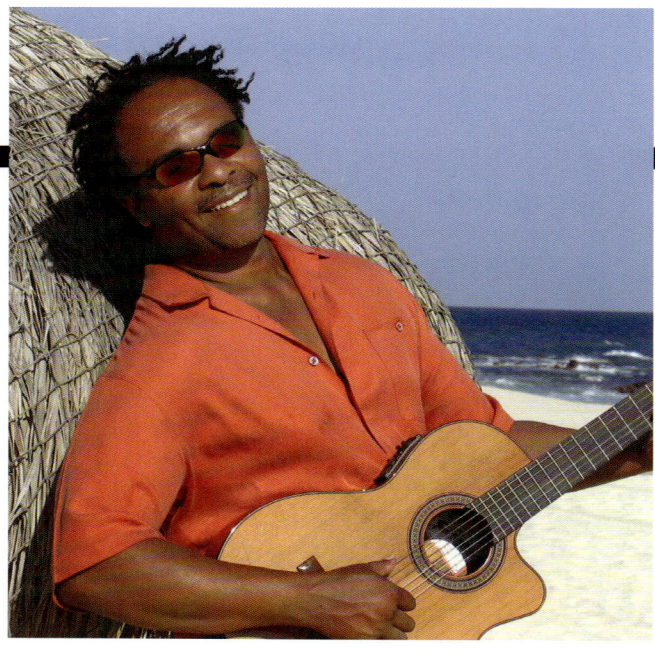

Born Ray Erskine Parker Jr. to Ray and Venoia on May 1st, 1954 in Detroit. He was raised in Detroit and attended Northwestern High School before starting his music career in Detroit. Ray wrote songs and did session work for some of the biggest Detroit performers including the Temptations, Spinners and Steve Wonder. Parker's biggest hit single was *Ghostbusters*, the title track for the movie soundtrack of the same name. Ray now lives in California and is still performing and producing music, his home is located just under a block west of Dexter.

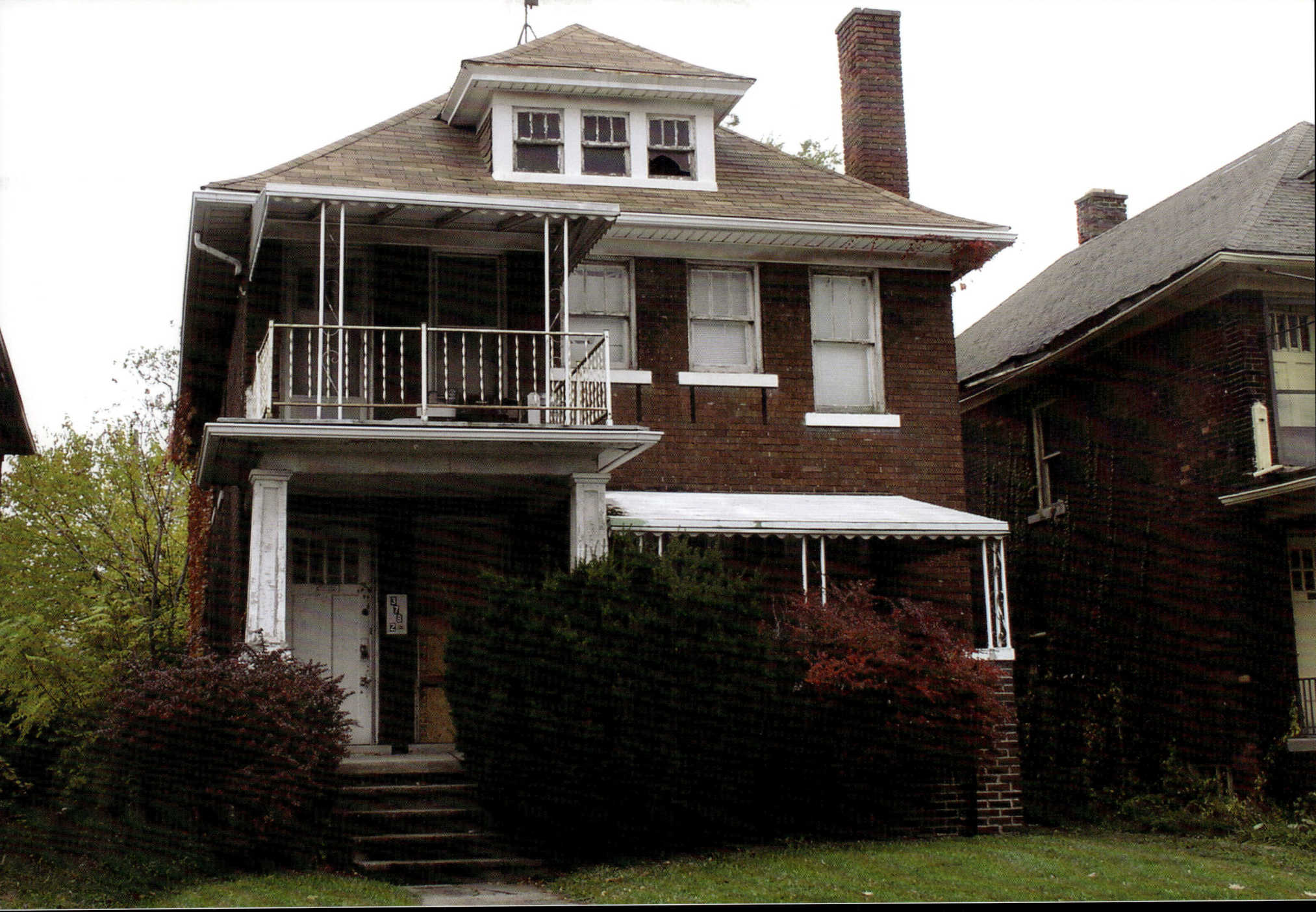

3780 Virginia Park

Jack White

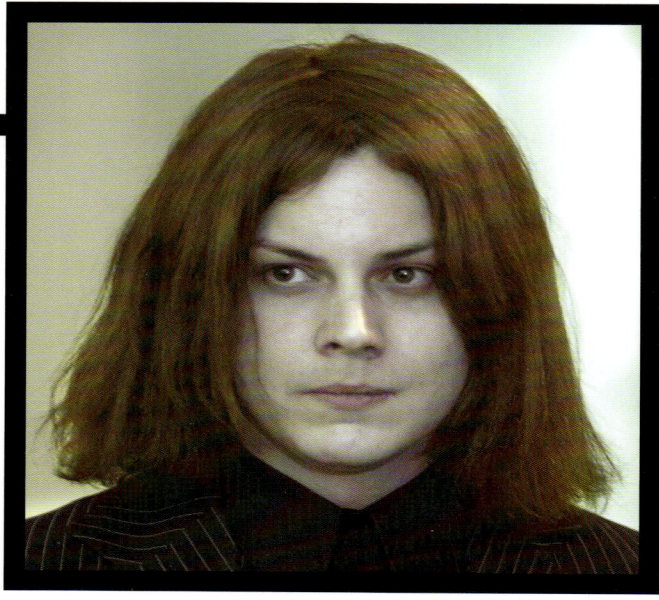

Musician, John Anthony Gillis, was born on July 9th, 1975 in Detroit to Gorman and Teresa Gillis, both of whom worked for the Archdiocese of Detroit. Jack attended Cass Technical High School and almost became a priest but decided not to go to the seminary because he couldn't take his amplifier. He met Meg White in 1994 and the couple married two years later, unconventionally, Jack took Meg's surname, White.

Together, they became the "White Stripes," but divorced after six years of marriage. They have stayed together as a musical group and Jack recently married model Karen Elson, Meg White was the maid of honor. Jack turned the pictured home into a recording studio and produced several albums at the home located in the Mexican Village neighborhood in southwest Detroit.

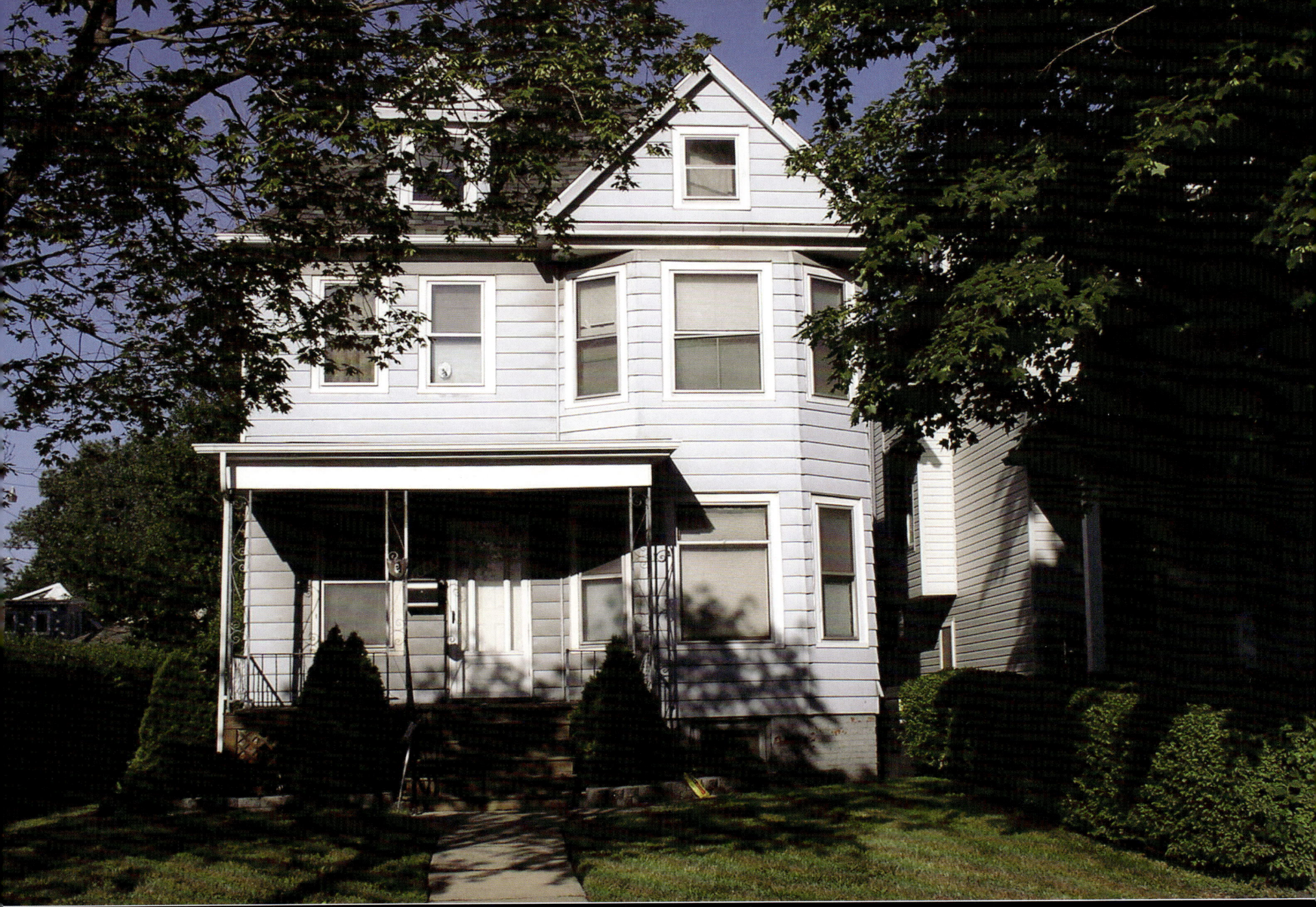

1203 Ferdinand

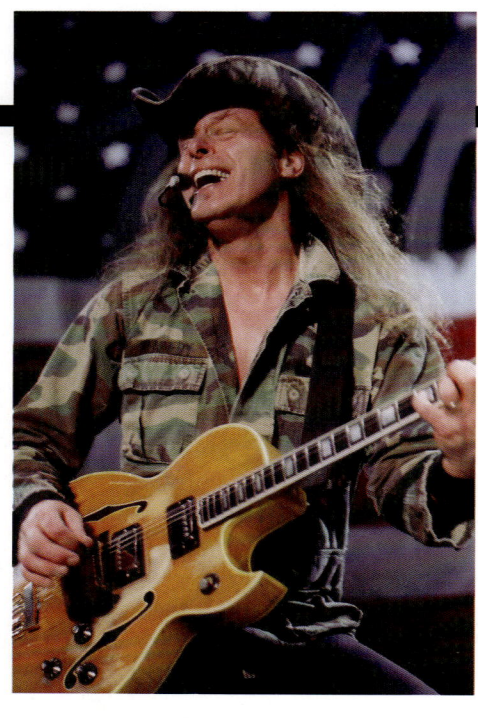

Ted Nugent

Ted was born on December 13th, 1948 in Detroit; his intensity and electric personality has carved him a permanent place among the legends of rock. Ted's talents and onstage antics quickly earned him the moniker of "Motor City Madman." Recognized as one of the world's leading guitar showmen, Ted's career spans four decades of multi-platinum hits.

Ted's hits include the ground breaking Amboy Dukes' *"Journey to the Center of the Mind,"* to classics like *"Stranglehold"* & *"Cat Scratch Fever,"* to the Damn Yankees chartbuster *"High Enough,"* and the classic *"Fred Bear,"* Ted continues to sell out venues around the globe. He lived at the pictured home located east of Telegraph and south of McNichols when he was ten years old but later moved to the Chicago area where he attended high school.

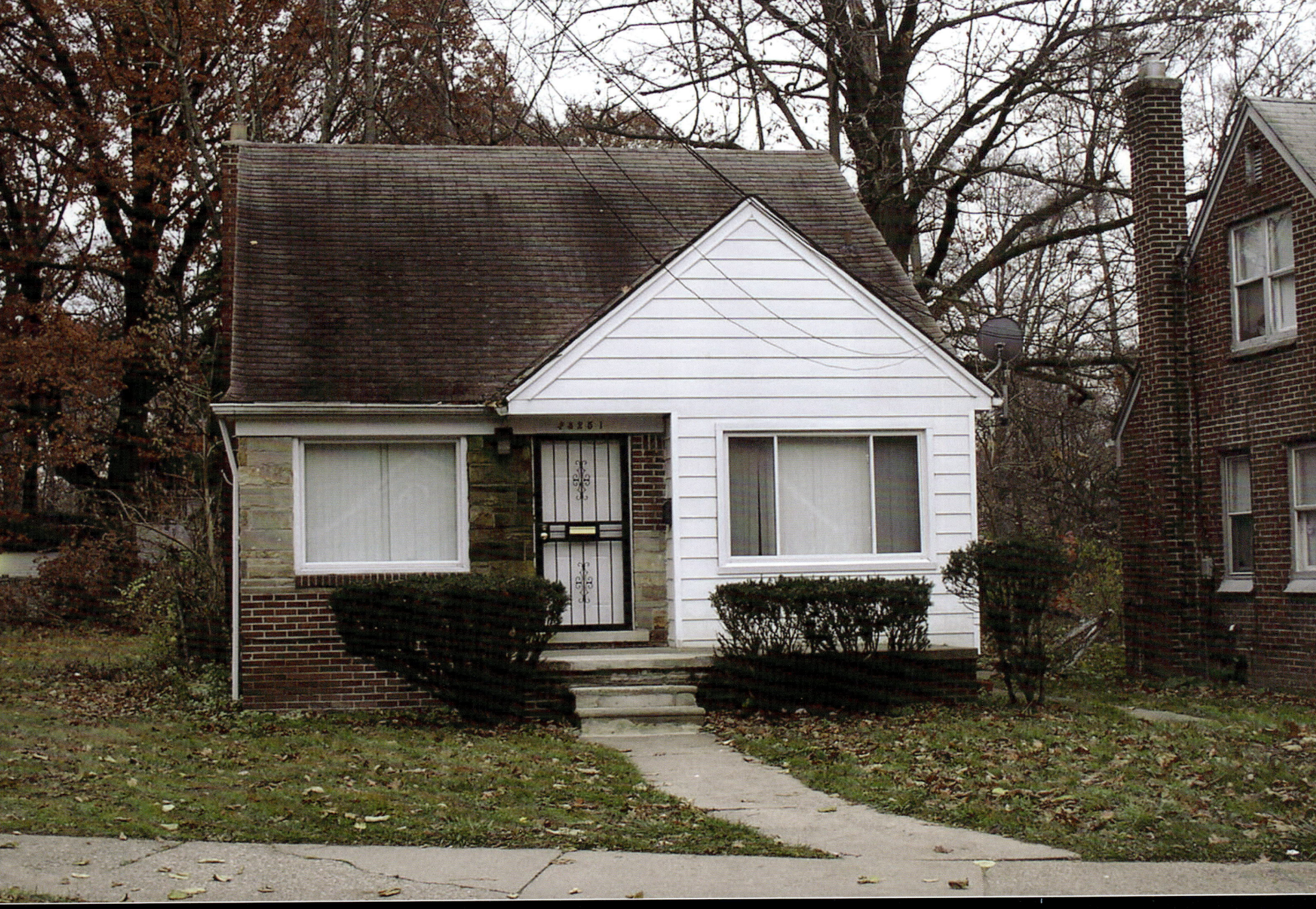

23251 Florence

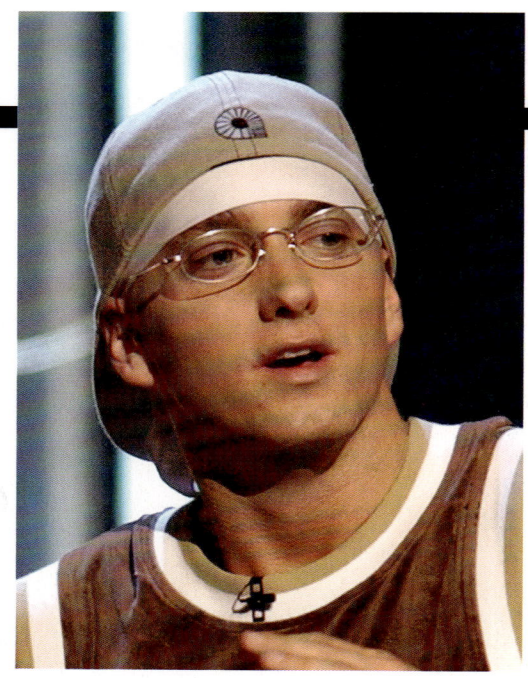

Eminem

Grammy and Oscar award-winning Marshall Bruce Mathers, a.k.a., Eminem, was born on October 17th, 1972 outside of Kansas City, Missouri. His single mother, Debbie Mathers, raised him and his childhood included constant moves, living in public housing, and under the care of relatives. After he dropped out of high school, he struck up a friendship with the late rapper Proof and started his music career. Marshall was discovered by Dr. Dre and hit stardom with his debut single *My Name Is*.

In 2002, Marshall starred in the movie, *8 Mile*, which portrayed his rise in the music industry and was filmed in the Detroit area. The only printed documentation I have for Eminem is a phone number, with no address, for the northeast part of Detroit where the pictured home on Dresden is located. This is also the home pictured on *The Marshall Mathers LP* cover, said to be one of his childhood homes. If that story is true, this is where he lived.

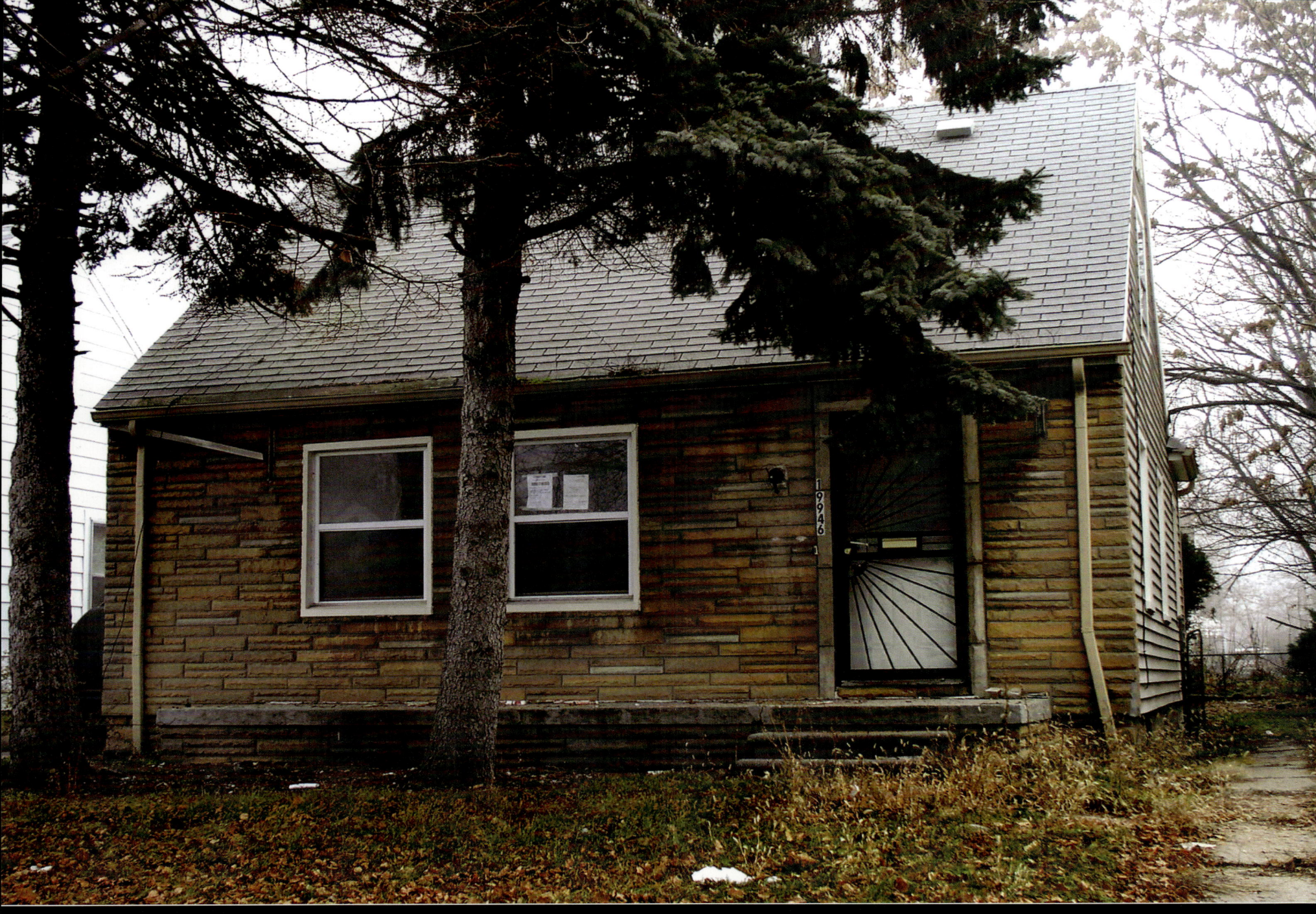

19946 Dresden

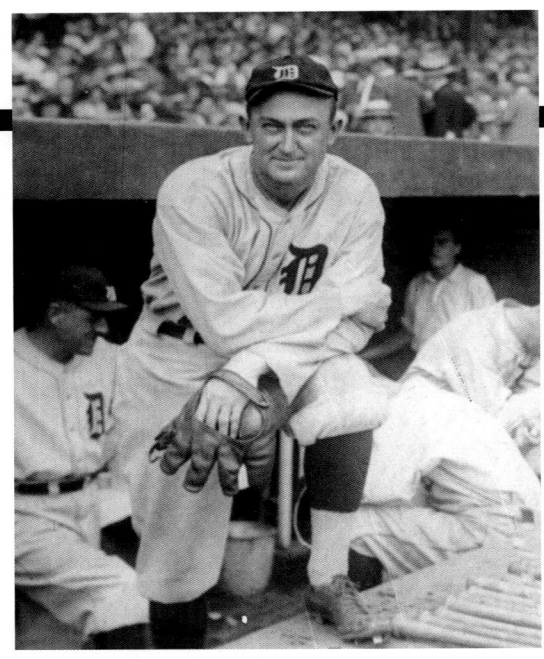

Ty Cobb

Born Tyrus Raymond Cobb on December 18th, 1886 in Narrow, Georgia, his nickname was the "Georgia Peach" and he is arguably the best baseball player who ever lived. Ty played, and or managed, the Detroit Tigers from 1905 through 1926. Ty lived in this house located in the historic Boston-Edison neighborhood in 1926, legend has it that Ty played baseball with the neighborhood kids in Voight Park, located two blocks north of this house. Ty was elected into the Baseball Hall of Fame in 1936 and passed away on July 17th, 1961 in Atlanta, Georgia.

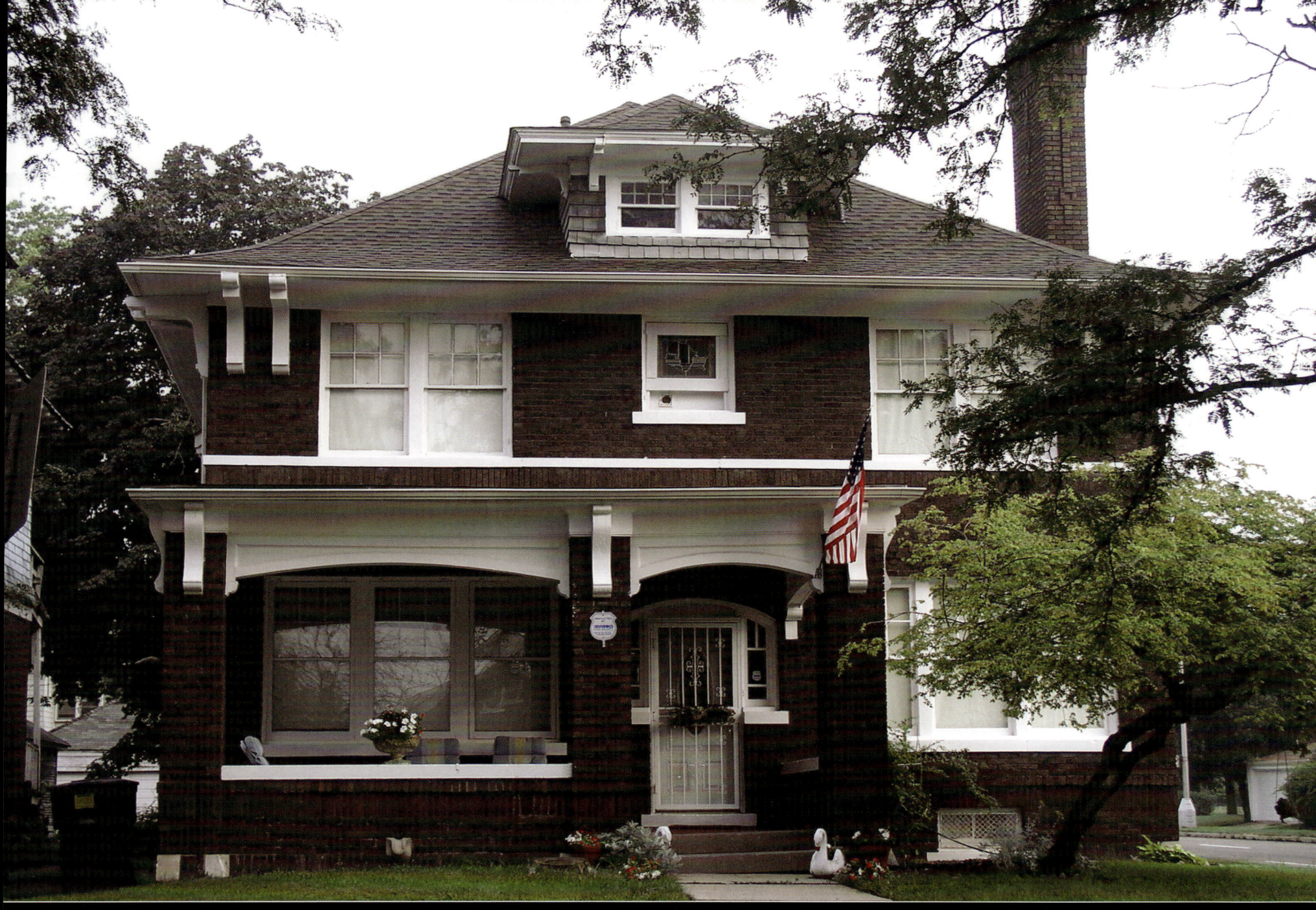

800 Atkinson

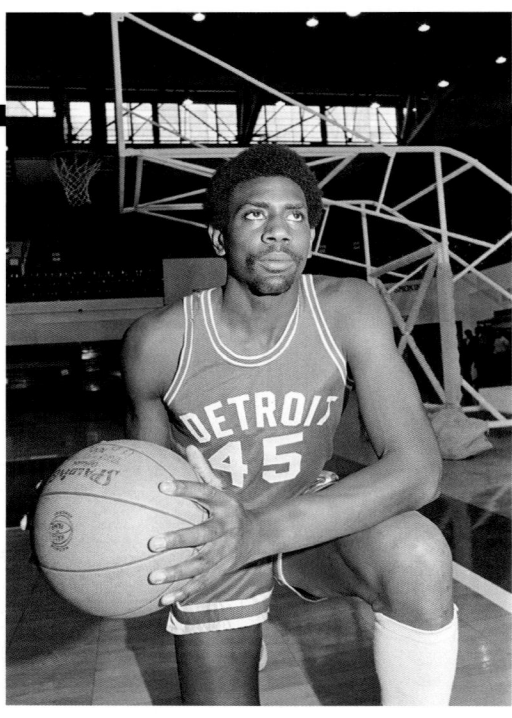

Spencer Haywood

Born on April 22nd, 1949 in Silver City, Mississippi, Spencer came to Detroit around 1964 where he attended Pershing High School. He lived with James and Ida Bell, who were his legal guardians along with legendary basketball coach Will Robinson. While Spencer attended Pershing, he worked with Detroiter and world famous self-help author Dr. Wayne Dyer, a counselor at the time, who helped Spencer become a stellar student.

Spencer went on to play basketball at the University of Detroit and led Team USA to a gold medal in the 1968 Olympics in Mexico City. Spencer left college after two years to start a professional career that lasted 14 years. The Bell's former home is located five blocks southeast of Pershing High School.

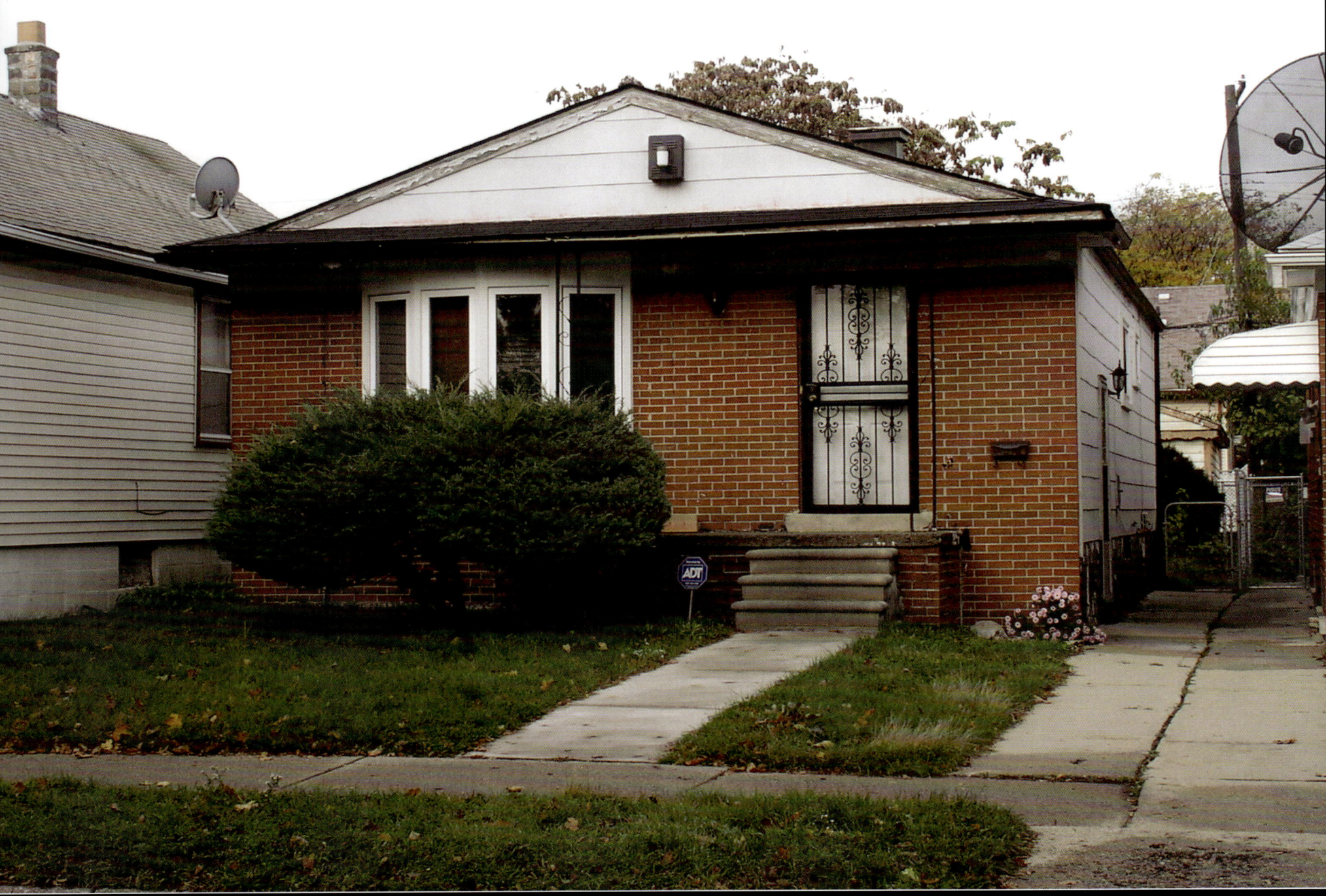

18421 Sunset

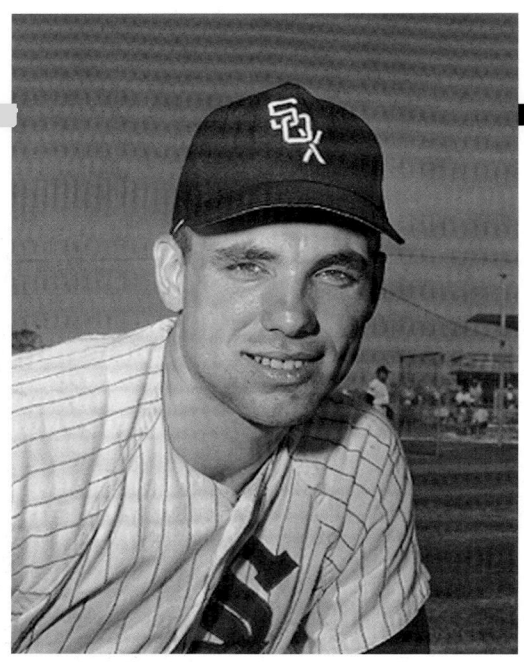

Dave DeBusschere

David Albert Debusschere was born in Detroit on October 16th, 1940. He graduated from Austin High School and went on to the University of Detroit. He was drafted by the Detroit Pistons and become the youngest player-coach in league history, at the age of 24, with the Pistons. He then went to the New York Knicks and was a member of the 1969-70 championship team. Dave also was a pitcher for the Chicago White Sox during the 1962-63 season. He lived at the pictured home on Evanston, located just north of the I –94 freeway, during his early childhood and then moved to 3827 Courville on the city's east side, that house is no longer standing. Dave DeBusschere died of a heart attack in 2003, at the age of 62.

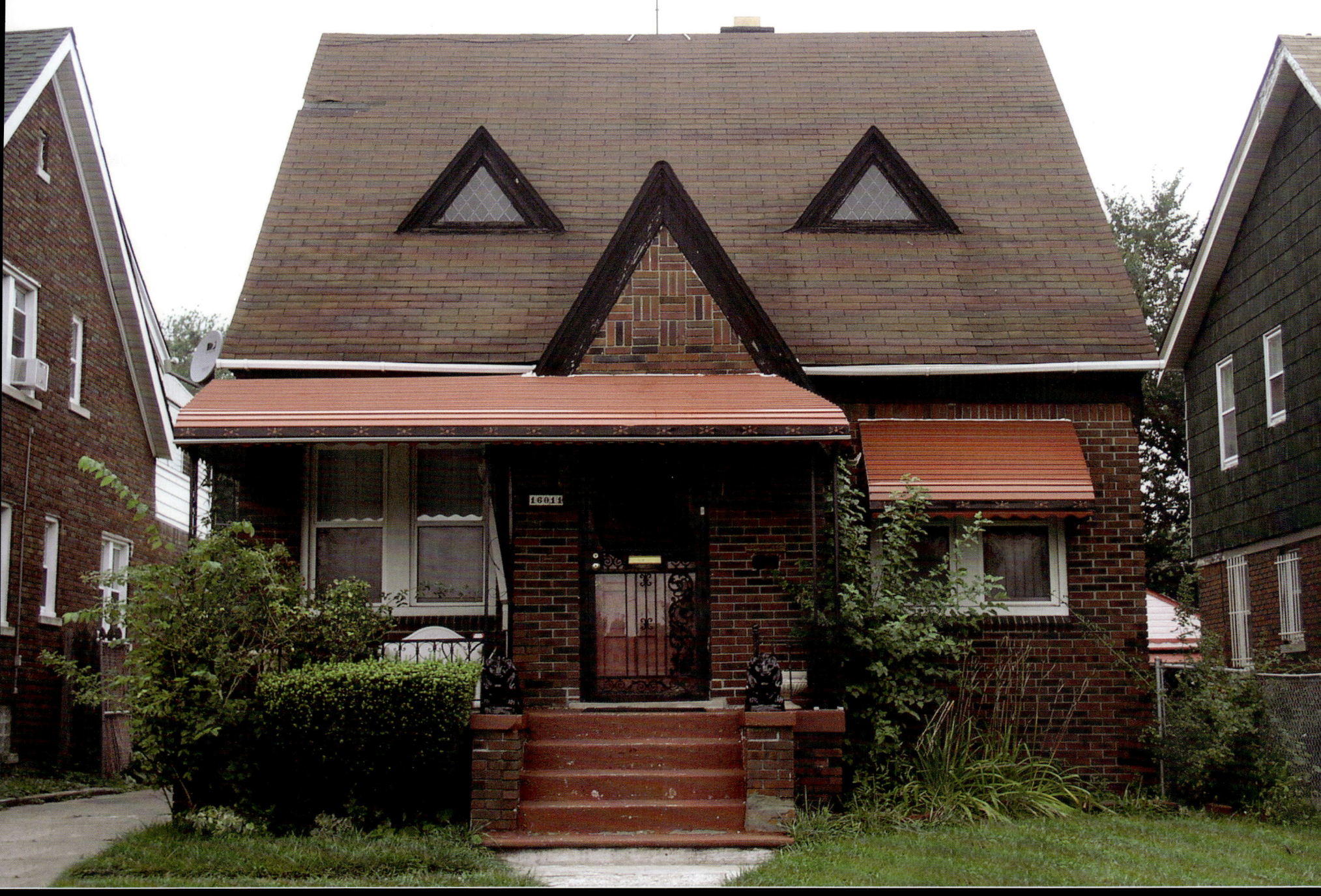

16011 Evanston

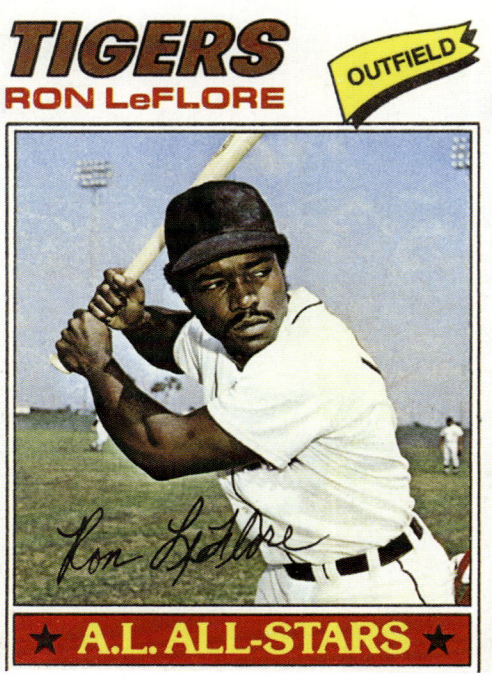

TIGERS
RON LeFLORE

OUTFIELD

A.L. ALL-STARS

Ron LeFlore

Ron was born to John and Georgia LeFlore on June 16th, 1948 in Detroit. He was in and out of the criminal justice system at an early age and was sent to Jackson Prison for burglary in 1970. While in prison, he was discovered by then Detroit Tiger manager Billy Martin. In 1973, LeFlore was a 26-year-old rookie in the Tigers' farm system and in 1974, he was in the major leagues. His book, *Breakout, From Prison to the Big Leagues,"* became a made-for-TV movie, *One in a Million, the Ron LeFlore Story,* starring LeVar Burton. Ron's home is located on Detroit's east side, just west of the historic Indian Village neighborhood.

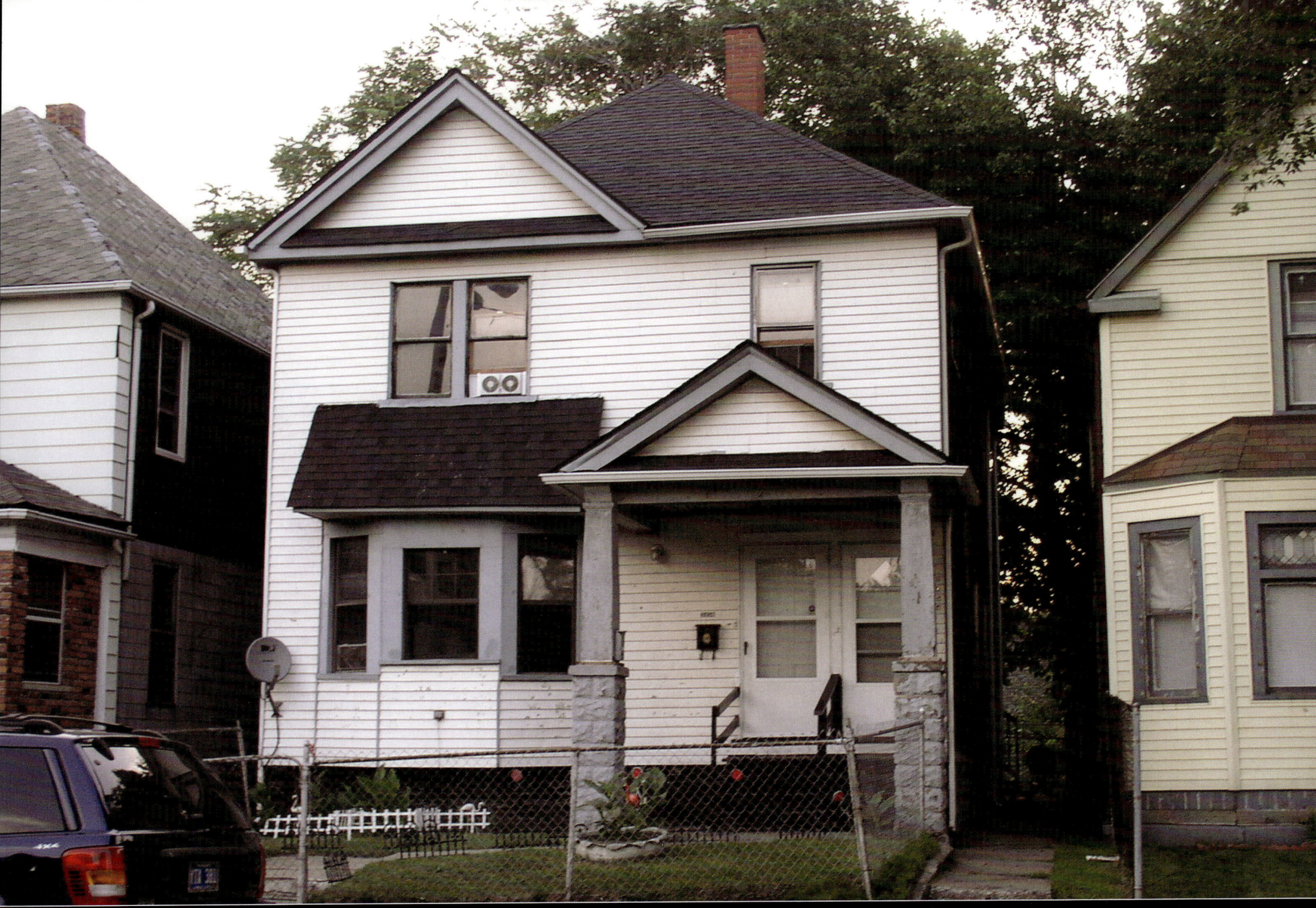

3454 Van Dyke

Rudy Tomjanovich

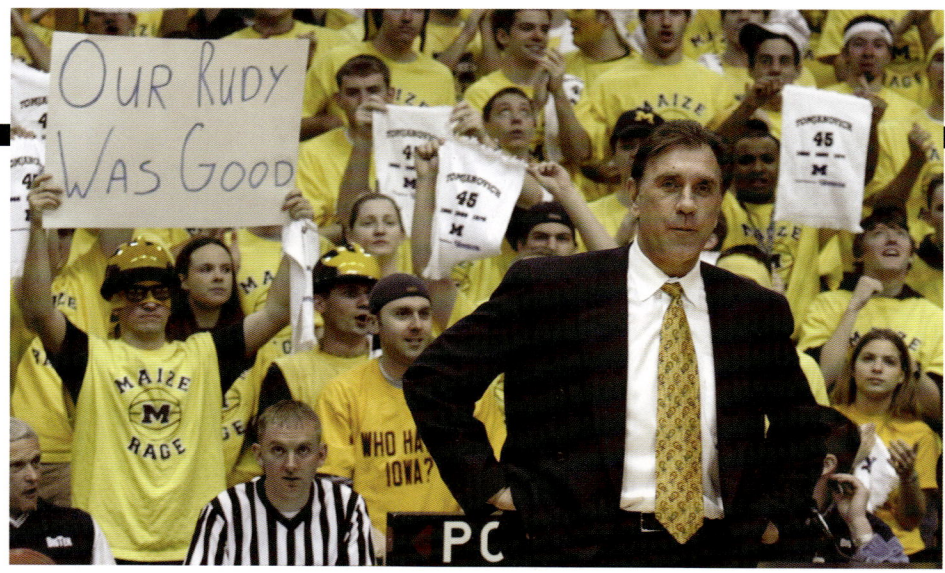

Rudy T. was born on November 24th, 1948 in Hamtramck, Michigan, a small city with a large Polish population contained entirely within the borders of Detroit. Rudy graduated from Hamtramck High School and went on to play basketball at the University of Michigan. He had a stellar NBA career, which was marred when Kermit Washington punched him during a game in 1977, which resulted in injuries that would sideline him for five months.

Rudy made a full recovery and played a total of 11 years for the Houston Rockets and later coached the team to two NBA championships, in 1994 and 1995. He lived his early childhood at 11428 Nagel but had to move down the street to the pictured 12147 Nagel when part of the neighborhood was demolished for the construction of the I-75 Chrysler Freeway. The pictured home can be seen while driving on I-75; it is located east of the freeway on the service drive, just north of Caniff Road.

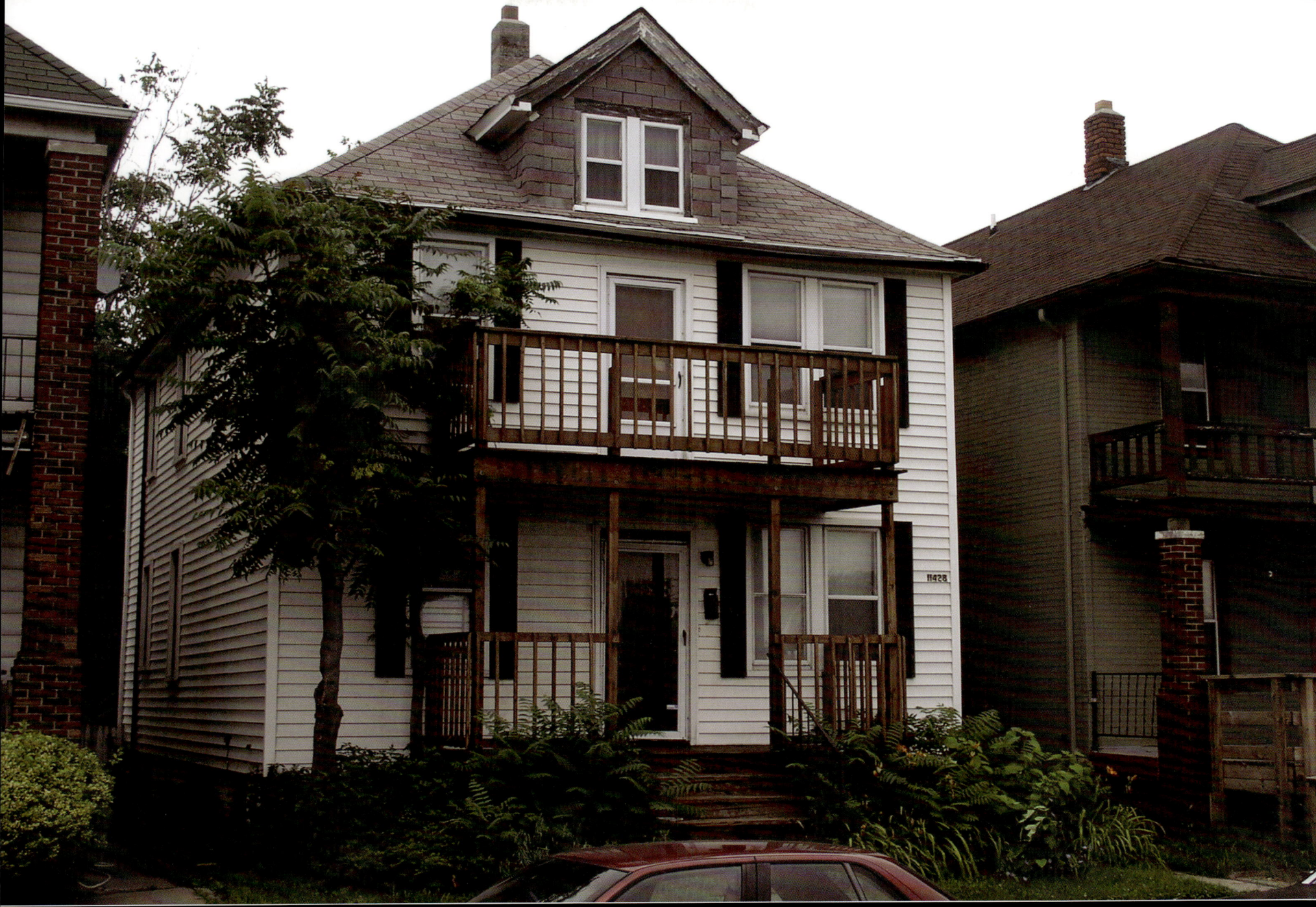

11428 Nagel

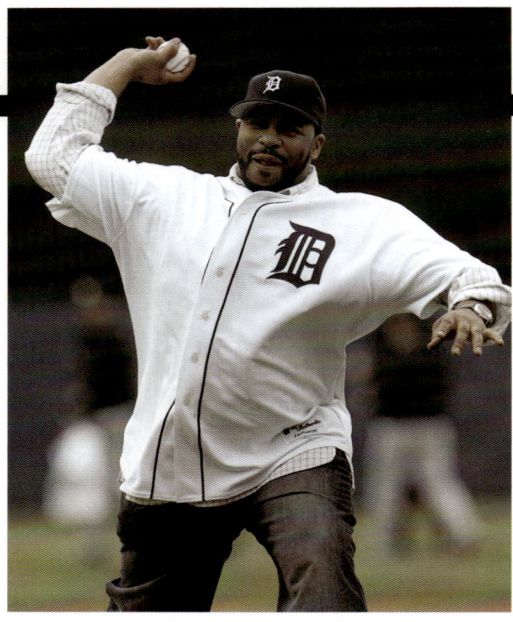

Jerome Bettis

Jerome Abram Bettis (nickname, The Bus), was born on February 16th, 1972 in Detroit. Jerome lived most of his childhood in the pictured home on Aurora just north of Mackenzie High School, from which he graduated. Jerome went on to play football at Notre Dame, where he finished his Notre Dame career with 1,912 yards and an average of 5.7 yards per carry. He was drafted by the Los Angeles Rams and was later traded to the Pittsburgh Steelers in 1996.

Jerome became an integral part of the Steelers team for the rest of his career, culminating in a Super Bowl Championship played at Ford Field in Detroit. Jerome is now retired, focusing on housing developments in Detroit and several charitable causes including the Jerome Bettis "The Bus Stops Here" foundation.

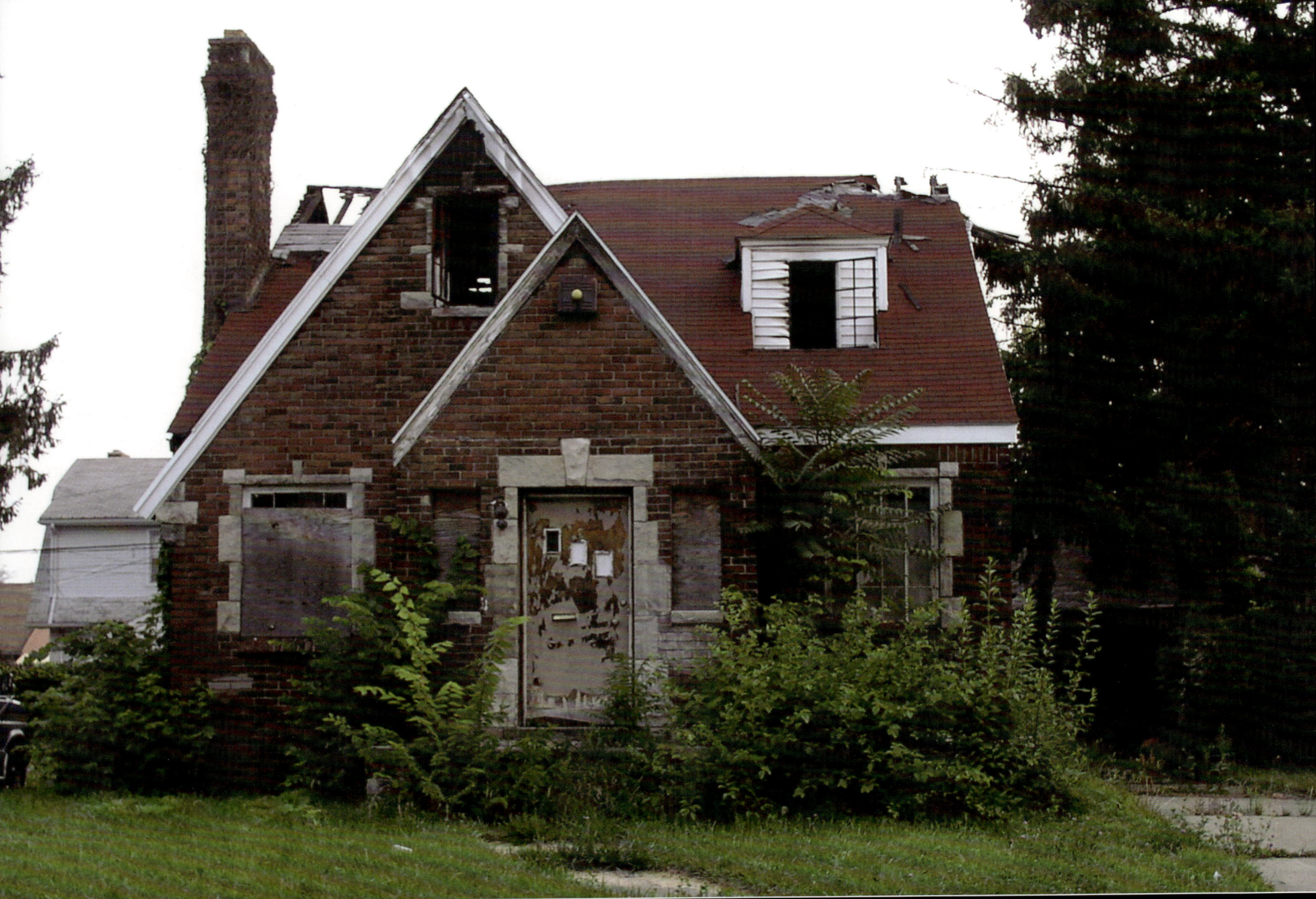

10384 Aurora

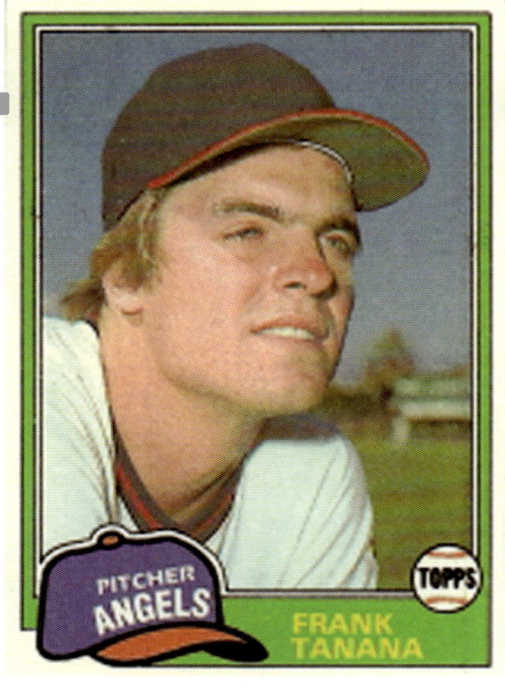

Frank Tanana

Major League Baseball player, Frank Daryl Tanana, was born in Detroit on July 3rd, 1953 to Frank and Dolores Tanana. Frank attended Detroit Catholic Central and was a first-round draft pick of the California Angels. He was a three-year All Star and later pitched for the Detroit Tigers. He was the winning pitcher when the Tigers defeated the Toronto Blue Jays in the last game of the year that clinched the 1987 divisional championship. Frank's father, Frank Sr., was a Detroit Policeman and played baseball for several years in the minor leagues. Frank's home is located in the southwest portion of Detroit, just a few blocks from Dearborn.

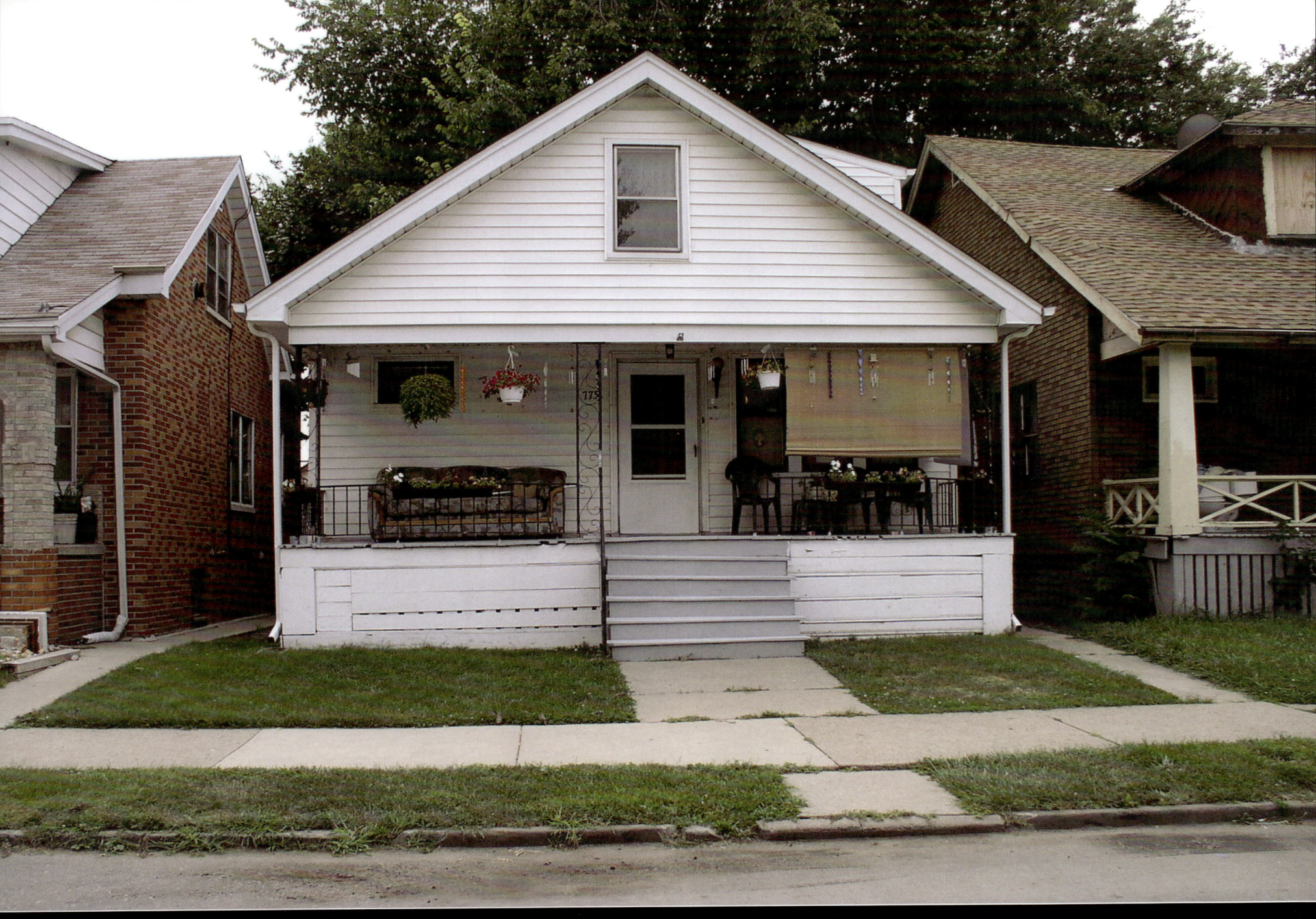

7751 Dayton

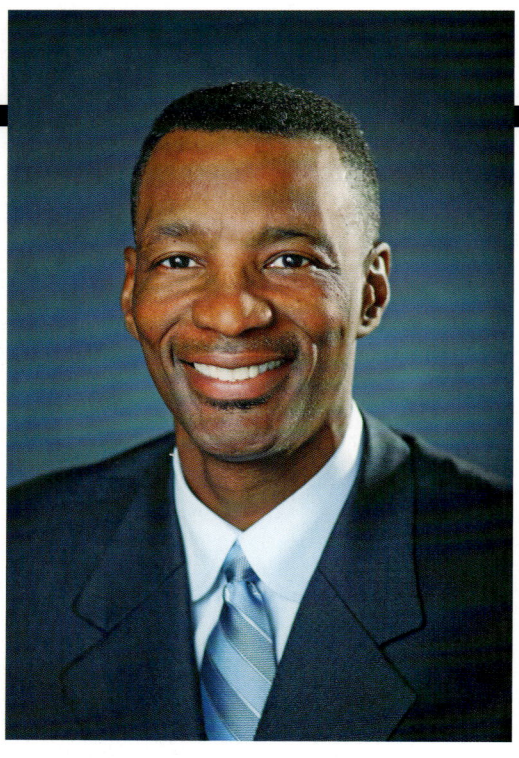

Greg Kelser

Greg Kelser was born on September 17th, 1957. After graduating from Henry Ford High School, Kelser went to play at the Michigan State University and teamed with Earvin "Magic" Johnson to lead the Spartans to the NCAA National Championship in 1979. He was drafted by his hometown Detroit Pistons, but was later traded to the Seattle Supersonics for Vinnie "The Microwave" Johnson.

Greg lived with his parents, Walter and Verna, in the pictured home on Cooley, near Lahser and Eight Mile Road. After his playing career, Kelser went into broadcasting as a sports analyst for college basketball and the Detroit Pistons, he is one of the best in the business.

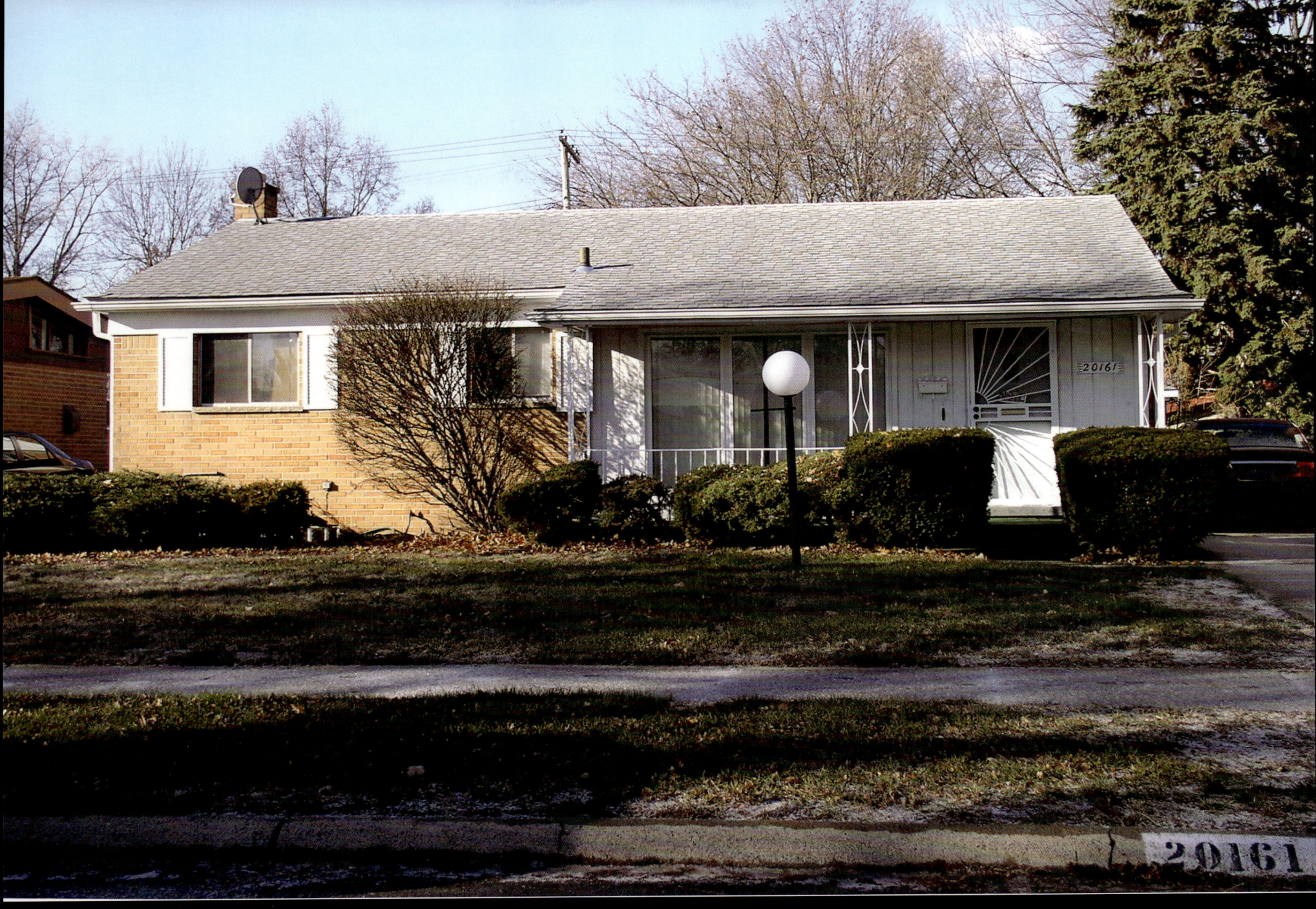

20161 Cooley

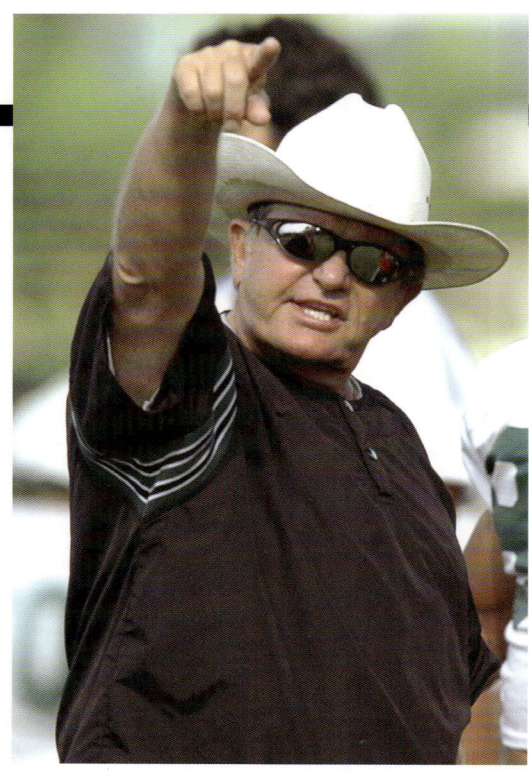

Jerry Glanville

Former NFL coach and TV analyst Jerry Glanville was born in Detroit on October 14th, 1941 and lived in Detroit until he was fourteen. Jerry played college football at Northern Michigan University, where he is a member of the school's Hall of Fame. Jerry lived in a housing complex on the city's east side before he moved to the pictured home on Edmore located just south of Eight Mile Road and west of Kelly.

Jerry then moved to Perrysburg, Ohio, which is located just outside of Toledo, where he attended high school and was friends with current Detroit Tiger manager Jim Leyland. Jerry came back to Detroit as a Special Teams and Defensive Assistant coach for the Lions in 1974; he is currently the head football coach at Portland State.

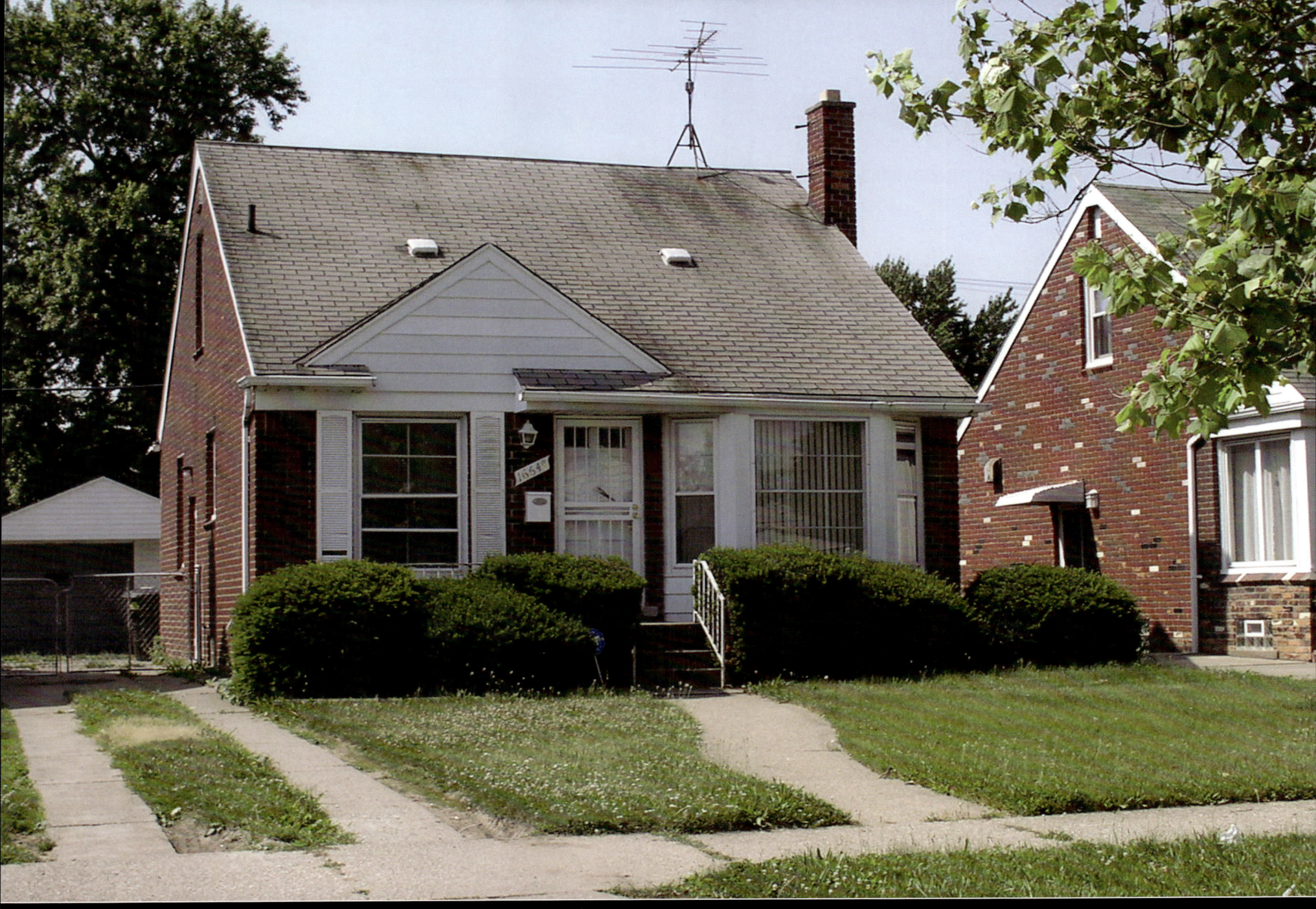

16648 Edmore

Chris Webber

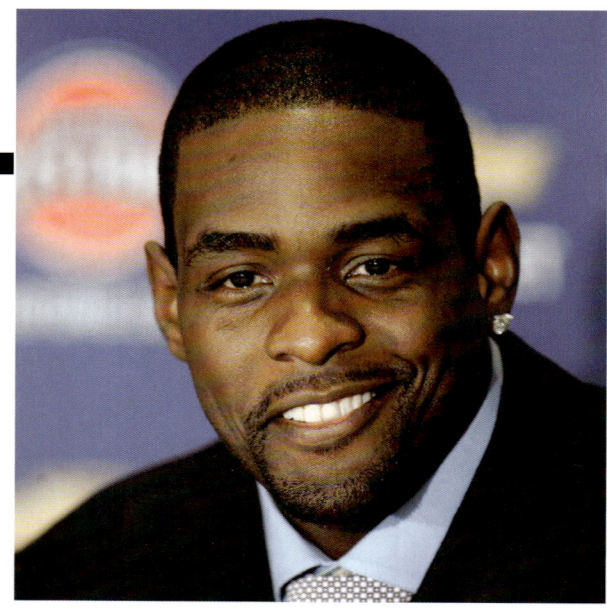

NBA standout, Chris Webber, was born Mayce Edward Christopher Webber III on March 1st, 1973. Webber played his high school ball at Detroit Country Day and went on to the University of Michigan, where he led the "Fab Five" to two NCAA finals appearances. Chris pleaded guilty to the charge of criminal contempt for lying to a federal grand jury about taking money from University of Michigan booster, Ed Martin, which led to the Michigan basketball team being placed on probation. Chris had a homecoming of sorts when he signed with the hometown Pistons in 2007, after the Philadelphia Seventy Sixers bought out his contract. His home is located just northwest of Cooley High School, on the west side of Detroit.

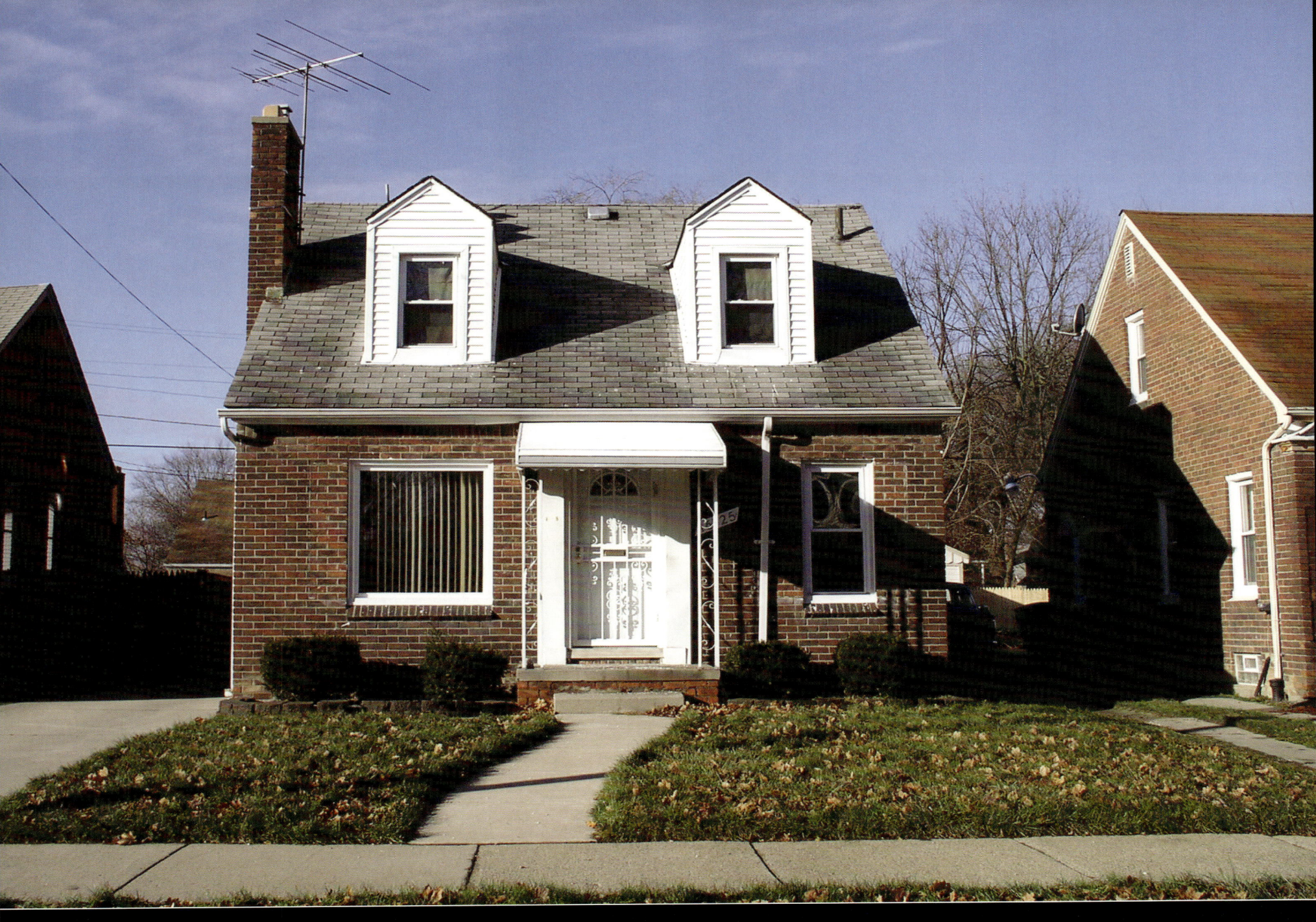

16725 Biltmore

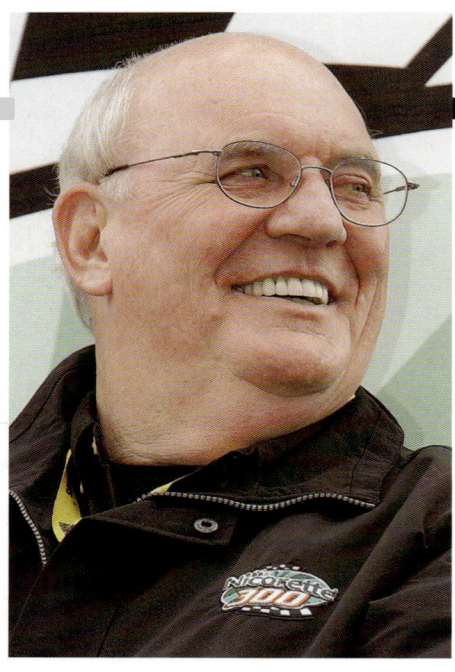

Benny Parsons

Born to Harold and Hazel on July 12th, 1941. When Benny's mother and father moved to Detroit in the late 1940s, Benny stayed behind in North Carolina and was raised by his grandmother Julia. Benny would come during the summer to live with his parents, but did not move to Detroit permanently until 1960, after he graduated high school.

Benny was a cab driver before entering his first race in 1963 at the Mt. Clemens Speedway that lead to a NASCAR career, which included 21 wins and 20 pole positions. He then went on to become one of the best racing color commentators. Unfortunately, Benny lost his fight with cancer on January 16th, 2007 at the age of 65.

Benny lived at 64 E. Montana, which is no longer standing. The pictured vacant lot where Benny's home stood represents all of the homes, and their memories, that are no longer standing in Detroit.

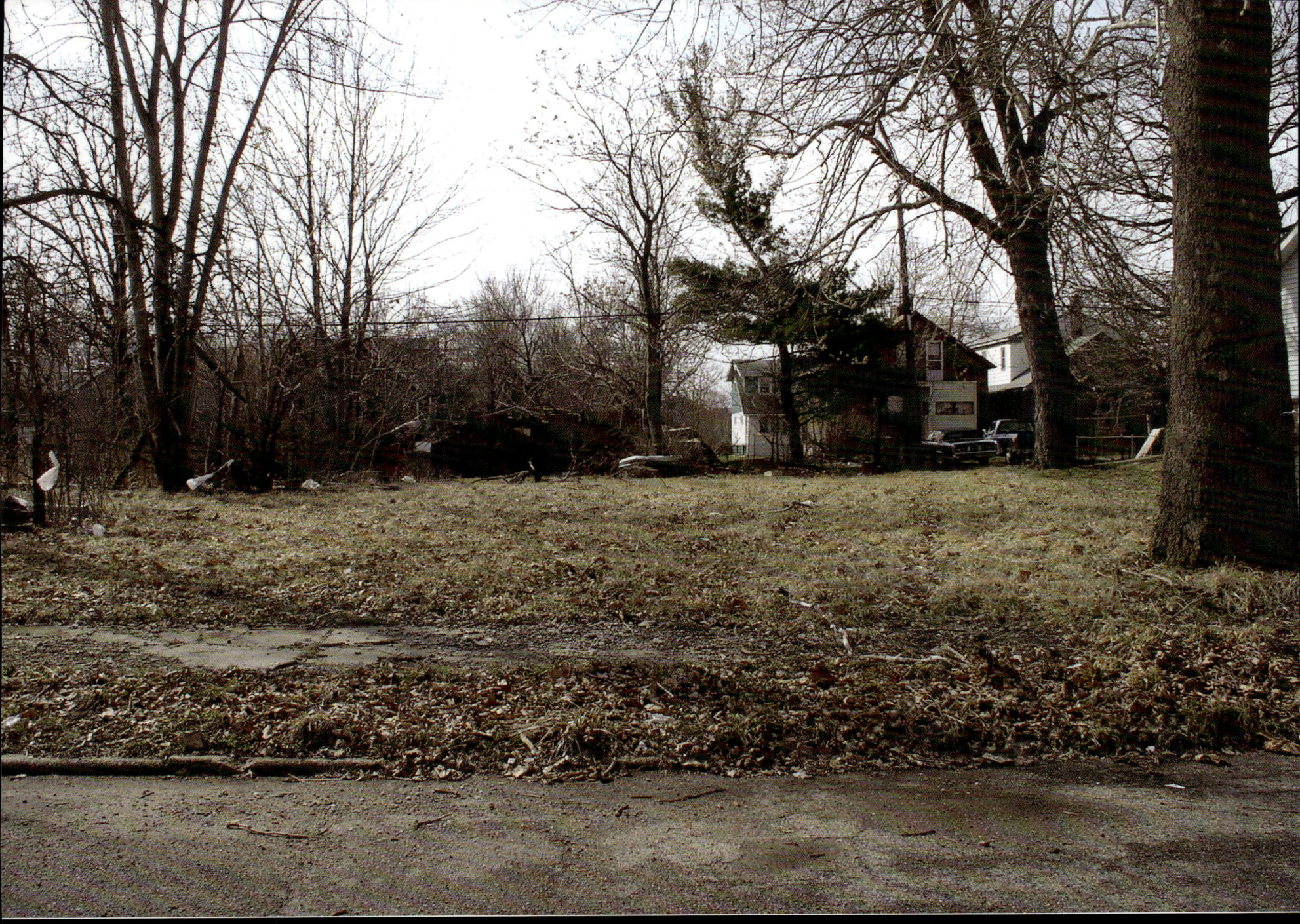

4 E. Montana

Index